Curtain
CALL

Curtain
CALL

Charm & Deceit

JENNIFER ALLEE *and*
LISA KARON RICHARDSON

WHITAKER
HOUSE

CURTAIN CALL
Charm & Deceit ~ Book Three

Jennifer AlLee
Web Site: www.jenniferallee.com
E-mail: jallee725@hotmail.com

Lisa Karon Richardson
Web Site: www.lisakaronrichardson.com
E-mail: lisa@lisakaronrichardson.com

Authors are represented by MacGregor Literary, Inc., and The Steve Laube Agency.

ISBN: 978-1-62911-007-3
eBook ISBN: 978-1-62911-031-8
Printed in the United States of America
© 2014 by Jennifer AlLee and Lisa Karon Richardson

Whitaker House
1030 Hunt Valley Circle
New Kensington, PA 15068
www.whitakerhouse.com

Library of Congress Cataloging-in-Publication Data (Pending)

1 2 3 4 5 6 7 8 9 10   20 19 18 17 16 15 14

Dedication

From Jen
To Magdaline Soos Ellsworth,
an amazing woman and my best friend forever before anyone
knew what a BFF was.

From Lisa
To Bethany "Beppy" Carter,
my sweet sister, who makes me happy to be her sister, and makes
me laugh because there's nothing she can do about it.

Acknowledgments

We are, as ever, immensely grateful to our agents, Sandra Bishop and Tamela Hancock Murray, who continue to guide our careers with great skill. We also owe a huge debt of gratitude to the wonderful team at Whitaker House. From designing the cover, to editing, to marketing, they are a dream to work with, and we appreciate all of the effort they put into making our stories a success.

Chapter 1

August 22, 1868
Manhattan, New York

Emily Forbes let the cadenza spill uninhibited from her lips. Caught up in the beauty of the aria, she let her folded hands break apart from one another, finding expression in motion. While wrapped up in the music, she felt free and…whole. In her imagination, she became the waif raised from ashes and cinders to marry a prince. As she sang the final aria of *La Cenerentola* in Italian, the words translated in her head and touched her heart.

> *No more sighing by the fire*
> *to be singing alone, no!*
> *Ah, it was a streak of lightning, a dream, a game*
> *My long life of fear.*

With a final vocal flourish, she brought the passage to an end. Overcome by emotion, she sank into a deep curtsy. It wasn't until she tried to push herself upright that she realized what a dire mistake she'd made. Her left foot slid, bringing her closer to the ground and throwing her precariously off balance.

How could she have gotten so carried away? Heat scalded her cheeks as she focused her gaze on a spot on the stage floor. Her mind whirled as she tried to figure a way to save a portion of her dignity, the squeal of wood against wood cutting through the air. Miss Clara had pushed back the piano bench and abandoned the instrument. She was at Emily's side in a flash, clapping her hands as she went. One arm slid around Emily's back, and she wrapped the fingers of her other hand around her upper arm. Then the woman leaned her head close so that her mouth was beside Emily's ear.

"I've got you," she murmured. Without appearing to do so, she practically lifted Emily from the floor.

Once Emily could plant her wooden limb against the floor, she nodded to Miss Clara, shifting her weight away to signal that she didn't need any more assistance. Miss Clara nodded back, then stepped aside, presenting Emily with a one-handed flourish. Emily pasted on the smile she knew she was expected to wear onstage. All the while, she fought against the humiliation that covered her like a shroud. None of this would work. No one would want her, awkward and deficient as she was. It had been ridiculous to ever hope.

Taking refuge in the familiarity of discipline, she again clasped her hands at waist level and focused on keeping her breath steady. Chin high, she awaited the verdict.

Another pair of hands began clapping, and footsteps clattered on the stage. "That was extraordinary." Leonard Jerome approached. He extended his hands to Emily, the ends of his bushy walrus mustache shivering with the speed of his movement. "It's been so long since I've heard *bel canto*, you made my heart ache." Indeed, his eyes were slightly red around the edges. He clasped Emily's hands in his and raised them to his lips. "I didn't even realize how much I missed the style. These modern singers aim for volume, but they forget artistry."

He released her and turned to Miss Clara. "When I received your telegram, I knew you wouldn't have contacted me unless you'd come across an exceptional talent." He linked his arm through hers. "The Academy must put on something to showcase her voice." Together they strolled off the stage. His voice drifted back to Emily. "I think Rossini."

Emily couldn't move from the spot. A bubble of disbelief expanded in her chest until it popped, and joy fizzed through her. She hadn't ruined things after all. He wanted her.

Mr. Jerome stopped and peered over his shoulder at her. "Is everything all right, Miss Forbes?"

She grinned. "Wonderful." Moving with as much speed and grace as possible, she caught up with him and Miss Clara.

When she reached his side, Mr. Jerome draped an arm over her shoulder. "My dear, you are going to captivate the city with that voice."

Miss Clara cleared her throat. He glanced at her, then shifted, offering Emily his arm instead. Miss Clara beamed. "Were you thinking *La Cenerentola?* Or perhaps *The Barber of Seville?*"

"No, something special. Something different."

He turned to look at Emily once again, scrutinizing her from head to foot. She shifted her weight uneasily. "There is something fey and sweet about your protégé, don't you think?"

He put a finger under Emily's chin and turned her head this way and that. "She needs something that will show off her voice. But it should also show off this youthful beauty."

Cheeks aflame, Emily pulled back slightly. As flattering as Mr. Jerome was, he made her feel a little like a prize horse on the auction block. Any minute now, she expected him to inspect her teeth.

"Perhaps *La donna del lago?*" Miss Clara said.

Mr. Jerome's eyes sparked. "That's it. That's it." He grasped Emily's hands and raised them to his lips once more. "A romantic masterpiece. You will make a delightful Lady of the Lake."

Miss Clara looked at her over his shoulder and winked. This certainly explained why she'd insisted Emily practice Elena's role from *La donna del lago* incessantly for the last two weeks. The sly thing had orchestrated it perfectly.

Emily didn't try to hide her smile. Mr. Jerome escorted them out through the stage door of the Academy of Music. His coachman pulled up, and Mr. Jerome handed Miss Clara inside. Emily, moving with great caution so as not to repeat her earlier faux pas, shifted her weight to her wooden leg, accepted his hand, and stepped up. She managed the maneuver without mishap.

Now she just had to worry about getting out of the carriage without falling on her face. Or, worse, falling on her new patron.

He hopped in after them, as limber as a man half his age. "Will you ladies join me for a bite of lunch at Delmonico's?"

Emily barely kept a squeak from escaping. Delmonico's. It was only the most sophisticated, fashionable restaurant in New York—in the whole country, for that matter.

"That sounds lovely," Miss Clara said. "It's been years since I've tasted their famous potatoes."

Mr. Jerome's smile lifted the edges of his thick mustache. "Jenny Lind used to eat there after every performance. In fact, every *prima donna* I've ever known has adored Delmonico's. So I know you will enjoy it, as well, Miss Forbes."

Emily's cheeks tingled. All her hard work over the last six years was paying off. She could not wait to write her brother, Carter, and his wife, Juliet. Her whole life was about to change.

⌒

Samuel DeKlerk snapped open his pocket watch. The stubborn hands hadn't budged.

His friend Robert Romijn stood beside him, drink in hand. He made a grunt of disapproval, then nudged him in the ribs with his elbow. "Bad form, Sam."

Sam sighed and tucked the watch out of sight. "I can't help it. These parties are so dull."

Robert pursed his lips in thought. "And what would you do if you weren't here? Hide away in that clinic of yours, I suppose?"

"As a matter of fact, yes. You have no idea how much work is waiting for me."

"You've obviously never seen my desk at the Museum." Robert raised an eyebrow. "The work will still be there in the morning."

"That's what worries me. I think the documentation must breed when I turn my back on it."

"Gentlemen, that is hardly fit conversation for a soiree." Ward McAllister approached them. Sam supposed the man's expression was meant to be both conspiratorial and reprimanding, but the result was that he merely looked spoiled.

Sam managed a weak smile for his mother's sake. She lived in fear of McAllister and his infernal list—*the* list, which dictated who in New York was worth knowing. Left to his own devices, Sam would have offered the pompous old snob a few creative suggestions regarding what he could do with his list. He had no use for society's Four Hundred. Not anymore.

After listening for what seemed an eternity to meaningless posturing, Sam disengaged himself from McAllister's clutches as gently as he could. When he was lost in the crowd, he once again reached for his watch. Surely he had served enough time by now that he could politely withdraw without sullying the DeKlerk honor.

No such luck. The hands of the stubborn watch had marked only twelve minutes since the last time he'd checked them. He raised the device to his ear to make sure it still ticked.

"I'm surprised at you, Doctor. All these lovely young ladies around, and you listening to sweet nothings from your pocket watch."

Feeling the slightest bit guilty, Sam focused on Leonard Jerome. Unlike McAllister, the fellow positively brimmed with bonhomie, making it impossible to take offense. Breaking into a smile, Sam extended a hand. "Jerome, good to see you."

"Likewise, Doctor, likewise. And may I introduce my newest discovery? This is Miss Emily Forbes and her chaperone, Miss Clara Wray."

For the first time, Sam noticed the young lady standing beside and just a bit behind Jerome. She was slight, with hair the color of winter sunlight, framing eyes of toffee brown. Hers was a change-able face, passing from serene elegance to pixie-like cheer the instant she smiled at him and her dimples appeared. He bowed briefly over her extended hand. "Miss Forbes, it's a pleasure."

"Likewise, Doctor..."

"DeKlerk," Jerome supplied. "The good doctor's family is one of the oldest in New York. I'm fairly certain his ancestors were the ones carting in the baubles used to buy Manhattan from the Indians." The fellow prattled on, seemingly oblivious to his guest's reaction.

Miss Forbes had gone pale, her smile dissolving. She stared at Sam so intently, he glanced down at his jacket to see what he had spilled there, but his lapels and shirt front were as clean as when he'd dressed three hours earlier.

"Is something the matter?" Sam ventured, breaking into Jerome's soliloquy.

Miss Forbes blinked. "No, not at all. My—it's just that my brother once worked with a man named Gordon DeKlerk."

"He's my father." Sam was unsure yet if he should continue the conversation or make a run for it. Father had made plenty of ene-mies in business. The last thing Sam wanted was to be harangued by the sister of one of his disgruntled cronies. "Perhaps he would remember your brother?"

"I doubt it. Their encounter was several years ago now." She smiled, and her dimples reappeared, shooting an electric spark right through him. "It's a pleasure to meet you Mr.—I mean, Dr. DeKlerk. I do hope you enjoy the singing."

"Singing? Oh! You're the mezzo-soprano." Feeling like an idiot, he fumbled his invitation from his pocket. "Mademoiselle Forbes, I am greatly looking forward to hearing you."

She still smiled, but one corner of her mouth tilted up, as if she knew he hadn't had the slightest intention of staying to listen but wouldn't hold this fact against him. And suddenly, the desire to leave faded. It wouldn't be so terrible to spend an evening away from the clinic. It would do him good to think of something else for a change. That way, when he did attack his work the next day, he could do so with a clear mind and refreshed spirit.

"Speaking of singing, it's time we allow Miss Forbes the opportunity to dazzle us." Jerome led her away.

Her chaperone—whose name Sam couldn't recall—gave him a polite nod as she passed, but he had a feeling she hadn't missed a single thing about him. He had been fully weighed and measured, and likely found wanting.

While most of the guests jockeyed for seats as part of the never-ending social game, Sam was content to prop himself against the wall between a pillar and a potted plant.

After a mercifully short introduction from Leonard Jerome, the chaperone seated herself at the piano. Jerome held his hand out to Miss Forbes, and she walked to him, arm extended.

They joined hands briefly, then he released her, and she turned to face her audience, her cheeks a becoming pink. The music began, and she closed her eyes for a moment. The familiar introduction of *Une voce poco fa* filled the salon. When Miss Forbes opened her eyes again, it was as if she had transformed into the elated, determined Rosina who had just fallen in love with a man through his serenades.

Sam straightened. The piece was fiendishly difficult, yet she made it sound effortless, like a natural outburst of girlish excitement. The undercurrent of whispered conversation that usually went on during such presentations stopped; all around him, the other guests gave Miss Forbes their undivided attention.

It wasn't just her voice that captivated the audience. It was her presence, something undefined. Sam stared, trying to put his finger on the source of her magic. Someone tapped his shoulder. He scowled and turned sharply away from Miss Forbes.

Robert stood beside him, grinning. "I call first try," he whispered.

Sam summoned his society face and put it on. While he found Miss Forbes intriguing, admitting such would only ensure that Robert would pursue the young woman with extra vigor. "No need to report to me."

His friend smirked. "None at all. But I've noticed that you haven't pulled your watch out for at least ten minutes."

"That's because something finally happened worth paying attention to. She is good."

"Very good." Robert nodded. "I imagine we will not be alone in our pursuit. Old Jerome is looking as wolfish as I've ever seen him."

Sam shook his head. "Don't underestimate that chaperone of hers. She appears to take her job seriously."

"Hm. That could be a problem."

"I'm sure you'll think of a way around it," Sam whispered in a clipped tone, hoping Robert would take the hint and be quiet.

Miss Forbes came to the end of the aria, and the room erupted with applause. She smiled brilliantly, but instead of dropping into the customary curtsy, she bowed. It wasn't much of a bow—more an inclination of her head, a swaying of her torso—but it was unexpected. Sam liked it. She wasn't fluttery with false humility, nor even surprised at the response. She was herself.

She would be worth seeing more of. Even though Sam wasn't accustomed to such fanciful thoughts, he had already decided Robert would not have a clear playing field. Miss Forbes was something special.

Chapter 2

Bow, *don't curtsy.*

Keeping her face professionally pleasant, Emily controlled her enthusiasm and bowed slightly at the waist. She reminded herself that the applause wasn't really for her. Without a masterful score, without a talented musician, without Miss Clara to coax out whatever natural talent God had graced her with, she was nothing.

Her eyes swept the crowd and halted when they came to Dr. DeKlerk, almost hidden by a pillar. She couldn't believe it was really him. It was like meeting a woman with long golden hair and discovering that Rapunzel was real. Perhaps she should have anticipated the possibility of meeting members of such a prominent New York family, but the idea had never crossed her mind. Another man was beside him, whispering something. Dr. DeKlerk scowled at the man, who shot a look at her, then turned back to the doctor and laughed.

Heat ignited in Emily's cheeks. She was certain the other man had mentioned her lack of grace. Somehow, he'd discovered her handicap and was remarking on her deficiencies.

With as much poise as she could muster, she turned to Miss Clara at the piano, raising her hand to direct the applause her way. The next moment, Mr. Jerome was at her side, his hand resting lightly between her shoulder blades, rotating her around to face the audience again.

"It's my pleasure to announce tonight that the Academy of Music will be staging a production of *La donna del lago*, with Miss

Forbes giving voice to Elena. Once she is hailed as a *prima donna assoluta*, you may all boast how you were present at her first New York appearance." He lifted his free hand in the air, encouraging the audience to resume their applause.

Now that the surge of excitement that came with performing was over, Emily felt conspicuous on the stage, like a prize heifer being presented at the state fair. More than anything, she wanted to melt into the crowd and regain a level of anonymity.

As the applause sputtered and died, Emily rested her fingertips at the base of her throat. "I'm terribly parched," she whispered to Mr. Jerome.

"Of course, my dear. I ought to have realized." He offered his arm and ushered her from the small stage and across the room toward the punch bowl.

Their trip was impeded by their hostess, the exquisitely dressed Mrs. Marietta Stevens. "Miss Forbes, I assumed you could sing because Leonard brought you to me, but I must admit that you exceeded my expectations."

"You are very kind, Mrs. Stevens." Emily smiled and inclined her head, acknowledging the lukewarm compliment as graciously as she could. Mr. Jerome had warned her that Marietta Stevens was one of the social arbiters in New York, one whose favor Emily needed to win.

A glitter shone in the older woman's eye. "Not at all. I believe in calling a spade a spade. I do hope you enjoy your stay at the Adelphia." The hotel, which she had inherited from her husband, gave her the ability to prove her patronage of the arts by providing Emily and Miss Clara with a three-room suite. She tapped Emily's arm with her folded fan. "And don't worry, dear; in time, you shall get over your awkwardness."

She swept away, leaving Emily's mouth drier than ever. She would not get over her awkwardness. She was permanently scarred. Permanently not quite good enough. In silence, she allowed Mr.

Jerome to lead her to the refreshments table and pour her a glass of punch.

Miss Clara joined them, a triumphant smile in place. "You've left them all abuzz. They are speaking of the success of the production as if it is *fait accompli*. The only thing left to decide is who shall play Malcolm and King James."

Emily squeezed her hand. The old dear was nothing if not supportive. "Let's not get ahead of ourselves. I'm afraid any minute now I shall wake to find this was all nothing but a lovely dream."

"A dream, yes, but not one you will wake from. Just look around you." Mr. Jerome gestured expansively. "You've won over the cream of New York. Everyone else will fall in step for fear of not being fashionable enough. I was thinking of trying to get Benedetta Lanzieri to play Malcolm. She is wonderful in trouser roles with that rich, full contralto of hers." He paused in mid-flow. "Will you excuse me? I see someone I must speak with."

Emily turned to survey the room and nearly collided with Dr. DeKlerk. Punch sloshed up the side of the glass, but, as it was almost empty, the liquid merely spattered her evening gloves.

"My apologies, Miss Forbes." Red-faced, the doctor took the glass carefully from her and set it on the table. Then he pulled a snowy handkerchief from his pocket and, with the intense concentration of a surgeon performing the most delicate of operations, took her hand in his and dabbed at the spreading stain.

The warmth of his hands, the gentleness of his touch…it was curiously intimate. Emily's palm began to tingle, and a warm flush swept up her arm and spread through her chest.

Dr. DeKlerk glanced up from his self-appointed task, and their eyes met with a clash that jangled Emily's nerves like the crash of cymbals. His eyes were much bluer up close—certainly not the gray she had taken them for originally.

"Dr. DeKlerk, I believe the patient will survive." Miss Clara's sweet voice managed to be congenial and commanding at the same time.

Emily pulled back her hand, feeling a moment of loss as her fingers slid free of his.

"I *am* sorry, Miss Forbes. I have a regrettable tendency to clumsiness."

"Then we have something in common." The tingly warmth in her chest had turned into a blaze and now spread to her cheeks. But she easily found a smile for him.

His responding grin was just as quick. "My friend, here, had asked if I might be able to provide him an introduction."

For the first time, Emily realized that another gentleman stood at his side. The fellow was strikingly handsome, but it was apparent he knew as much. His smirk seemed to expect all and sundry to admire him. It was the same man who had been whispering with the doctor during her performance.

Dr. DeKlerk turned his palm up and waved it between them. "Miss Forbes, may I present Mr. Robert Romijn, one of the curators at the New-York Historical Society. He's on the board of the Academy of Music, as well."

With the mandate to be charming echoing in her mind, Emily inclined her head and extended her hand. "Mr. Romijn, it's a pleasure."

Despite her first impression, he took her hand gently in his and held it neither too long nor too short.

A wide grin on his face, Dr. DeKlerk nudged his friend in the ribs with his elbow. "Like me, Robert's descended from some of the original Dutch settlers. So, though his name sounds like 'ro-mine,' it's spelled r-o-m-i-j-n." By the end of this overly jovial inanity, the doctor's cheeks had grown a dull red.

"Well." Emily raised both eyebrows in what she hoped was a fascinated look. "That's certainly interesting. I've heard very nice things about your museum."

Mr. Romijn was slightly more suave. "I'm glad to hear you say so. I hope you will do me the honor of allowing me to give you a tour sometime. We are a first-rate institution, no matter what John Jay and his cronies may imply."

Emily had no idea who John Jay was. Her gaze slid to Dr. DeKlerk's again for an explanation. But the doctor remained silent, staring miserably at the punch-stained handkerchief he held in his hand.

Romijn stepped in, having apparently realized she was at a loss. "I'm sorry. A bit of a *bête noire* for me. One of New York's legal luminaries has gathered a band of well-intentioned but misguided folk to help him start another museum in the city."

"I see."

"I keep telling you, there's no need to be so defensive." Dr. DeKlerk's tone made it sound as if they'd had this particular discussion many times before, and he'd long ago grown tired of it. "Whatever they do won't cause the end of the Historical Society."

"You had better believe it won't. The Society is a venerable institution with an impeccable pedigree. These upstart parvenus haven't a chance of displacing us." Judging by the whiteness of his knuckles as he clutched his punch glass in a strangle hold, the subject evidently meant a great deal to him.

A fashionable young woman, in a dress of cream silk decorated with swags of fruit created from gorgeously vibrant velvet, passed nearby and fluttered her fan in their direction. Emily stared after her, and so did the gentlemen. Not that she could blame them. The girl was lovely, with the lush, pink-cheeked, blue-eyed beauty that men seemed to adore. There was power, and the knowledge of that power, in the sway of her hips and the set of her chin.

Mr. Romijn broke off in mid-sentence and, muttering something vague, excused himself.

"He seems...passionate about his work." Emily tried to remain politic.

Dr. DeKlerk shook his head. "You have no idea." Then he too excused himself.

Emily tried not to feel slighted. She hadn't come to New York to find a beau. In fact, she had given up thoughts of beaus long ago. She was here to pursue her dream. This little encounter had been a perfect reminder of that fact. It was a warning that she needed to guard against distractions.

"You seemed quite taken with the good doctor." Miss Clara raised her punch glass to her lips and gave Emily a significant glance over the rim.

Emily put a spin on the significance and volleyed it back. "Dr. DeKlerk is the son of Gordon DeKlerk. That means Sarah DeKlerk must have been his sister."

Clara frowned, and then understanding widened her eyes. "That poor girl who was murdered?"

"Yes." Emily glanced around to make sure no one was eavesdropping, though the tragedy was hardly likely to be news to these people. "It was Carter's case. The one he was never able to solve, because he was pulled into war work and other duties."

Clara shook her head. "You stop right there. I can see the wheels in your head turning. Nothing good can come of raking up some old tragedy. And besides that"—her voice dropped to a hiss—"the murderer was never caught. He's still out there somewhere and wouldn't look kindly on any closet skeletons being rattled."

"I know." Emily had spent enough time with her Pinkerton brother to know the hazards involved in tracking down a criminal. Still, the idea of looking into Sarah's murder and helping Carter wrap up his one unsolved case held great appeal. After all, whoever the killer was, he had to have known Sarah to get close to her. It would make sense for the culprit to have run in the same social circles back then, and he probably still did.

Miss Clara pulled her shoulders back, prepared to bring out the big guns. "You've got enough on your plate trying to become a

prima donna. You don't need any distractions. Especially dangerous ones."

"I know," Emily repeated. "It's not as though I'm a Pinkerton
who's going to start an official investigation and line up suspects."

Miss Clara was right—she didn't have the resources or the
time to investigate. But there was nothing to stop her from poking
around a little as she went about her business in the city. What
harm could there be in asking a few discreet questions here and
there? And wouldn't Carter be proud if she uncovered a clue for
him? The case had nagged at him like an infected tooth for years.
With a nudge in the right direction, perhaps he could solve it once
and for all.

In a way, family duty compelled her to look into the case. It
would be negligent of her *not* to ask questions. But she'd be so careful, there couldn't possibly be any danger.

Minutes later, Emily paused outside the police station and
looked both ways. Gaslights illumined the street and had made
it easy for her to find her way the three blocks from Mrs. Stevens'
home to this place she had spied on their journey to the soiree.
Once the idea of investigating had taken root, she'd decided she
needed a place to start, and what would be better to begin with
than the police report of the murder?

She looked back the way she had come once again and then
hurried inside. If Miss Clara hadn't been so disapproving, she
would have brought her along; but, as it was, she had decided to
come alone.

Inside, a burly officer stood at a high desk. Emily approached,
but he didn't look up. She cleared her throat.

"Yes?" He looked over her gown. "Robbed or here to bail
someone out?"

"Excuse me?"

"Were you robbed, or are you here to bail someone out?" He
enunciated each word as if she were a simpleton.

"Neither. I'd like to obtain a copy of a police report."

Once again his eyes swept her frame. "Sorry. Not gonna happen."

Emily thought she knew where she'd gone wrong. "I should have clarified. The case is closed. It has been for ten years."

"Still not gonna happen."

"But it's a public record, isn't it?"

"There's public, and there's public, miss. Ain't nobody gonna give you one of our reports. And you ain't got no business askin'."

Emily bit the inside of her cheek, then drew in a calming breath. "I'd like to speak to your superior."

"I'm as superior as you're gonna get tonight." His grin held no humor. "Now, scat before I have you thrown in the clink with all the other tarts what ought to be home abed this time o' night."

Grinding her teeth, Emily turned, swept from the room, and began the walk back to the party. Hopefully she'd get back before anyone had even missed her. As she walked, she considered her options. There had to be another way to get a peek at the report. And even if there wasn't, she was not going to be dissuaded by a little setback. She'd just have to come up with a new approach.

Chapter 3

Forbes. The name was so familiar, but why?

If only Robert hadn't pulled him away when he did, he could have continued his talk with Miss Forbes. But every time he tried to approach her, she was surrounded by effusive social climbers hoping to attach themselves to a possible rising star. When Sam finally left the soiree, he was still trying to place the name.

The mystery nagged at him as he walked down Madison Avenue toward home. With his hands deep in the pockets of his overcoat, Sam hunched his shoulders against the brisk evening air. His posture might seem passive, but he kept his head high, taking in his surroundings and making eye contact with the other pedestrians as they passed. He had learned the importance of never letting one's guard down during his time as a battlefield surgeon. Even though he had spent endless hours bent over the wounded, digging minie balls from bloody flesh and amputating limbs too mangled to save, he had always been aware of what was going on around him, and who was doing it. Those had been uncertain times. But there were areas in New York that weren't much safer.

When he reached the clinic, he unlocked the front door and stepped quickly into the foyer. As he fastened the door latch, he considered his choices. To his left was the entrance to his office, where the ever-present mountain of medical documents awaited him. And up the stairs was the solitude and peace of home. There was nothing difficult about the decision.

Sam trudged up the stairs, and with each footfall, the question played over and over in his head.

Forbes....

Forbes....

Forbes....

Why did he know that name?

Once inside his apartment, he shrugged out of his coat and hung it on a hook by the door. Everything in the small, two-room space was designed for function and efficiency. His parents never could understand why, with all the family money, he would choose to live such a Spartan life. But Sam couldn't justify spending money on frivolities when there were so many important things it could be used for instead.

Squeezing past the tall bookcase that took up half of the short hallway, he brushed his fingers across a daguerreotype of a young woman with a serene smile. His sister would have understood. She had enjoyed the finer things, but she'd also known what truly mattered in life. Sarah had cared little about society's rank and file. She'd been more interested in the character of those around her. Until her death—

Sam froze in his tracks. That was why he knew the name Forbes. He was that incompetent Pinkerton agent in charge of the investigation. The man who'd never been able to catch up to her murderer.

And Emily Forbes was his sister.

The realization left a sour taste on his tongue. He had no interest in any member of the Forbes family, not even one who had the voice of an angel and a smile to match. Robert had called first try, and Robert could very well have her. In fact, if Robert hadn't insisted he attend the gathering at the Stevens Mansion, Sam wouldn't even have met her. He was a doctor, a man of science. He had no time for trifles like the opera.

He pulled open the cupboard where he stored his food. After placing a hunk of bread and a piece of cheese on a plate, he took the meager meal downstairs to his office. There was work to do. That would put all thoughts of the Forbes family out of his mind.

⌒

Emily was exhausted by the time she and Miss Clara returned to their hotel. As she climbed carefully out of the vehicle, she managed to smile and thank the driver. It had been kind of Mr. Jerome to send them home in his carriage, and she wanted to make sure her appreciation was known.

"Come, dear." Miss Clara linked arms with her. "It's been a long day. That bed will feel mighty good."

Emily put her hand atop Miss Clara's arm as they entered the hotel. Anyone observing them would believe she was helping her aged friend, but the truth was entirely different. Miss Clara was a stabilizing force, assisting Emily to make her way with a minimum of difficulty.

And it was indeed difficult. Unaccustomed to standing for such long periods of time, the stump of her leg felt raw where the padding had rubbed away and it rested against the wood of the prosthetic limb. A nice, long soak in warm Epsom salts, followed by an application of liniment, would help. But Emily knew from experience that it wouldn't eradicate the pain. Only time would do that.

"Here we are." Miss Clara fished the key out of her purse and opened the door. "What a blessing that Mrs. Stevens procured a ground-floor room for us. I would hate to face a staircase every evening."

Emily smiled her agreement. She appreciated the woman's attempts to make her feel normal. There were times when it even worked, but tonight was not one of those times.

Miss Clara frowned as Emily limped past her into the room. "You should have said something if you were in pain."

"And interrupt the gaiety of the evening?" Emily waved dismissively as she collapsed on a settee. What she truly yearned for was the soft comfort of the bed, but it was in the other room, and she couldn't go another step.

Kneeling in front of her, Miss Clara took hold of the hem of Emily's dress. Heat flamed in her cheeks, but Miss Clara had helped her before, and right now, Emily was too tired to argue.

Miss Clara pushed up the pale blue silk skirt and layer upon layer of muslin petticoats. As Emily's intricate appliance came into view, a gasp escaped Miss Clara's lips.

"Merciful heavens, child. You're bleeding."

"What?" Emily tried to sit up and look, but the crinoline beneath her back left her feeling as graceless as an upside-down turtle.

"Lie back and relax. Don't move." Miss Clara wagged a warning finger before getting to her feet and hurrying away. She came back a moment later with the water basin and a towel.

"Please, Miss Clara, I can take care of it myself. You shouldn't—"

"I shouldn't what? I shouldn't help a friend in need?"

There was no arguing with that line of reasoning. Miss Clara knelt back down beside the settee, and Emily closed her eyes against the pain she knew was coming.

"You know, this reminds me of the story in the Bible when Jesus washed the feet of the disciples." Miss Clara chattered away as she tended to Emily. "Not that I consider myself equal to our Lord. Gracious, no. But I like to think of following His example."

It was Miss Clara's sweet but ineffective attempt to distract Emily as she unbuckled the leather straps on the appliance and pulled it away. A ring of fire encircled the skin just below her knee where the edges of the prosthetic had dug in. Jaw clenched, Emily hissed in a breath between her teeth. There was always a level of pain when the device came off, but it hadn't been this bad in a very long time.

She opened her eyes and once more attempted to get a glimpse, but the heap of material from her skirt and crinoline completely blocked her view. "How does it look?"

"Hold on, dear one." Miss Clara dipped one end of the towel into the water and gently dabbed at Emily's stump. "It doesn't look good. The skin is rubbed raw in several places and broken in two others." She touched the towel to the place that hurt the most, just below the knee.

Emily groaned. The only way to let her injuries heal would be to keep the prosthetic off. But she couldn't very well do that. She had an opera to prepare for—the next step in becoming a *prima donna assoluta*. It would never happen if she had only one good leg to stand on.

Miss Clara wrapped the towel around the stub of her leg and then stood. "You stay right here. When I get back, I'll help you out of your crinoline and into bed."

Emily pushed up on one elbow. "Where are you going?"

"To ask the concierge to send for a doctor."

"But—"

"No arguments, if you please. Your brother entrusted you to my care, and I will not endure his wrath if he discovers that you were injured and I stood by and did nothing."

Without another word, Miss Clara whisked out the door. Despite the situation, Emily smiled. Carter's wrath, indeed. Her brother was a kindhearted, even-tempered man, which Miss Clara very well knew. Just as Emily well knew that, even though she had no desire to be examined by a doctor, it was probably the best thing.

Her leg throbbed, the pain traveling past her knee and up her thigh. She had to think about something else.

Her mind went again to Carter, and from there she thought once more of Dr. DeKlerk. He seemed intensely serious. Surely it would help him, too, if she could discover who had murdered his sister. She began dredging up events in her memory, searching to recall everything Carter had ever mentioned about Sarah DeKlerk's murder and about how he had conducted the investigation.

The first thing she should do was try to understand the people she would be dealing with—their pasts, their problems, their prospects. From there…well, from there, she'd have another idea about how to proceed.

Chapter 4

Sam rubbed bleary eyes. He'd fallen asleep at his desk once again. He straightened his back, stretching out the stiff muscles. The thought of his bed beckoned. He would strip off his sweat-stained clothes and stretch out with the window open. It wouldn't be cool, exactly, but it would be cooler than he was now.

A knock sounded at his door. He let his head fall back and stared at the ceiling. Why him? Why now? Come to think of it, it might have been a knock that had woken him.

Scratching his back, he tromped down the stairs and cracked open the door. "What?"

A pimply-faced lad in hotel livery a size and a half too large for him raised his lantern and tilted his head, as if trying to gauge whether the door had been opened by a man or a troll.

Sam opened the door another inch and cocked his eyebrow.

"Oh. Uh, sorry, sir. Are you Dr. DeKlerk?"

Sam just barely kept himself from asking the young man who else might be answering the medical clinic door at this time of the night. "Perhaps. What do you want?"

"We've got a guest who needs a doctor, sir." The boy swallowed, his overlarge Adam's apple bobbing up hard against his collar. "That is, at the Adelphia, sir. They asked for someone with experience tending to amputees."

Sam started to shut the door. "Check with Dr. Harris."

"Already did, sir." The lad sounded desperate. "He told me to check with you."

"Perkins?"

The boy nodded. "Him, too."

Sam murmured a prayer for strength as he scrubbed a hand across his face. "Give me a moment."

The boy perked up. "Yes, sir!" He looked awfully small against the black of the street.

With a growl, Sam swung the door open wider. "You might as well wait in here."

"Thank you, sir."

Sam gathered his medical bag and reached for his frock coat. He was tempted to leave it behind and pretend he'd forgotten it in his haste, but it would hardly be professional. And someone staying at the Adelphia should have money—money he might be willing to part with, for a good cause. A good cause, such as a clinic operated by a doctor to whom he was grateful.

Spirits buoyed by the thought, Sam was only slightly cranky as he allowed the boy to lead the way with the lantern held high.

The oppressive humidity felt electric, threatening a storm. Not the kind that would rinse away the stink of the city and cool tempers, but the flash and bang of a heat lightning storm. All of New York seemed on edge, waiting for the show to start. Shadowy figures moved just beyond the periphery of the lantern. The fine hairs on the back of Sam's neck rose, and he stayed alert. He'd had more than one tussle with would-be thieves when he was on a late-night house call. He reached inside his jacket pocket and touched the butt of his pistol. He'd learned it was best to be prepared for all eventualities.

He was relieved to arrive at the hotel. The concierge managed to greet Sam warmly while implying that the bellboy was going to get it for having taken so long about his errand. The lad sighed.

Unaccountably protective, Sam returned the concierge's handshake. "I wouldn't have come at all, except that this young man was most persuasive. I understand he had been turned down by two other physicians and he wasn't going to accept the same answer from me."

His efforts were rewarded with a nod from the fellow and an appraising look for the boy. Then a bell rang on the wall behind him and they were dismissed.

The bellboy motioned for Sam to continue following him. "The lady said to come on in, because she wasn't sure she would hear, and of course the other one can't get up to answer the door." The boy gave a cursory knock, then ushered Sam into a guest suite. The gaslights in the sitting room had been turned low. A slight figure in a frilled dressing gown sat on a settee, head resting against the back.

He hadn't expected his patient to be a woman. The idea hadn't even crossed his mind. As he was trying to adjust to this new circumstance, the lady stirred, and her face caught the light. Sam stopped in his tracks. It had to be some sort of wicked trick.

⌒

Emily's eyes were gritty with sleep, though she could only have dozed for a moment or two. Ignoring the burning that encircled her leg, she glanced down hastily to ensure she was decently covered as the concierge ushered in the doctor. An instant later, Miss Clara entered from the bedroom with a dampened washcloth in her hand.

"Let's put this on to help with the—why, Dr. DeKlerk, what a pleasure to see you again. And so much sooner than anticipated."

At the sound of his name, Emily's head jerked up. *It can't be.*

And yet it was. He stood just inside the door, scowling as if he'd been offered rancid meat.

Heat seared Emily's cheeks and stung her eyes. She must repulse him, for him to look at her like that. Her chest ached suddenly with the effort of breathing. But she would not cry. Absolutely would not.

"I'm here to treat a patient." He sounded stiff as iron and twice as cold.

Miss Clara glanced from Emily to Dr. DeKlerk and back again. "Yes. Miss Forbes is your patient."

"But I was told I would be attending an amputee."

Once again, Miss Clara glanced at Emily, her eyes warm with sympathy. She spoke softly. "Yes."

Emily wanted to strike her. If it hadn't been for her insistence on sending for a doctor, none of this would have happened. Emily couldn't even flee his terrible scrutiny. She was trapped.

Dr. DeKlerk remained in the doorway for an interminable moment. Emily could no longer bring herself to look at his face. Instead she glared at Miss Clara's back as the woman excused the bellboy and handed him a handsome tip.

With the boy's departure, Dr. DeKlerk seemed to wake from a dream. He squared his shoulders and entered the room.

"Madam Wray, perhaps you can tell me what the problem is?"

"She was on her feet too long today, I fear."

"I can speak for myself." Emily regretted the waspish words as soon as they had stung their way out of her mouth. Now she would have to talk to him. And not just talk, but talk about her deformity. This could not get worse.

He made no remark on her tone. "Of course. My apologies." He approached and took a seat on the ottoman, setting his medical bag on the floor beside him and opening it with a practiced motion. "May I see the wound?"

She had been completely and utterly wrong. It could get worse. A great deal worse. He would see her leg, or what was left of it, up close. Before, he had only been able to guess about her disfigurement, but now he would be intimately acquainted with it. She didn't know what to do.

Miss Clara was no help. She hovered at his shoulder. "Should I have her lie down?"

The doctor's gaze scoured Emily's face, but she refused to allow him to catch her eye. He gave a wan smile. "I don't think that's necessary."

Emily stared fixedly at the mantel.

"Miss Forbes?"

She remained paralyzed by indecision.

His voice gentled. "Miss Forbes, please allow me to help you. It's the only reason I came out in the middle of the night."

Her chin began to tremble. She could fortify herself against his disdain, but not his kindness. Fingernails digging into her palms, she fought for composure.

"If you wish to be at your best for rehearsals, you must have your leg tended to." Miss Clara's words cut through the fog of her distress.

That was the life preserver she needed. She could focus on that and not the moment. Sucking in a deep breath, Emily raised the hem of her nightdress and dressing gown. Taking care to keep her whole leg covered, she revealed the angry red of her injured stump.

As if he knew what the gesture had cost her, Dr. DeKlerk stopped trying to pin her gaze and turned his attention to her limb. "Thank you, Miss Forbes." His words were so soft, she might have missed them, had there been any other sound in the room. Louder, he said, "Can you flex and extend the knee?"

She did so.

"Good. Madam Wray, might we get a little more light?"

Miss Clara hurried to turn up the gaslights. Another sort of privacy ripped away.

He scrutinized the area carefully, then grasped her knee in strong but gentle hands. "Hmm. A bit warmer than I'd like, but this weather means that everything is warmer than I'd like."

She could not manage a smile for the weak witticism. But he didn't seem to notice. In fact, he seemed to be speaking more to himself than anyone else.

"Does it feel swollen to you?" he asked.

"Just the end."

"Does it cause you pain for me to hold it?"

"Only if you touch one of the wounds."

He nodded and released her. "Very good. There doesn't appear to be any infection, which is good news."

"Thank heavens." Miss Clara was vehement.

"My advice would be to stay off your feet for the next week or so."

Emily's shoulder muscles tightened. "That isn't possible."

He shook his head. "Somehow I thought you'd say that." He bent to rummage in his medical bag and then pulled out a jar. He opened it and scooped out some sort of cream.

Emily wrinkled her nose at the awful smell. "What is that?"

"A kind of salve that will help speed the healing." He applied it to her leg, and the sudden coolness made her shiver. Next, he pulled a length of bandage from his bag and expertly wrapped the wound.

"Whatever padding you were using in the prosthetic should be replaced. Sheepskin covered in silk is the best. Use clean ones every day, and when they get worn, discard them and buy new ones. It will help to prevent a recurrence."

Miss Clara jerked her head up and down in agreement. "Is there anything further, Doctor?"

He handed the jar of salve to Miss Clara and snapped his bag shut. "Just that I repeat my advice for her to stay off her feet as much as possible."

Now that his job was done, it seemed he could hardly wait to depart.

Miss Clara walked him to the door. "What do we owe you for the call?"

"No charge." He nearly bit the words off, he said them so quickly.

"But—"

A perfunctory smile tipped up the corners of his mouth, and then he was gone before Emily could manage a thank-you. Assuming, of course, that she would have tried a thank-you.

Miss Clara closed the door behind him, and before she had time to turn back, Emily's rage and humiliation bubbled over and spewed in her direction. "How could you let them bring him?"

"I simply requested a doctor," she said with a frown. "How was I to know the boy would fetch Dr. DeKlerk?"

The reasonableness of this statement did nothing to assuage Emily's fury. She fumbled for her crutches, which were tucked beneath the settee. Miss Clara stepped forward to help, but Emily rose on her good leg and swung herself out of the room without acknowledging her.

How could she ever look Dr. DeKlerk in the face again?

She dropped onto her bed and let the crutch thud against the wall. She rubbed her eyes. She would prove to him that the look of repugnance he had given her was unjustified. Her body might be maimed, but there wasn't a thing wrong with her mind. If she could find his sister's murderer, or even just pick up a new lead in the investigation, maybe he'd forget what he'd seen. At the very least, the memory would fade. It was a long shot, but it couldn't hurt.

Chapter 5

Emily groaned and smacked the alarm clock by her bed, cutting off the jangling clatter of the bell.

It was official. She was no debutante. Those young ladies were able to sleep in after late-night parties. Then again, they had much less interesting things to do. Emily sat up and stretched. Last night had certainly been interesting. And, more than interesting, it had been productive. One of the gentlemen she'd been introduced to was Charles Prescott, the newspaper mogul. And that had given her an idea.

Despite her determination to dig into Sarah's case, Emily had a problem: She simply didn't know enough about the players in this drama. She needed to acquaint herself with everyone and everything associated with the murder. If anyone could help her with that, it was Mr. Prescott. Or, if not him, his newspaper.

She reached for her artificial leg and a fresh piece of padding and silk. One look at her still-swollen stump made her hesitate and grit her teeth against the thought of the pain that would come from strapping on the wooden leg. She sighed. There was no use for it. As much as she wanted to leave it behind, she couldn't manage going about New York without it. The crutches just wouldn't suffice. Decision made, she dressed hurriedly and didn't bother to ring for breakfast. There was no time. At the suite door, she paused and looked back over her shoulder.

Her hastily scrawled note to Miss Clara sat propped on the mantel, where it could not possibly be missed. She nodded once, then opened the door. Miss Clara would be spitting mad that she'd ventured alone into the wilds of New York City, but she would recover.

The doorman hailed a hansom for her, and almost before she knew it, she was on her way. The drive to the offices of *The Examiner* wasn't far, and as the horse trotted along, Emily lifted her face to catch what little freshness was to be had in the city air this time of year.

At the corner, an oysterman with his cart was already doing brisk trade with office workers headed to their places of business. A newsboy with papers held high called out the day's headlines in hopes of attracting customers. An omnibus packed tight with morning commuters pulled close beside Emily's cab, and a bowler-hatted fellow with a whip-thin mustache that drooped at the ends waggled his eyebrows at Emily. She rolled her eyes in response and looked away.

She had considered taking an omnibus in order to save money but had elected not to because she wasn't familiar with the system and didn't want to end up in the wrong place. Now she was glad to have her judgment reinforced in that regard, at least.

The newspaper was housed in an impressive limestone-faced building replete with architectural flourishes of swags and lions' heads and other embellishments she didn't know the names of.

Inside, a man at an imposingly tall desk squinted through his spectacles at her as she approached. "May I help you, miss?"

"I'm here to see Mr. Prescott."

"I'm afraid he's not in yet. Do you care to wait?" He gestured to a row of stiff, anemic-looking chairs lining one wall of the long foyer. All but two of them were already occupied by men who wore expressions of varying degrees of boredom.

Emily smiled, thankful she had another option. "In that case, he told me to ask for Hiram Davis."

The man appraised her anew. "Certainly." He snapped arthritic fingers at a group of boys outfitted in green jackets. "George, take this young lady up to see Mr. Davis. Smartly, now."

One of the lads hopped to attention and tipped his cap. "Yessir." He directed a broad smile at Emily. "This way, miss."

Emily followed him up a marble staircase that swept upwards with a kind of urgency. It was slow going, but she managed to keep from wincing much. The boy stopped at the third floor and led the way down a long hall lined with doors inset with opaque glass windows that bore stenciled names and mystifying titles: *Copy Editor. Sub Editor. Copy Sub Editor.* The last door on the right was labeled merely *Editor.*

George tapped on the door, then poked his head in without waiting for a response. "Lady to see you, Mr. Davis."

"Who is it?" a querulous voice demanded.

George looked back at Emily.

"Emily Forbes. Mr. Prescott sent me."

"Emily Forbes. Mr. Prescott sent her."

There was a heavy sigh. "Send her in."

George held the door open wide and ushered her through, but she stopped on the threshold. The office looked as if it had suffered an avalanche of paper. It was on the tip of her tongue to ask if there had been any survivors. But the gentleman presiding over the chaos had the pinched appearance of a man with too many things to do and a lack of appreciation for all things humorous. How did he manage to work for the jovial Mr. Prescott?

Mr. Davis stood grudgingly. "What can I do for you, Miss Forbes?"

"I was hoping to look at some old issues of the paper. Mr. Prescott said that you keep copies of everything you print."

"How old?"

"Ten years or more."

His face lightened. "George, take her down to the archives and help her find whatever she wants. Make sure you put it all back when she's done."

"Yessir." George clicked his heels together and appeared to stop himself just short of saluting.

Now that his unexpected visitor was no longer his responsibility, Mr. Davis sat back down with a relieved air.

Emily retreated from the office, more than happy to have the company of cheerful George rather than the dour Davis. She only wished she'd known the archives were on the lower level before she trudged up three floors of stairs.

George led her down and down and down again, into the building's basement. The grandeur of the public floors gave way to the grubbiness of realms occupied only by those lowest on the paper's totem pole.

Finally she was introduced to a small room with a table in the center. Tall arrow windows set high in the wall let in light that was filtered through a coat of grime. She could make out the ankles of passersby as they hurried along the street outside.

George lit a couple of lamps. "What do you need, miss? Just tell me, and I'll go fetch it."

"Society pages, starting...." She pursed her lips. "Let's start fifteen years ago."

"All right, Miss Forbes. I'll be right back."

Emily set her handbag on the desk and tried not to fidget. It was highly doubtful she'd solve the mystery by looking at old newspaper articles, but it would give her some context for understanding all these people and how they related to one another.

A little chill of apprehension swirled in her stomach. If Sarah's murderer had been one of the people she knew, that person had been going around doing perfectly ordinary things for the last ten years, with no one the wiser. Emily could be reading about him and wouldn't even know it. How would she ever narrow things down? And what would happen if she did?

An hour and a half after she'd begun her research, Emily emerged from the bowels of the newspaper office and blinked against the bright sun as she made her way to the hansom cab stand. Her eyes were gritty, and her mouth felt as though it were stuffed with cotton. Still, her mission had been a success. She now had a much better understanding of Sarah DeKlerk and the circumstances surrounding her death.

"Cab, miss?"

Emily had been so deep in thought, she hadn't realized she'd reached the front of the line of cabs. Before she could answer, the driver jumped down and held the door open.

"Thank you." Grimacing at the croak of her voice, she stepped up and settled herself on the worn leather seat. She was going to need a nice cup of hot honeyed tea before attempting to sing a note.

"Where to?" The driver had one hand on the door.

"The Academy of Music, please."

The fellow swung the door shut, then jumped into the driver's seat. With a cluck to the horse and a slap of the reins, the cab jerked forward and swerved into traffic. Emily clutched her purse tightly in her lap. There had been so much information to dig through, she'd been afraid she would forget the important bits, so she'd taken notes with a pencil and paper provided by the pleasantly helpful George. Now those sheets were carefully tucked away until she could spend more time going over them.

As the cab rolled on through the congested street, Emily's mind mulled over the facts that were impossible to forget. Sarah DeKlerk had been quite the debutante. There hadn't been a single article about the events of that season in which she wasn't prominently featured. From what Carter had said about the young woman, Emily suspected the mother had been the driving force behind Sarah's partygoing. Nevertheless, Sarah had been firmly ensconced in society's upper crust. So it was no surprise that her murder had been covered in great detail.

Emily tapped her finger against her pursed lips. What did surprise her was to find out that Sarah had been engaged, and to none other than Dr. DeKlerk's friend, Robert Romijn. According to Carter, Sarah had been in love with the gardener and planned to elope with him the night she was killed. It hadn't occurred to Emily that Sarah might have had a fiancé. What if he'd found out about her plans that night? Emily had spoken only briefly with Mr. Romijn, but he didn't seem the sort who would resort to violence. Still, there was no telling what a man would do if his affections were spurned, especially if he felt the fool.

Another person who popped up quite a bit in the society sections was Alice Geddes. From what Emily could tell, it seemed she was a close friend of Sarah's. If that were true, Miss Geddes would undoubtedly be a treasure trove of information about Sarah and the circumstances surrounding her murder. Emily would have to look her up.

When it came to the investigation itself, the majority of the journalistic fingers pointed in one direction: at the gardener, Grant Diamond. There had been no witnesses to the crime, making all the evidence in the case circumstantial. One reporter, Jamison Parker, had gone so far as to report on Mr. Diamond's difficult childhood, as if the fact that he was an orphan who'd been raised by nuns made him not only capable of murder but peculiarly fit for it.

The hansom cab jerked to a stop, pulling Emily from her thoughts. She clutched the edge of the seat to keep from sliding off. The driver hopped down, opened the door, and assisted her out. After paying the fare, Emily moved as quickly as her injured leg would allow, going around the building to the stage entrance. She hadn't meant to, but she'd spent far too much time at the newspaper office. Hopefully, Miss Clara was in a good mood.

That hope was dashed as soon as Emily entered her assigned dressing room. In a chair directly opposite the door sat Miss Clara, arms folded over her chest, back straight as a fire poker, and cheeks red as glowing embers. When she spotted Emily, she sprang from the chair. Emily opened her mouth to explain, but it became clear that she would first have to do the listening.

"What in the world possessed you to venture out into the city on your own?" Miss Clara's fingers gripped Emily's upper arm and pulled her into the room. "A young lady like you has no business traipsing around New York without a chaperone."

Emily came to a sudden halt, nearly jerking Miss Clara off her feet. "A lady like me? You mean, a cripple who isn't fit to care for herself?"

Miss Clara huffed out a breath in frustration. "No, a lovely, innocent young lady, who is the perfect target for any number of the scalawags and flimflams who roam the streets."

"Oh." Emily chided herself for being so sensitive. "I'm sorry."

"You should be." Miss Clara tugged on her arm and got her settled on the small settee. "And you should have spent the morning preparing for a long day of singing, instead of…." For the first time, Miss Clara took a good look at Emily's face and the bodice of her dress, both of which undoubtedly held their share of dust and newsprint ink. "Heavens, you look a fright. What have you been doing?"

Emily bit down on her lip. Once again, she had acted without thinking the situation through. It would be easy enough admitting to having gone to the newspaper office, but then she would have to explain why. If Miss Clara was unhappy about Emily's trip through the city, she would be apoplectic at the discovery that Emily was investigating a murder. Best to tell the literal truth. "I went to the newspaper office. I was trying to learn about some of the New York society families. It will help me know how to interact with them." She smiled and pulled off her ruined gloves. "Wouldn't it be better to do a little research in advance rather than commit some faux pas?"

Miss Clara gave her a long, calculating look. "And why would you need to sneak out at the crack of dawn for that?"

"If I had meant to sneak out, I wouldn't have left a note telling you I'd gone and would meet you here."

Miss Clara looked skeptical but seemed willing to forgo the pleasure of further reproaches. "Promise me you won't do it again."

Emily raised her hand and solemnly promised not to run off again and leave a note. Her conscience twinged a little. She knew Miss Clara thought her promise was not to venture into the city alone.

"Now sit and let me take a look at that leg. I can only imagine how it's faring." Miss Clara reached for the jar of salve. "And you'll gargle with throat spray. You sound dreadful."

Emily sighed as she lifted the hem of her skirt. It promised to be a long, tiring day.

Chapter 6

Trudging up the street, Sam tried to shake off the wretched despair of Five Points, but hopelessness clung to him, its bony fingers refusing to loosen their grip. Mr. Dickens had written about the slum, declaring that "all that is loathsome, drooping, and decayed is here." Sam was of the opinion that Mr. Dickens had been entirely too kind.

His friends thought him mad for venturing into the gang-controlled neighborhood. In truth, there were times he doubted his own sanity. But Five Points was home to more than criminals and ruffians. There were women and children there, scraping to survive. And there were soldiers, too—men who gave all for their country, only to return home and find nothing left of the life they used to know, or the men they used to be. Sam would prefer to treat them in his clinic, but they wouldn't come. Pride or fear, or a combination of both, kept them away. So he went to them, once, sometimes two times, a week.

It was never pleasant, but today was particularly disheartening. He'd tended the usual assortment of patients, repeating his entreaties to keep wounds clean and to take the medicine he gave them rather than sell it. By the time he'd set the broken arm of the last woman, who claimed to have tripped and fallen but whose bruises and scars told another story, he was mentally and physically exhausted.

With every step he took, he turned his thoughts toward home. He lived a meager existence compared to that of his parents, but it was by his own choice. And even though his apartment was small, it was warm, dry, and clean—conditions that simply didn't exist in Five Points.

Sam walked past a dilapidated structure that looked more like a jumble of rotting wood than a house. A figure darted out of the shadows and stopped directly in his path. The man's clothes were soiled, his hair was matted, and, from the smell of him, it was doubtful he had more than a passing acquaintance with soap.

Sam's breath caught in his chest, but he forced himself not to show fear. Shoulders back, he looked the man in the eye. "May I help you, sir?"

"You the doctor?" When he spoke, he revealed the absence of several teeth.

"I am." Sam's fingers tightened around the handle of his black leather bag.

"I need ya to tend my mate."

If this had been a robbery attempt, Sam would have stood his ground. But he couldn't refuse treatment to the ill and injured. "What's the nature of his problem?"

The man shook his head, eyes darting from side to side. "He's bleedin'. Bad."

No doubt the result of a gang war, judging from the man's reticence to share details. What was Sam walking into? "Lead the way."

The man turned back toward where he'd come from, and Sam followed him through a narrow passage between the buildings. It led to a labyrinth of makeshift shanties and lean-tos. The smell of refuse and excrement assaulted his nostrils. He turned his head, as though he might be able to find a pocket of clean air. Instead, he saw two bone-thin children squatting down in the dirt, playing with what looked like a tiny cat. Only, it wasn't a cat. It was a large rat. Sam's stomach clenched. No human should live in such squalor, let alone a child.

The man stopped in front of a three-sided structure with a holey blanket serving as both roof and door. He pulled back the blanket and pointed inside. "This here's your patient."

It was worse than he'd imagined. "He's only a boy."

"Aye." The man's voice cracked with unexpected emotion. But when he looked at Sam, his eyes were hard, displaying no weakness.

Crouching low, Sam moved into the narrow space where the boy lay. Now, he saw a woman kneeling there, too, her back against the wall. The piece of cloth she held against the side of the youngster's head was soaked with blood that had seeped onto her fingers. Blood also smeared the bodice of her dress and the side of her face, undoubtedly from hugging the child to her and kissing his cheek. She might be his mother, or maybe his sister. The harsh conditions of Five Points had a way of making everyone look old and haggard. But one thing was certain: the boy was this woman's family.

She looked at Sam with swollen, red-rimmed eyes. "I don't know what else to do." Blinking, she gulped back a sob. "Help him."

"I'll do what I can." Going down on his knees, he leaned forward to examine the wound, but the woman wouldn't budge. He smiled gently, then said in a firm voice, "It's all right. I need to take over now."

She clenched her bottom lip between her teeth, then pulled her hand away. Sam opened his bag and prayed silently. Head wounds were notorious for heavy bleeding, but even if the boy's injury turned out to be minor, infection was still a possibility.

As always, Sam was keenly aware of his own inadequacies. No matter how hard he worked, he could never save them all. But he would save as many as he could.

⌇

"What has happened to my Elena?"

The music stuttered to a stop as the rehearsal pianist looked with wide eyes at Mr. Jerome. He stormed the stage with such intensity, Emily found herself gripping her crutches in fear he might barrel into her.

Her foray into the city had been more arduous than she'd expected, breaking open one of the half-healed wounds and making her stump swell. When Miss Clara had seen it, she'd insisted Emily keep the artificial limb off for a while, to give the leg some relief, leaving her with no choice but to use the crutches. How she had hoped her benefactor would stay away from the Academy until her leg was healed enough for her to wear the limb once more. She should have known that would never happen. A man like Mr. Jerome wanted to be involved in every aspect of the production.

Before Emily could utter a word of explanation, Miss Clara stepped out of the wings and came to Mr. Jerome's side.

"I'm afraid Emily had a mishap. But there's no need to worry." She laid her hand on his arm and smiled warmly. "She'll be right as rain in a couple of days."

His eyebrows drew together in a frown. "Are you sure? Has she seen a doctor?"

"Of course. She's under the care of Dr. DeKlerk."

The two continued talking about Emily's condition as though Emily herself had ceased to inhabit the room. Frustration heated her cheeks. Miss Clara meant well, but Emily didn't appreciate being treated like a child, especially in front of the man who could make her career. Turning carefully with her crutches, Emily addressed Mr. Jerome. "I am perfectly able to answer for myself, sir."

He quirked an eyebrow and looked down at the hem of her skirt. Emily held her breath. The dress was fashionably long and full, allowing not even the toe of her single shoe to be seen. There was no way he could know her secret unless she told him.

Mr. Jerome looked up and nodded. "Of course you can. I insist you return to the hotel at once."

Now she'd done it. She'd offended him. "Mr. Jerome, forgive my rudeness."

He waved a hand at her. "Nothing to forgive, young lady. You have Elena's fire. I knew I chose well with you, which is why I will not take any chances with your health."

"I assure you, sir, I'm fine."

"Not another word." His eyes bore into hers, making her intended argument impossible. "You will spend today resting and come back tomorrow ready to sing."

There was nothing to do but nod her agreement.

"Very good. If you'll excuse me, I have something to tend to." He turned to Miss Clara, tapped the brim of his hat with one finger, and then hurried off the stage almost as quickly as he'd come.

Emily watched him retreat up the auditorium's center aisle. Her arms began to shake. If she didn't sit down soon, she might very well crumple into a heap, despite the crutches.

She had failed. Her first day of rehearsing the role of her life, and she'd been told to go home.

"Come now, dear." Miss Clara spoke in her soothing way. "You'll get some well-needed rest. Things will look better tomorrow. You'll see."

If Emily opened her mouth, if she attempted to speak, she knew there would be no holding back the tears. So, she nodded, swung the crutches forward, and made her way slowly, painfully, off the stage, while the eyes of all the other cast members bored into her back.

⌒

The boy was alive, for now. There was no guarantee he would survive the healing process, but Sam had done all he could. The man who'd summoned his help showed his appreciation by escorting Sam safely to the edge of Five Points, a kindness he greatly appreciated.

It was days like this that made him long for some of the luxuries of his parents' home. How glorious it would be to sink into a tub filled with hot water. But no use wishing for something that couldn't be. He would go upstairs, fill the pail, set it on the fire to heat, and enjoy a quick sponge bath.

But as he turned the corner, his hopes of a quiet evening were dashed. Leonard Jerome stepped out of a carriage stopped at the curb and moved swiftly to the door of the clinic. The chances were exceedingly good that the man wanted to see him concerning Emily Forbes.

The one woman he hoped not to see again was the one he couldn't seem to escape.

Chapter 7

Emily stared at her reflection in the looking glass. Her eyes were still red and watery. But she was done crying. She was tired of feeling weak and helpless. She was going to take charge of her future. No more moping about her leg. She didn't need two legs to sing, and if Mr. Jerome changed his opinion of her because he suspected that she was missing a limb, then God would provide some other opportunity.

"Miss Clara?"

"Yes, child?" The woman's voice held a note of concern, and Emily could hear her struggling to extract herself from the deep cushioned chair near the fireplace. "Are you all right?"

"I'm fine." Emily grabbed up her crutches and moved quickly from her room. She was nothing if not an expert with the supports by this time. "Let's get to work."

"And what of your rest?" Miss Clara planted her hands on her hips.

"My leg is resting simply by not having the appliance on. My soul will rest if I can practice."

Miss Clara smiled as if Emily had given the correct answer at a spelling bee. "That's my girl. This has all been a bit overwhelming, but I knew you wouldn't let this get you down."

"Well, I'm not going to let it keep me down, anyway."

Miss Clara settled herself at the piano that had made this suite at the Adelphia so very desirable. "Let's begin with *Tanti affetti*. Your transition from the high note was uneven."

Emily nodded.

Miss Clara placed her hands on the keyboard, and Emily inhaled. The words came easily. She knew this aria. Knew that she could sing it. That she could be Elena. She closed her eyes, allowing the music to soothe her. It swelled in the room, wrapping around her and rocking her gently. This was right. This was comforting. No, she didn't need two legs to sing.

A knock sounded at the door.

Emily's eyes snapped open.

Miss Clara struck a discordant note and stood. "If it's not one thing, it's another."

Emily moved to sit down. In spite of what she'd told Miss Clara, wisdom dictated she allow her body to rest as much as possible.

"Mr. Jerome?" Miss Clara stepped back to allow the top-hatted man to enter.

"Did I hear Miss Forbes?" When he caught sight of Emily, he stopped. "Miss Forbes, I thought I told you to get some rest."

Emily straightened her spine. "Mr. Jerome." She nodded in greeting, bringing to bear all the hauteur she could muster.

There was movement behind him, and then Dr. DeKlerk entered. He held his hat in his hands, and his eyes roved the room. Dark circles shadowed his eyes, and his complexion was tinged gray. His friend Robert was right. He worked too much and cared for himself too little.

Emily yanked her attention back to Mr. Jerome. "I appreciate your concern for me, but I am not an invalid."

"I've had a conversation with Dr. DeKlerk, here, and it would appear that you are an invalid." He frowned mightily. "Much to my chagrin."

Emily rose as evenly as she could. She could not bear to have him looking down on her in that supercilious way. "I am *not* an invalid." She took care to enunciate. "I am a cripple." The word tasted bitter, and her cheeks flamed, but she felt a certain amount of power, too. "I may not have two legs, but I do have a voice. And that's what an opera singer needs, isn't it?"

It was Mr. Jerome's turn to look chagrined.

"Would you fire a jockey because he couldn't sing? No, because he doesn't need a voice to ride. Well, I don't need two legs to sing, *and* I can still ride."

"And argue." Mr. Jerome raised a hand. "I'm not going to fire you. I'm only concerned you'll try to do too much and hurt yourself further."

Emily sank slowly back onto the settee. "You're not going to get rid of me?"

"No." Mr. Jerome raised an eyebrow and gave a significant look at one of the chairs.

"Please do be seated," Emily said, though it felt as though the words came from someone else. Someone distant and a little muffled.

"I do have a condition, though."

Emily didn't respond but eyed him warily.

"I've spoken with Dr. DeKlerk, and I want to make sure you continue to see him daily. It would be best if you didn't have to use crutches during the performances."

"Is that what he's doing here?" She looked at the doctor, who continued to stand near the door.

"Yes." Mr. Jerome patted her arm. "Now, don't worry about the expense. I've taken care of that. I just want you in tip-top shape, especially for the premier."

Emily nodded, waiting for the other shoe to drop. When Mr. Jerome continued to smile benignly and then turned to Miss Clara to pass a remark about the weather, she couldn't stop herself from interrupting. "Is that all?"

He raised his eyebrows. "That's all. Of course, you'll need to heed your physician's advice. If he instructs you to rest, for example…." He waggled his eyebrows now.

Relief that her career hadn't ended before it began washed over her, and Emily couldn't help but laugh. "All right. I shall be a good patient and obey his instructions to the letter."

"Good." With that, Mr. Jerome took up his cane again. "I'll leave you all to it."

Miss Clara hurried to see him out.

Dr. DeKlerk approached Emily then. "I need to examine your wounds to make sure there are no signs of infection."

"There aren't."

"Nevertheless." He tilted his head to the side, waiting for her consent.

She lifted her skirt to reveal the injured limb.

He squatted down beside her. Carefully, he removed the bandages and wiped away the salve that coated her stump. His brow creased in a frown. "This looks worse. You obviously haven't been staying off it as I instructed. What have you been doing?"

Emily gritted her teeth. How dare he use such a tone with her, as if she was a naughty schoolchild caught cheating on a test? He'd eat his words if he knew she'd aggravated her injury trying to help solve his sister's murder. But she couldn't tell him that. Not yet. Frustration and annoyance burst out of her, and she turned the mirror of accusation on him. "It wasn't your place to tell Mr. Jerome about my leg. What did it matter to you?"

He kept his eyes on the fresh bandage he was wrapping around the injury. "I didn't know it was a secret."

Somehow he managed to make her feel as if she were the one who should be ashamed. "Don't you afford your patients any sort of privacy? Will you answer questions about my affairs for anyone who asks?"

He looked at her as if she had stepped from the gutter to accost him. "I was speaking to your patron, not someone off the street. And I know more about your family that I could have shared, but I refrained."

Emily jerked her leg out of his hand. "What is that supposed to mean?"

He sat back on his heels, elbows on his knees, making no attempt to hide his contempt. "My sister, Sarah, was murdered. And your brother is the incompetent Pinkerton who let her killer get away."

"How dare you!" She wanted to hurl something at him. He was detestable. "For your information, I am well acquainted with that case, probably better than you are. Did you know that your father didn't want the murder investigated? He insisted that Carter chase after the gardener, which he did for three years. If the murder went unsolved, it is because your family was so insistent that the killer was a servant, when, all along, it was probably someone from your circle. *Someone with whom you still socialize.*" She flung the last words at him.

Beneath the gray pallor, his skin paled. "So, the Pinkerton shared the private details of my sister's case. Now who has been talking out of school?" He snapped his physician's bag shut and rose quickly to his feet. "I shall not trespass on your time any longer, Miss Forbes."

"Thank you for your ministrations, Dr. DeKlerk, but your services are no longer needed. And I'd appreciate it if news of my infirmity did not appear in the newspapers tomorrow morning."

He smiled coldly. "Rest assured, I'll refrain from speaking to any reporters. But you'll not be rid of me so easily. I'll be back tomorrow."

"But—"

"I promised Mr. Jerome I would attend you, and I shall, regardless of my personal feelings on the matter."

Emily crossed her arms over her chest. "I shan't receive you."

"Yes, you will."

"No—" She recalled her own promise to Mr. Jerome. She would have to see the doctor again, or he'd run and tell Mr. Jerome, and then she really would be tossed out of the production. There was no way around it. She had to cooperate with the doctor, at least to an extent. It wasn't as if she'd have to deal with him much. He'd check her leg for a few days, and then it would be healed, and they could part ways for good.

After that, Emily didn't care if she ever again laid eyes on Dr. Samuel DeKlerk.

Chapter 8

The woman was insufferable. Sam stalked down the street, spine stiff as an iron rod, his jaw clenched so tightly it hurt. And all the while, her words rang in his ears.

"It was probably someone from your circle. Someone with whom you still socialize."

The very idea that Sarah could have been murdered by someone he knew…. How dare Emily Forbes accuse one of his friends of such a heinous act? She was just trying to find an excuse for her brother's inept handling of the case. A case about which she knew far too much.

Why was that? His pace slowed. If the detective talked of his work with his sister, did that indicate a guilty conscience, or a man determined to track down the criminal? She had been right about Sam not knowing of Father's insistence that the gardener was guilty. Sam had always believed the Pinkerton's investigation had led him in pursuit of Grant Diamond. What else did Emily know that Sam didn't? And did any of it really matter now?

Sarah was gone—had been for ten years. Myriad questions surrounded her death, but there was one inescapable fact that Sam had never forgotten: If he had been home, he might have been able to save her. But there'd been no reason to believe his sister was in any danger. She'd been so proud when he'd told her of his intention to attend Harvard Medical School. Unlike his parents, who didn't understand why a man of his station would dirty his hands caring for the sick and wounded, Sarah had always encouraged him to follow his dream. She'd continued to do so as he studied, sending him regular letters full of positive words and news from home. Now, those letters, tied together with a hank of twine and safely tucked away in his apartment, were all he had left of her.

Sam slowed as he turned the corner and caught sight of the clinic. Thankfully, no unexpected visitor waited for him this time. It had been a long day, and he yearned for a little peace. But peace would be hard to come by tonight, since he couldn't stop thinking about the accusations leveled by the irritating Emily Forbes.

He unlocked the door, wary of any who might approach with yet another emergency. He didn't have the strength or the patience tonight. Scuttling inside as fast as if he were robbing the place, he shook his head at his own foolishness.

He inhaled the sharp, clean, antiseptic smell of the clinic, and some of the tension eased from his shoulders. *Home.* Sam ran a finger under his tie and pulled it loose. He trudged up the stairs, his footfalls sounding unnaturally heavy as they ricocheted off the walls of the small space. His stomach rumbled, registering its own protest against the relentless pace he had been keeping. But he was too tired to cook. The heel of a day-old loaf of bread and a knob of hard cheese would have to suffice tonight. It sufficed most nights.

His sole luxuries, a sturdy leather club chair and matching ottoman, invited him into their embrace, and he went willingly. Head tilted back against the cool leather, he sat for a long moment in the darkness. It was enough to be still and close his eyes for a few moments. A little rest would do him a world of good.

When Sam's eyes drifted open again, the world had grown the soft gray of impending dawn. He stretched out the kink in his neck, then pulled off his boots. Rubbing at the stubble on his cheek with his knuckles, he headed to bed. A little more sleep would help clear out the cobwebs.

Stretching out on the mattress felt a bit like he'd found paradise. Aah. He relaxed, allowing his mind to drift and carry him back to slumber.

"*Someone from your circle.*" Emily Forbes's words rattled around in his mind, as difficult to ignore as the lady herself.

Sam's eyes popped open. Why would any acquaintance of his family wish to harm Sarah? It was patently ridiculous. The DeKlerks didn't consort with blackguards and murderers. At least, they hadn't for the last hundred and fifty years. They had become the solidest of solid citizens, and their friends were no different. The Knickerbockers of New York were notoriously dull.

If Father had thought the murderer was that wretched gardener, then it likely was the gardener. But Sam had no illusions about his father. It was possible that he had leapt to conclusions. And if that were true—*if* it hadn't been the gardener—then someone else had murdered Sarah.

Sam rolled over and opened the little chest on his bedside table. He reached for the packet of letters from Sarah. Her last one had troubled him when he'd received it at college. He plucked it from the stack and read again the words he'd already committed to memory.

Dearest Sam,

I beg you not to be too disappointed in me. If anyone will understand, I think it will be you. After all, you know what it is to desire something other than the narrow existence prescribed by our station. I cannot tell you the details of my scheme. If you disapprove, you will feel compelled to inform Mother and Father. And if you approve, then you will still bear the guilt of knowledge, should they ask you about it. I shall spare you that, at least. You will find out soon enough what I am plotting, and when you do, I hope you can forgive me and believe me to be, always, your loving sister,

Sarah

It was such an odd letter, and he had never found out what she'd meant by it. His first horrified suspicion had been that she had committed suicide. But his parents and the officials had assured him that was impossible. He had refrained from mentioning the letter to anyone, for fear it would sully her memory. Was it possible that Emily Forbes knew more about what her brother had learned that could shed light on the mystery? And even if she did, would she tell him, now that he'd insulted her brother?

⌣

"How dare he!"

If she were wearing her artificial limb, Emily would be pacing around the room to work off her frustration. But, sitting on the bed with her leg elevated and her crutches out of reach, all she could do was gesture wildly with her hands as she told Miss Clara everything that was wrong with Samuel DeKlerk.

"First, he has the gall to share my personal medical information with Mr. Jerome. Then, he insults my family."

Miss Clara hurried to the side of the bed and removed a teacup and saucer just as Emily's hand slashed through the air beside them. "Mr. Jerome was concerned about you, dear. You should appreciate that fact."

Emily huffed out a breath and crossed her arms tightly over her chest. "That isn't the point. Why did the doctor have to tell him about—" She looked down at the stump below her knee. "Why did he tell him I'm crippled?"

"Oh, child." Miss Clara dropped onto the bed beside Emily and pulled her into her arms. "You are *not* crippled. You were the victim of a terrible crime. But look how God has used it."

Emily cringed inside. Ever since the robber's bullet ripped through her leg and shattered her bone, she'd doubted God's goodness. There had been times when she'd even doubted His very existence. "He used it to make me someone to be pitied."

Miss Clara's chest shook with her snorted laugh. "Right now, the only one pitying you is you." She gently pinched Emily's chin between her thumb and forefinger, then tilted her head back till they were eye to eye. "I do believe that, before the accident, you focused all your attention on the piano. Is that right?"

Emily nodded.

"And why did you stop playing?"

"It was too difficult to maneuver the pedals with the artificial limb."

"I see. Is it fair to say that you discovered your talent for singing only because you could no longer play the piano?"

"Well...." Emily gulped.

"Now, I'm not saying God caused the accident. But He certainly did use it to give you a wonderful gift. Wouldn't you agree?"

Emily moved gently away from Miss Clara and leaned back against the headboard. "I suppose you could be right. But I'd rather have kept both my legs and still have found my voice."

Miss Clara chuckled. "And I'd rather still be young and beautiful, but we can't have everything we want."

"No, that's certainly true."

Miss Clara squeezed Emily's hand. "Oh, but look at the wonderful future laid out before you. And, really, I believe this small setback with your leg is a blessing in disguise."

"In what way?" How in the world would Miss Clara find the silver lining on this black cloud?

"In the last two days, two people have discovered your secret. And both of them responded with understanding and compassion. Neither Mr. Jerome nor Dr. DeKlerk thinks less of you because of it."

Miss Clara was right. Mr. Jerome was certainly more interested in her voice than in whether she stood on two good feet or one. Dr. DeKlerk...well, he was another matter altogether. "The good doctor has entirely different reasons for thinking less of me."

"Yes, I overheard your conversation." Miss Clara's eyes narrowed. "Carter worried over Sarah DeKlerk's murder like a dog with a bone, and for years."

"And that insufferable man has the nerve to call Carter incompetent." Now that the subject had moved from Emily's own self-doubts to Sam's accusations, her ire was once again rising. "Can you imagine?"

"Obviously, Dr. DeKlerk doesn't know your brother." Miss Clara rose from the bed.

"If he did, he would understand how this unsolved case has eaten away at Carter."

Miss Clara shook her head. "And Carter didn't even know Sarah DeKlerk. Imagine how her brother must feel." She moved swiftly across the room. "I'll be back in a moment with our lunch, dear."

As the door shut with a click, Emily sunk lower on the bed. That Miss Clara—she loved to flip Emily's perspective right on its ear. She'd been so concerned about herself and determined to defend Carter's honor, she hadn't even stopped to consider how the doctor must feel. His sister had been murdered, and the killer never caught. He hadn't even seemed to consider that someone close to him might have committed the murder. He'd looked utterly shocked. Even now, she couldn't begin to imagine his grief.

"What a mess I've made." She rubbed one temple with her fingertips.

Thanks to Mr. Jerome, Dr. DeKlerk would be seeing her on a regular basis. And every time he did, it would be a reminder of the sister he'd lost. Emily winced at the remembrance of the words she'd thrown at him, accusing a member of his own circle of the murder. How could she make amends?

If Miss Clara was right, and God had brought her to this place on purpose, then surely there was a reason for meeting Dr. DeKlerk. Her thoughts began to whirl. The only answer was to continue trying. She'd keep looking for the real killer. That would help Dr. DeKlerk and clear Carter's name in one fell swoop. She seemed to know more about the actual facts of the case than the doctor. And now, through Mr. Jerome, she had access to the same social circle as the wealthy and powerful DeKlerk clan.

Unbidden, a snippet of a Bible verse came to mind. *"Seek, and ye shall find."* She had an idea that she was probably taking the instruction out of context, but it seemed apropos anyway.

The only way to give Dr. DeKlerk any kind of peace would be to find Sarah's killer. Even though she wished she'd kept her opinion to herself, it didn't make the idea wrong.

Carter would be furious if he found out she'd put herself in danger. But she didn't have to put herself in danger. After all this time, who would suspect a crippled opera singer of investigating a decade-old murder?

Emily took up the boar bristle brush beside her bed and began her hundred strokes for the evening. One way or another, she would help Carter and Dr. DeKlerk find the answers they needed.

Chapter 9

It was three days before Sam ran Miss Forbes to ground at the Academy of Music. If he didn't know better, he'd think she was avoiding him. The cast moved across the stage in a grand sweep of movements and sounds. They were almost all men. Sam could already see them as fierce Scottish clansmen. And ever since Queen Victoria had begun going to Balmoral, all things Scottish had become wildly popular. It was a wonder no one had thought of putting on this opera sooner. It was sure to be a hit, even if the singing was mediocre. Which, if he was any judge, it wasn't.

In the darkened theater, Sam found himself instantly caught up in the struggle being portrayed. Slender and tiny amid the brawny men of the chorus, Emily Forbes nevertheless managed to capture attention completely. Even James Gardiner's portrayal of King James and Benedetta Lanzieri in the role of Malcolm didn't hold a candle to Emily's magnetism. How did someone that size manage to project a voice so powerful and rich with emotion? Sam watched her with rapt attention. Her wound must be healing well, because she moved without the aid of crutches. If he hadn't known of her lost limb, he never would have guessed she was anything but entirely whole.

He owed her an apology for his outburst the other night. Even though he was probably still right about her brother's incompetence, she wasn't to blame for the fellow. She couldn't have been more than a child when the whole ugly business took place. And of course she would feel protective of her brother. No doubt she'd grown used to defending him over the years.

Pleased with his own magnanimousness, Sam strode to the middle of the theater and took a seat, waiting for a lull in the action on the stage. The plush seat wasn't as comfortable as his armchair, but it was certainly better than some of the places he'd rested in his time. He stretched his legs and slouched a bit, settling in for what might be a long wait. In the twilight gloom, his eyes began to drift shut.

He was brought to by a knock on his head. Not a hard blow, but enough to pull him to his feet, fists raised, as his eyes struggled to focus. The familiar sound of a chuckle registered, and he recognized the fellow standing beside him. He sighed. "Afternoon, Robbie."

His friend offered a cheeky grin and waved him to move over. Sam scooted to the right, and Robert Romijn settled himself in the vacated seat.

"So Sam, what brings you to the Academy of Music? Or do I even need to ask?" He waggled his eyebrows and gave a significant glance toward the stage.

Sam decided not to defend himself. "I could ask you the same."

"You could, but my motives are spotlessly pure. I am here as an advisor."

"An advisor?"

"Old Jerome has gotten a bee in his bonnet about making the production"—he mimicked the older man flawlessly—"'authentically Scottish.'"

Sam frowned. "What does that mean?"

"Considering that not one of the singers is actually Scottish, nor the setting, nor the costumes, I have no idea. But, since I have been to Scotland, he asked me to come and offer my opinion."

Sam shook his head. "I doubt you'd know a kilt if you were wearing one."

"Don't be so sure. The breeze would give it away."

Sam snorted. Robert had always been able to coax a laugh from him eventually.

"Now, just so you don't think you actually got away with changing the subject on me...." Robert stared fixedly at the stage. "What are you doing here?"

"I have to see a patient."

That got his attention. Robert raised an eyebrow. "Is there a madman loose in the opera?"

"Not that I'm aware of. Aside from yourself, of course."

Robert's face clouded over.

Sam raised a hand. "It was a jest. Don't ruffle yourself." He ought to know better than to try a joke. He was too heavy-handed and Robbie too sensitive. "It...uh...it's a different kind of patient. Not from the clinic."

"I see. Today's patient has a physical infirmity, not a mental one." Robert turned back to the stage, his interest waning. "So, how is the thankless job of trying to talk the crazies of the world back to sanity?"

Sam clenched his teeth. Robert knew precisely how to get under his skin, and he was paying him back for his thoughtless remark. But Sam could choose how to react to the dig. He chose to ignore it.

At last, the performers took a break. Sam nudged Robert with his elbow. "I'll see you later."

Robert nodded but didn't move. "Are you going to the Lorillard ball?"

Sam hesitated. "I don't—"

"Think about your work, Sam. If you want money for your clinic, you should be hobnobbing with the people who *have* money, not with every derelict and ruffian in this godforsaken city."

"I'll think about it." Sam hustled to his feet. He needed to get to the stage before Miss Forbes disappeared. He'd already wasted too much time on this errand as it was.

But apparently Robert wasn't going to let him go that easily. His friend stood and followed him down the aisle.

Sam smothered a sigh. The last thing he needed was more of Robert's sly insinuations, when he had no romantic interest in Miss Forbes whatsoever. Though he could hardly explain what his interest really was—not to Robert. It would be too painful for them both.

⌣

Emily gratefully accepted the damp cloth Miss Clara handed her, and wiped it across the back of her neck. Those who didn't know would never believe what strenuous work singing was, not to mention the emotional stress of mounting an opera. They were in the throes of the production now, the time when the amount of work still left to do made it seem an impossibility that it would all come together. But it would. She had to believe that. In the end, all the disparate bits would meld and become a wonderfully cohesive whole.

Either that, or it would be an unmitigated artistic disaster.

Since that absolutely, positively could not happen, it had to be a success. If hard work could achieve anything, then she was going to make certain she worked as hard as she could.

She nearly guzzled the lemonade that had been set out on a bench for her. She was parched.

"Miss Forbes?"

Refreshed by the sweet yet tart beverage, Emily turned with a pleasant smile. It withered when she saw Dr. DeKlerk. "Doctor."

Mr. Romijn stepped around the doctor and caught her hand, raising it to his lips. "Miss Forbes, it is a pleasure to see you again. We've been listening in on some of the rehearsal, and I'm convinced the production will be a triumph."

Emily felt as if someone had lifted twenty pounds from her shoulders. "Oh, do you really think so? There's such a difficulty.

You know, internally, in my head. I know what I envision, and I can't ever quite seem to live up to what I picture in my own mind."

"Very few of us ever do. But you certainly exceed the day-dreams I have conjured since our first meeting."

It wasn't at all what she'd meant, but Emily didn't know how to correct him. Nor did she know how to extract her hand from his hold without being rude.

Dr. DeKlerk cleared his throat. "Miss Forbes, I've stopped by your hotel room twice to check your injury."

"I've been here, for the most part." She spoke through lips so tightly pursed, it was a miracle any sound came out at all.

"Perhaps, since there is a break now—"

"You don't mean to tell me that Miss Forbes is your patient?" Mr. Romijn interjected, looking quite amused.

Dr. DeKlerk gave a short jerk of his head.

"Aren't you coy, Brother!" Mr. Romijn marveled. "This is a new side to you entirely."

"Brother?" Emily scrambled to find any topic of conversation beside her leg.

"Well, almost." Mr. Romijn's mobile features turned grave. "We would have been brothers. I was engaged—"

Dr. DeKlerk cleared his throat loudly.

Emily cast Mr. Romijn a quelling glance. "I'm sorry, what did you say?"

He glanced at Dr. DeKlerk as if he suspected him of teetering on the edge of insanity. Then he turned his attention back to her. "I said I was engaged to Dr. DeKlerk's sister, my sweet Sarah, but she died before we could wed."

He looked as downcast as if Sarah's passing a decade ago had been just last week. Impulsively, Emily patted his arm. "I am so sorry for your loss. That must have been quite a blow."

He nodded, lips pressed tightly together, but said nothing.

"You must have loved her very much if you've never married since."

"All right, Miss Forbes," Dr. DeKlerk all but forced his way between her and Mr. Romijn. "If we could please go someplace where I can examine your injury in private...."

Emily sighed. Why did he have to be so overbearing? And why was it that, every time he was around, some new person became privy to the fact that she had need of a doctor's care? First Mr. Jerome, now Mr. Romijn. It was almost as if he was trying to keep her off balance, metaphorically speaking.

"Come along." Miss Clara stepped forward, looking slightly amused. "The dressing room will more than suffice."

Before Mr. Romijn could move, the doctor turned to him and poked a finger at his chest. "You and your big mouth can wait here."

Emily frowned. Dr. DeKlerk was obviously still upset over the revelation that Mr. Romijn had been engaged to Sarah. In fact, he fairly bristled whenever Mr. Romijn turned his attention her way.

Could it be the doctor was trying to hide something?

Chapter 10

Sam glared back at Robert. The last thing he needed was to raise more questions about Sarah. He was trying to be discreet. Miss Forbes wasn't dense. She'd know he was fishing for information. Although, maybe he could sort of imply that she had dredged up all the old memories now, and he needed to find some way to settle them. He hadn't finished mapping out his campaign when Miss Clara ushered him into the dressing room.

He stepped aside so that Miss Forbes could precede him.

"I don't appreciate your coming to my place of work to treat me, Doctor." She spoke without deigning to look at him.

"If you'd allowed me to tend to you back at the Adelphia instead of running from me, I wouldn't have had to come here."

Her stride faltered for a moment. She turned and sat in a straight-backed chair, lifting her chin. "Be that as it may, if you come here again, I shan't receive you."

"You will if you want to retain Mr. Jerome's good favor."

Her eyes narrowed. "Because you will tell tales?"

With effort, Sam wrenched his temper back under control. He had to keep his goal in mind. If he could master his own anger, he could master the conversation. "No. No, I won't tell Mr. Jerome."

She opened her mouth as if she had a retort all ready, but when his words registered, she closed it again. "Thank you." She tilted her head, as if she was trying to make him understand, and softened her voice. "It's—I do not want the other cast members to think of me as too delicate."

It hadn't occurred to him, but she was right. By all accounts, the stage was a competitive place, and any weakness would be noted. Coming here had been a misstep. So, how to get things on a better footing?

Awkward silence blanketed the room. Sam finished his examination in record time. He stood, and she smoothed her skirt back into place.

Sam cleared his throat. "I'm very pleased with your progress. The wound is almost completely healed. Try to stay off your feet as much as possible over the next few days, and it should be good as new."

"All right."

He picked up his bag. "Don't forget to use the salve."

"I won't."

Waiting for an opportune moment to say what he wanted hadn't worked. If he wanted to leave here with fences at least partially mended, he had best simply jump in. "I—I'm sorry that I said what I did the other day...about your brother. I'm sure he's a fine man."

She rewarded him with a trembling smile. "Thank you, Doctor. I apologize for being so defensive. Carter has told me I can be too fierce at times." She laughed, and her hauteur faded into nothingness.

Sam found himself smiling in response. Miss Forbes wasn't unreasonable. She would gladly tell him all he wanted to know.

A knock sounded at the door. "Miss Forbes, you're needed on stage."

Miss Clara swept toward the door and opened it. "Thank you for stopping by, Dr. DeKlerk. We will let Mr. Jerome know how we appreciate your care."

He raised a hand to protest. He hadn't had a chance to ask any of his questions.

"I am sorry, Doctor. I must run along." With a wave of her hand, Miss Forbes was off, followed by her ever-present companion, leaving him standing alone in the empty dressing room. She'd done it again—dashed away without giving him the satisfaction of answers.

Coming to the theater had been a mistake, for multiple reasons. This was her territory, making it easy for her to scurry off and avoid him when she pleased. Next time would be different. The next time he saw her, he'd be sure it was in a place where he'd have the advantage.

She couldn't avoid his questions forever.

⌒

"Do you think I'll ever stop being overwhelmed by these grand mansions?"

Miss Clara chuckled at Emily's whispered question. "I suppose there will come a time when you'll stop noticing the opulence and simply see someone's home."

Emily wrapped her fingers around Miss Clara's arm. "When did that happen for you?"

"Hasn't yet," she said with a shake of her head. "I'm still bowled over at how the cream of society lives."

The Lorillard mansion was grander than anything Emily could have imagined, and they hadn't even gone beyond the foyer. "It's like a scene from one of the operas come to life."

A throaty laugh sounded behind her. "I used to feel the same way, dear."

Emily turned. The woman was poised and elegant in an elaborate gown of ruby red silk. Strands of silver threaded through her chocolate-brown hair, which was arranged in an artful configuration of braids and ribbons. Had it not been for her warm smile, she would have been thoroughly intimidating.

Miss Clara's hand pressed against the small of Emily's back, no doubt to ensure she didn't run the other way. "Mrs. Lorillard, it's an honor to visit your home."

Emily gulped. "Mrs....oh, my." She was acting like an oaf in front of their hostess. Drawing on whatever reserves of composure might be lurking beneath her skin, she pulled herself together. "It's a pleasure to meet you."

Mrs. Lorillard leaned forward ever so slightly. "And you as well, Miss...?"

Heat bloomed in Emily's cheeks. "Emily Forbes. And this is Clara Wray."

Mrs. Lorillard's eyes grew wide with delight. "Ah, Miss Forbes. Leonard has been simply giddy over the discovery of his promising new ingénue. You, my dear, are the talk of the town."

"That's very kind of him."

"Nonsense. Leonard only brags about talent where it exists. If he says you have the voice of an angel, then I expect God Himself is present whenever you open your mouth to sing."

At that moment, Emily's mouth was so dry, her lips felt pasted together. If God was nearby watching, He was likely chuckling to Himself.

"I certainly hope I can convince you to share a song with my guests tonight, Miss Forbes." Mrs. Lorillard smiled in the expectant way people do when they aren't used to their requests being denied.

Having momentarily lost the power of speech, Emily simply nodded.

"You'll have to excuse her, Mrs. Lorillard," Miss Clara spoke up. "We were just discussing the beauty of your home, and I believe it has quite taken Emily's breath away."

Mrs. Lorillard nodded. "Yes, it can be a bit much to digest, I'll grant that. Which is why I commissioned the mural."

Emily and Miss Clara followed their hostess's gaze. The mural she indicated was of a lush paradise. Boldly colored tropical flowers bloomed among deep green, broad-leafed plants. And hanging from the branch of a tree was a snake, its forked tongue testing the air.

"It's the garden of Eden," Emily said.

"Precisely. Imagine living in such a beautiful place, with everything one could want or need at one's fingertips, yet Satan was still able to tempt them." She turned back to Emily and Miss Clara. "That mural is meant as a daily reminder that, no matter how much or how little a person has, life is always fraught with temptation, and we must guard against it."

A sound from the entry caught Mrs. Lorillard's attention. "Excuse me, ladies. Mayor Hoffman has arrived and will be terribly hurt if I don't personally welcome him." She winked and added quietly, "He's amazingly thin-skinned for a politician."

Their hostess whirled so quickly, her skirts nearly wrapped around her ankles. Then she was off, already motioning to the next guest.

Miss Clara chuckled. "That woman is a force of nature."

"Amazing." Emily looked again at the mural. Mrs. Lorillard was right, of course. In the grand scheme of life, material possessions were of little importance. Still, it was easier for people who had so much to espouse such a philosophy, than for those who had nothing.

Emily shook her head. This was no time for such deep thoughts. Once again, she'd been called upon to perform, but she was totally unprepared. She squared her shoulders and turned to Miss Clara. "What shall I sing?"

Miss Clara tapped her lips with her finger. "Something romantic, I think…something timeless." She threaded her arm through the crook of Emily's elbow and compelled her forward. "We must speak to the musical director. Perhaps the orchestra is already planning to perform something you know."

As they moved through the arched entryway into the grand ballroom, Emily's eyes swept the crowd. So many sophisticated, well-fixed people. Soon, the music would start, and the couples would whirl and glide across the dance floor. Mrs. Lorillard didn't realize it, but she'd done Emily a great service. She would far rather sing, under any circumstances, than have to spend an evening standing on the sidelines, pretending she had no interest in joining the dancers.

"Oh, look. There's Dr. DeKlerk."

Emily's head whipped around. Sure enough, there stood the doctor, talking to his friend Robert Romijn and a willowy young lady dripping with stunning jewelry.

"What's he doing here?" Irritation had crept into her voice.

"The same thing you are, I imagine."

She arched an eyebrow. "Mingling with the upper crust of society to further his singing career?"

Miss Clara smiled and gave her cheek a playful pinch. "Sassy girl. From what Mr. Jerome has told me, Dr. DeKlerk is no more a fan of these functions than you are. But he attends in order to gain support for his medical practice."

"Why does he need to do that? His family is quite well off."

"I don't believe his family approves of his chosen profession, so the good doctor makes do on his own."

Emily's opinion of Dr. DeKlerk rose a bit. It spoke well of the man, that he would follow his passion rather than his family's fortune. "That is admirable."

Miss Clara nodded. "Indeed. And let's not forget the wonderful care he's given to you over the last week."

There was no denying that. He'd prescribed a new type of ointment that had soothed her chaffed and broken skin. And, thanks to the additions of extra padding to the artificial limb and a protective stocking over her stump, the limb no longer rubbed her raw. "Perhaps I've been too hard on him."

"There will be plenty of time for mending fences later." Miss Clara patted her arm and steered her toward the area where the orchestra was set up. "First, you have a song to sing."

Emily turned and nearly ran straight into a wall in human form.

She gasped as strong hands grasped her upper arms, bringing her to a halt and avoiding what would have been an embarrassing collision. She looked up. And up. And finally met the eyes of a gentleman who had to be the tallest man in New York.

"Easy there, miss." Amusement laced the tenor voice, matching the smile quirking his lips.

"Oh, dear. I'm so sorry."

"No need for apologies. It's quite the crush of humanity in here. Are you all right?"

His gaze swept quickly from her head down to her toes and back up again. It was the act of someone concerned for her welfare, nothing more, but it still left a flush of embarrassment in its wake.

"I'm fine, thank you."

His hands fell from her arms, and he gave the briefest of nods. "In that case, let me properly introduce myself. Harrison Kerns, Alderman."

"Emily Forbes."

He bowed courteously over her hand, his lips brushing across her silk-covered knuckles. "Ah, Miss Forbes. I should have known. You've been the talk of many a lively dinner conversation of late."

"Me?"

"You are the shooting star in New York's firmament at the moment...a singer with the voice an angel, and a beauty to rival Venus herself." He inclined his head, giving her a knowing look. "People are always fascinated by the newest thing. And right now, my dear, that thing is you."

She didn't know whether to be embarrassed by his compliments or offended at being referred to as a "thing." Finally, she did neither. "I wish only to use the gifts God has given me, to His honor."

He nodded, then continued as if she hadn't spoken. "My interest in you is for an entirely different reason."

The muscles in Emily's shoulders tightened, and she lifted her chin, while Miss Clara stepped closer and opened her mouth. Their reactions drew a laugh from Mr. Kerns.

"Nothing nefarious, I assure you." He glanced sideways, as if checking for eavesdroppers. "It's your name. I knew a Pinkerton agent by the name of Forbes years ago when I was Police Commissioner, and I've wondered if you're any relation."

Emily blew out a sigh of relief. "Yes, Carter Forbes is my brother."

Mr. Kerns nodded in a way that conveyed he'd known all along he was right.

Now that an opportunity had presented itself, there was no way Emily could let it slip by. "Carter worked on the murder case of Sarah DeKlerk."

"Ah, yes. Dreadful thing, that." His forehead creased, and his ice-chip-blue eyes seemed to darken. "It's such a pity that your brother was never able to apprehend the villain who murdered Miss DeKlerk. We'd all sleep a little bit better knowing Diamond had been brought to justice."

Biting back a protest, Emily weighed her options. It was doubtful that the former police commissioner would appreciate any implication that his men were inadequate, but this was too good an opportunity to pass up altogether. Best to start slow. "Were you involved in the investigation?"

"Almost from the start. It was a difficult case, emotionally, but of course there was never any real doubt as to the culprit."

"Really? What made everyone so certain?"

"Who else could it have been? And besides, the fellow ran away."

"People *were* chasing him." Emily softened the pointed state-ment with a belated smile.

"Ah, but the guilty flee where no man chases, and he had to have already been packed and ready to go before anyone knew Sarah had been murdered." Kerns gave her a look that had an effect equal to an indulgent pat on the head. "Will you excuse me? I'm afraid I must speak to the mayor for a moment."

Cheeks hot from the effort of holding back the retorts that fought for voice, Emily stretched her lips into what should pass for a smile and inclined her head. Suddenly she had an additional reason to find the real killer—the pleasure of seeing Kerns' face when he was shown up as an incompetent lout. And the next person to patronize her risked a fat lip.

⌒

"And then, Sir Victor reached over and bit the silk flower right off of her hat!"

Robert roared with laughter, then leaned closer to Mildred Wainwright. "Imagine that. You'd expect far better behavior from a thoroughbred."

Sam had been holding a forced smile for so long, his jaw ached. Miss Wainwright was full of anecdotes about her father's race-horses, and she apparently intended to share each and every one of them. If not for the fact that James Wainwright III had shown interest in Sam's work, he would have excused himself four tales back.

Just when he thought he couldn't stand another moment, the orchestra began to play, and Miss Wainwright flounced off to find someone who had made her "absolutely promise to give him the first dance."

"What a delightful creature," Robert said.

With a finger pressed against his temple, Sam glared at him. "You and I obviously have different definitions of 'delightful.'"

Robert slapped him on the back. "Buck up, old boy. There are worse ways to spend an evening."

At the moment, Sam was hard-pressed to think of any.

One day, Robert would invite him to one of these soirees, and he would flatly decline. But that day was a long way off. As long as the clinic needed funding, Sam would hobnob with the elite.

"Ah, now I see why you have no interest in the other ladies tonight." Robert's elbow dug into his side. "Your little songbird is here."

Sam frowned. "What are you talking about?"

Robert pointed toward the orchestra.

Emily Forbes stepped to the front of the stage, hands folded together at her waist. An odd chill skittered across Sam's shoulders. The woman frustrated him, but there was something about her that drew him in and captured his attention, despite himself. Compared to the other women in attendance, she was simply dressed, but her sea-foam-green gown perfectly complemented her creamy complexion. She possessed an elegant simplicity that far outshone everyone else.

Sam shook his head. "How would I have known she'd be here?"

"Come, now. You spend more time in her company than you have with anyone else in the last five years. It's apparent you have a relationship with the woman."

"She is my patient," Sam huffed. "The only relationship we have, if you can even call it that, is purely professional."

Before Robert could poke any further into his personal life, the orchestra began a new song, and Emily's clear soprano filled the room. She commanded the attention of every person.

Robert leaned closer to Sam. "She's just your patient, eh?"

"Yes."

"You work too hard. You need to learn to play a little."

As if to prove his words, Robert moved to the closest available woman. A moment later, he was claiming half a dozen dances on her dance card.

Sam shook his head. Robert played a good game, but Sam knew his devil-may-care attitude existed merely on the surface. Sarah's death had affected him deeply, but he had dealt with his grief by developing a cavalier approach to relationships, and a much too personal relationship with alcohol. Sam, on the other hand, had taken the opposite path. Connections of the heart were to be avoided at all costs. If Sarah's death hadn't proven it to him, his time serving on the battlefield had cemented it.

As Emily Forbes sang of a love that transcended time, Sam turned and walked away, reinforcing the wall around his heart as he went.

Chapter 11

Emily wandered out onto the terrace and gazed at the tiny, perfectly manicured garden lit by strings of bright Chinese lanterns. Only a few couples dotted the walks, and the air was fresher. All in all, she was glad to have found the oasis of peace before someone cornered her and asked her to dance. There were probably benches in the garden. She'd find a nice secluded spot to rest her leg, and when a respectable amount of time had passed, she would find Miss Clara so they could go home.

"Miss Forbes, that was delightful."

Emily turned her head to find Mr. Romijn approaching. "Thank you. I was not as prepared as I would have liked, so I am doubly pleased that you enjoyed it."

"Would you care to walk with me?"

Grateful that he hadn't asked her to dance, Emily accepted with alacrity. He gave her his arm, and she nestled her hand in the crook of his elbow.

"It's a fine night. Not as hot as it has been." The weather? She had nothing better to discuss than the weather?

He smiled down at her, one eyebrow cocked, as if he knew she was a witty conversationalist and he was waiting for the clincher. "But quite warm enough."

"Yes, quite." Having failed to find a way to turn the observation into anything remotely amusing, she decided on another gambit. "Did you hear of the suspected rebellion in Arkansas? Rebels are said to have murdered a member of the legislature, and the governor has taken Union troops to suppress the outbreak." *Wonderful. From the weather to murder and mayhem, with nary a stop in between.* Truly, she had no social graces.

Mr. Romijn frowned. "I had heard that. I fear the war is still with us, in many ways."

"Did you fight?"

"I did. In the Sixth New York cavalry regiment."

"Were you an officer, then?"

"I was."

"Then, surely I should be calling you 'Captain,' or something rather than 'Mr. Romijn'?"

"To be honest, I prefer plain old 'Mister.' I'm not usually one to let go of any honors that are due me, but when it comes to the war, I'd as soon forget it ever happened."

Emily nodded sympathetically. "I lived in the capital throughout the war. I know a bit of what our men endured." She shook her head. "Battle certainly didn't bring the glorious triumphs we'd all anticipated, did it?"

His eyes appraised her again. "Most ladies think I am overly sensitive and that I'm reluctant to claim the title because I don't think I'm good enough. They seem to think it makes me more of a hero."

"Does it?"

"No. Just more honest."

To her mind, his honesty was quite refreshing. "Why did you join up?"

"Patriotic fervor. The hunt for glory. It was something to do. Take your pick."

"A bit of all of those?"

"Most likely. After Sarah died, I was lost. I rattled around New York, aimless as a dropped coin. I didn't know what to do with myself. The one good thing about the war was that it gave me a purpose."

"Because you had something you were fighting for?"

He shook his head. "Because all I could think of was getting out of the army. I started to paint rosy pictures for myself of how it would be after the war, and since it's been over, I've put an awful lot of energy into making those pictures a reality."

Emily nodded, and they walked in silence for a few moments. "You must have loved Sarah DeKlerk very much."

He gave her an inscrutable look but then nodded. "She was something special."

Those terms were hardly equivalent. Emily made a mental note of the discrepancy. But how to pry more, without seeming to pry? "Yet you still call Dr. DeKlerk 'Brother.' You must have remained close, despite her passing."

"We have. Don't let Sam fool you. He tries to make everyone think he's a hopeless curmudgeon, but really he's as softhearted as they come."

"I gather that her death affected him greatly."

Mr. Romijn nodded. "I think the worst part for him was that he wasn't there. He felt that if he had been around, he could have prevented the gardener from ever getting close to Sarah. He's tormented himself with the idea for years. Of course, it doesn't help that the fiend was never brought to justice."

Now they were getting to the heart of the matter. "How is it that everyone was so sure of who committed the murder?"

"It wasn't too hard to figure out." The words came out of him with a knife-like edge. "The fellow ran away. Why would he have done that if he wasn't guilty?"

Emily kept her thoughts on that particular notion to herself. "But why should he have wanted to murder the daughter of the man he worked for?"

Mr. Romijn shook his head. "The lower classes can be depraved. But, as for his particular kind of madness, I don't know. You'll have to talk to Sam about that. Sometimes I think his preoccupation with diseases of the mind was sparked by Sarah's murder and not by the war, as he likes to assert."

"There you are, Robbie, lad, and Miss Forbes," a gruff, barking voice broke in. "I have been looking everywhere."

Dr. DeKlerk materialized from the shadows, as if a magician had conjured him from the night. He did not look at all happy.

Emily tightened her grip on Mr. Romijn's arm, but he didn't seem concerned about the doctor's scowl.

"I didn't realize my whereabouts were of such great importance," he said with a laugh.

"To me, they're not. But a certain Miss Farthington is pining at the loss of your company." Dr. DeKlerk motioned over his shoulder with a jerk of his chin. "It seems the party is deathly dull without you, and she will simply wither away unless you do her the honor of a dance."

Mr. Romijn's laugh rumbled up from deep in his chest. "Never let it be said that I would leave a lady in such distress." He looked down at Emily and patted her hand. "If you'll excuse me, Miss Forbes. I greatly enjoyed our stroll. Hopefully next time, we can avoid any interruptions."

With a two-fingered wave, he sauntered away, leaving Emily alone in the garden with the scowling doctor.

She gulped down a breath of cool evening air. "I should find Miss Clara. Good night, Doctor."

As she moved away, his hand shot out, fingers wrapping around her upper arm and pulling her to a stop.

"Not so fast, Miss Forbes." His brow was furrowed in consternation. "I have some questions. And this time, you're going to answer them."

Chapter 12

For a brief moment, panic coiled around Emily like a serpent, squeezing the air from her. It must have shown on her face, for the doctor's grip loosened, and his frown relaxed. Now, instead of furious, he simply looked mildly annoyed.

"What is it you want to know, Dr. DeKlerk?" It was a testament to her vocal training that she managed to keep her voice steady when her insides quivered like jelly.

"Why is it that you continue to interrogate Robert about my sister?"

Emily's fear abated as indignation took its place. "I did not interrogate him. We were having a pleasant conversation, nothing more."

"My sister's murder is hardly what I consider a pleasant topic."

She'd said the wrong thing again. And it wouldn't help to tell him that, considering how the conversation had started out, Sarah's demise was not the most unpleasant subject they'd covered.

"Forgive me, Dr. DeKlerk. I didn't mean to trivialize what happened to your sister. I simply meant that we talked as we walked, and the conversation moved along of its own accord."

He stared at her for a moment, then nodded, as if he accepted her explanation. Emily moved forward and winced as she stepped on a rock, which made the artificial limb dig into her stump. She hoped the doctor hadn't noticed, but, of course, he had.

"You've been on your feet too long." He frowned and looked around them. "Come. There's a bench beside the hedgerow."

His fingers slid down her arm to her elbow as he led her off the path and across the neatly manicured lawn. It felt wonderful to sit, although she wouldn't give him the satisfaction of admitting it.

Before Emily could say anything, the doctor angled his body toward her. "Why are you so fascinated with my sister's murder?"

Well, that was direct. And he deserved the same from her. "I never knew your sister, Doctor, but I feel as though I've lived with her ghost for years."

He frowned. "Because of your brother."

"Yes. You probably think that Carter had no personal stake in solving the case, but that isn't true. Carter chased Mr. Diamond across the country for years. And when it became obvious that Grant wasn't the murderer—"

"Wait." Dr. DeKlerk held up his hand. "You speak as if you know the man. Do you?"

"Not personally, no. But my brother got to know him quite well." An idea sparked in Emily's mind. If Dr. DeKlerk knew what kind of a man Grant Diamond was, then perhaps he'd be more apt to believe in his innocence. "Carter tells quite a colorful story of their encounter in Eureka, and how Mr. Diamond met the woman who is now his wife."

"Is that so?" It was difficult to make out the doctor's face in the dim light of the garden, but his hard tone communicated volumes. "Your brother is friends with the man who murdered my sister?"

Emily fisted her hands in her lap. This was not working how she'd hoped. "No, that's what I'm telling you. Mr. Diamond was not responsible for Sarah's death. On the contrary, he mourned for her. He loved her very much."

Dr. DeKlerk turned away, as though he had decided that not another word from her mouth could be believed. There had to be a way to make him see the truth.

"Doctor, I know how painful this is for you."

"You can't know," he growled.

"In fact, I can. My parents were killed in a robbery, and the culprit was never apprehended." She reached out and gently rested her hand on his shoulder. "It's one of the reasons Carter became a Pinkerton agent. He swore that no other family would go through the pain we did. That's why being unable to solve Sarah's case weighs so heavily on him."

Slowly, Dr. DeKlerk turned around. He looked down at her leg and then up again, meeting her eyes. "Is that when you were injured? During the robbery?"

"Yes."

"Miss Forbes, I—"

"Emily." If there was any chance that he would agree with her intended proposal, they needed to move beyond stiff formality. "Please, call me Emily."

His lips twitched, as though his attempt at a smile was too difficult to complete. "And you must call me Sam."

She nodded. "I know how much pain Sarah's passing brought you. It touched my family, as well. If there's any way I can help bring the criminal to justice, then I want to do so."

"I don't understand. You think you can investigate her murder?"

"I know I have no special training, but I do believe that whoever killed her knew her well. Right now, I don't know whom to suspect. Besides you, Mr. Romijn is the only person I've talked to who was close to Sarah."

Leaning forward, elbows to his knees, Sam gripped his hands tightly together. "It's too late. If a Pinkerton couldn't solve the crime, what hope do a doctor and an opera singer have?"

"Maybe none, but the least we can do is try. We have the benefit of hindsight, after all. We know that the prime suspect in the case was innocent. And you knew Sarah better than anyone else did. If we share information with each other, who knows what we might discover?"

Sam didn't speak, didn't move. Emily began to wonder if she should simply stand up and walk away, but then he straightened his spine and looked at her. "You really believe that, don't you?"

Conviction surged through her. "I do."

His shoulders shook in a mirthless laugh. "You're either the most optimistic woman I've ever met or the most naive. But, as lunatic as it sounds, I think you've convinced me to try."

Emily let out a quick, short breath. "Where do we start?"

"I'm not sure. But I know when, and it's not now." He rose to his feet and held out his hand to her. "If we don't return to the ball, Miss Clara may come looking for you, and I don't want to be on her bad side."

Emily laughed as she slid her hand into his. "A very smart decision, Doctor."

The decision to speak to Emily in his own territory may not have been the right one, after all.

They'd agreed to meet following her rehearsal, and she'd arrived at the clinic at four o'clock. As luck would have it, that was also when Randall Wade stumbled through the doors for an unscheduled appointment.

The man barreled past Emily, nearly knocking her down, then rushed to Sam, blabbering incoherently the whole time.

"So loud! So loud! The flowers, all dead. Dry and dead!" Randall pressed down the matted hair on the side of his head with the heel of his left hand, while the fingers of his right picked compulsively at the ragged edge of his filthy jacket.

Emily stood just inside the door, her back plastered against the wall, her face pale from shock. It was a miracle she was still in the room. Most people would have fled rather than share the same space with Randall.

"Dry and dead. Dry and dead."

Sam focused all his attention on the agitated man. "Yes, Randall. But new flowers will grow in the spring."

With his arms down at his sides, hands open, palms facing out, Sam moved slowly toward him. Randall was no longer hitting his head, but his left eye blinked furiously.

"Why? Why do they die?"

"Nothing lasts forever. All God's creation dies. There's no way around it." Sam kept his voice low and soothing. "Remember what we talked about?"

Randall jerked his head up and down. "God gives. God takes."

"Yes. And God sees all. He knows that none of it was your fault."

Tears tracked their way through the grime on Randall's cheeks. "But so many...so many dead." He sucked in a gasping breath, once, then twice. His body jerked, and he gasped again.

"Randall." Sam spoke firmly, but there was no response. "Randall." Louder, yet still no reaction. "Lieutenant Wade! Attention!"

At Sam's gruff order, the man pulled himself up straight as a poker. The shaking and the tears stopped, although his breathing remained labored. "Yes, sir," he croaked out.

"Get ahold of yourself, Soldier. If you hadn't done what you did, no one would know of the bravery of your unit. Do you understand that?"

"Yes, sir." The words were barely a whisper.

"Good man." He grasped Randall by the shoulders, squeezing them firmly. "Your life is a gift. But death is not punishment."

Randall blinked. He didn't argue, but Sam knew it would take a long time before those words rang true for him—if they ever did.

"Randall! Randall!" A woman burst through the still-open door. Perspiration wetted her brow, and her hair had come loose from its pins. She looked as though she'd run for miles. When she saw Randall, she stopped short and flattened her palm against her heaving bosom. "Thank heaven he's with you, Doctor."

And thank heaven Randall's sister had found him. "No need to fret, Charlotte. He knew to come somewhere safe. That's progress."

"I don't know what happened. He's been fine for nigh on a month. But today...." Her voice trailed off into a sob.

"He said something about a loud noise."

Charlotte's eyes grew wide with realization. "The guns. There was shooting behind our tenement."

Sam didn't dare ask what the shooting was about, lest he be pulled into another crisis situation. "That must have triggered it. Do you have any of the laudanum I gave you?"

"Yes, some."

"Good. Put a little in his tea, and he should be calm for the night. When he's coherent, bring him back, and we'll have a chat."

Charlotte put her arm around her brother's shoulders and pulled him to her. "Thank you, Dr. DeKlerk." She looked at Randall. "We're going to go home now, and you can have a big piece of pie."

A spark of life flickered in Randall's eyes. "Apple?"

"Of course. I made it for you, special."

Charlotte carefully steered her brother out into the street. Sam shut the door behind them, then turned to Emily. "I apologize for that scene. He's a patient."

"I gathered as much." She pushed herself away from the wall and looked toward the door. "That poor man. Did you call him 'Lieutenant'?"

Sam nodded. "He fought in the war—valiantly. But he came home a totally different person from the one who left."

"Now I understand what Mr. Romijn meant when he said you deal with diseases of the mind." It was a compassionate statement, free of judgment or censure.

"I hope you'll still entrust the care of your leg to me," Sam teased, hoping to lighten the mood.

"Oh heavens, yes. It would be too much trouble to train a new doctor now." Her dimpled smile let him know she jested in return.

"In that case, let's get that out of the way." He opened the door to the examining room and ushered her in.

"Yes, let's. And then we can get down to the business at hand."

As she swept past him, a whiff of lavender tickled his nose. Emily Forbes had his attention, for more reasons than he cared to admit. "Is Miss Clara here?"

She looked at him over her shoulder, chin high, eyes meeting his in a challenge. "Miss Clara would not approve."

"Uh." He glanced back out the door he had not yet closed, as if the older woman might still appear, if he wished for it hard enough. "Do you think that's wise? I don't wish to injure your reput—"

"Is my virtue in danger here?"

"No. No, not at all." He shut the door reluctantly. "Not from me."

"I thought not."

"But if this should get out, it would be extremely compromising."

"Then I shall have to rely on your discretion."

Sam shook his head. A part of him condemned her foolhardiness, while another part admired her courage, and yet another wondered what she was really after.

Chapter 13

The doctor's office was small and a bit cluttered but surprisingly cozy. It seemed lived-in, loved. The wooden desk was free of dust, and the brass on the lamp gleamed. Books, a sure way to make any space homey, lined the shelves along one wall. A patterned rug softened the bare boards of the floor. A rather good rug, if Emily was any judge. If the doctor's patients had an idea of its value, they would have looted the place ages ago. The mantel held an ormolu clock, and a fine watercolor of the seaside decorated one wall. Even the most uncultured ruffian would recognize these items as having value, and yet they remained unmolested. Emily reappraised the doctor as he shifted a foot-high stack of papers from his desk to an empty chair. He pulled another chair close to the desk so that Emily could sit.

"Would you like something to drink?"

He was nothing if not well mannered.

Emily shook her head.

At last, not having anything else to fidget with, he took his own place behind the desk. He clasped his hands together, then dropped them into his lap. Leaned forward and then back. One would think he was the one who had risked his reputation and his future to take part in this conversation.

Somehow his nervousness made her calmer. At last, she took pity on him. "Dr. DeKler—Sam, perhaps you could start by telling me what you remember of what happened to your sister."

"The problem is that I was so far removed from what was going on here. I don't know what she was doing her last days. I received a telegram at school. I was called out of class. Very unusual, I assure you." His voice was tight, controlled, as if he had rehearsed what he would say but still found it no easier to release the words into the air. "The telegram said simply that she had passed. It didn't even hint at murder, but I caught the first train home. I didn't pack anything. Didn't get leave of my professors or even tell anyone farewell." He raised his eyes from his scrutiny of the desktop, his mouth curved in a rueful, heartbreakingly sad smile. "I think a part of me hoped they had been mistaken, that my newfound physician's skills could save the day."

Emily's fingers ached to smooth away the lines of grief that scored his face. The poor man looked as if he had forgotten what happiness felt like. She folded her hands in her lap, planting them firmly where they could not get her into trouble.

"They didn't even want to let me see her when I arrived, but I insisted. It is...." He drew in a breath. "It is something I regret to this day. I would have been better off without that image in my mind, but I was so stubborn."

"Did you notice anything unusual?"

He sighed. "It's not a subject for a lady. Suffice it to say that it was obvious she had been throttled."

Emily decided she wasn't sure she wanted to know what had made it obvious.

He carried on. "My father showed me where she'd been found. The area had been searched thoroughly, but nothing had turned up. By this time, the gardener's disappearance had been discovered, and a manhunt was under way. My father suspected that Sarah had caught him doing something nefarious and that he'd killed her in the fear of the moment."

"Did that theory make sense to you?"

He leaned back and looked down the length of his nose at her. "Why wouldn't it?"

She needed to tread carefully. "It does leave several things unexplained. For example, why was Sarah alone outside in the middle of the night?"

"What are you trying to imply?"

Carefully. Carefully. "I'm not trying to imply that Sarah couldn't have had a legitimate reason to be out of doors; I'm just asking what it was. We have to weigh all the evidence and question everything if we are to have any hope of getting to the bottom of this."

He rubbed his eyes. "You're right, of course. Tell me, though, why do you care? What do you hope to gain by this?"

"I want my brother to have peace. And, to be honest, I want to vindicate him. He did not handle the case inappropriately. He was assigned to chase down Grant Diamond, and he did. But when he was convinced that Diamond wasn't the murderer, he had to start trying to fit the pieces of the puzzle into a different pattern, and when he left out Diamond, he realized that an entirely different picture was beginning to emerge."

"What picture?"

"Well, if we set aside the certainty that Diamond was the murderer, perhaps we will realize there are more questions to which we don't have answers."

"What makes your brother—what makes *you*—so sure that Diamond didn't do it?"

Emily hesitated. "I told you that Grant Diamond loved Sarah. She loved him, too."

His face turned red, and she rushed on before he could explode.

"She did. They were supposed to elope that very night."

He shook his head. "That's not true."

"It is." She couldn't back down now. "Mr. Diamond had a note from her."

"How could you know it was genuine?" Sam glared at her, his gaze challenging.

It was time to hurry on. "I've seen it. He gave it to Carter, and Carter compared it to other verified examples of her writing. If you can allow that it was even a possibility she was willing to run away with him, what reason would he have to harm her?"

"Maybe she changed her mind." Sam squeezed his eyes shut, as though the answer to his questions could be found in the darkness. "Maybe she went out that night and told him she wasn't going to run away with him, after all, and he lost control of himself and attacked her."

"Did you know him?" Emily was curious.

His eyes snapped open, and he looked taken aback. "I—well, yes."

"Think back. Did he seem like the kind of man to murder a young woman?"

Her question did nothing to soften his visage. In fact, it only grew harder. "If I've learned anything in the last few years, it's that no one can tell what's in a man's heart."

Exasperation threatened to propel Emily to her feet and straight out the door. But instead, she gripped the arms of the chair and leaned forward. "Do you want to hear what he said happened or not?"

~⌒~

Blood pounded in Sam's ears as he clenched his jaw and waited.

"All right." Emily folded her hands primly in her lap. Surely, she wasn't as collected as she pretended to be. "Mr. Diamond claims he arrived at the garden at the appointed time and found her already lying dead on the ground. Just about that time, a light came on in the house, and the hue and cry was raised. He backed away and tripped over the bag she had brought with her. He couldn't believe what was happening, but he was scared, and it seemed to him that the timing wasn't a coincidence. It seemed as if someone wanted him to be found with her so that he'd be blamed for her death. So he ran."

"That's his story?" Sam indulged himself a snort. "How is that credible? Why not stay in the city and explain to the police?"

She frowned as if he had disappointed her. "Tell me, Doctor, do you find that the poor people of New York have a great deal of confidence in the police force?"

She had a point. Still, why would anyone believe that story? "He made up that ridiculous tale to save his own skin. No one made any mention of a packed bag or indicated that Sarah had taken anything at all outside with her."

Emily stood, a flush reddening her cheeks. "Why don't you ask your parents if there was a bag? Then you can decide whether you are serious about this endeavor or not."

Without another word, the ever-exasperating young woman turned and walked from the clinic, pulling the door shut behind her with a firm thud.

Emily Forbes was way off the mark. The idea that Sarah had planned to run away with the gardener was…well, it was inconceivable. Never in a million years would he believe such a fanciful tale. Still, as Sam lay in bed that night, with sleep nothing but an elusive desire, that fanciful tale was all he could think of.

Sam had been away from home for two years when Sarah was murdered. When he'd left, she was an innocent fifteen-year-old, more interested in her artwork than in boys or romance. But so much could change in two years. He remembered how she'd loved to take her easel out on the grounds of the estate and paint whatever struck her fancy. With all the time she spent outside, it was possible she might have started up a friendship with the gardener. But anything beyond that?

Abandoning the idea of slumber, Sam threw back the covers and sat up. Something nagged at him. He lit the lamp beside his bed and reached for the ribbon-bound packet of letters. Sarah's letters.

Starting at the beginning, he opened each one and read it carefully. The first had arrived three weeks after he'd left home for college. His absence had been hard on Sarah. Without him around to focus on, their mother's attention had shifted to her. At the time he'd received the letters, the accounts had seemed little more than the power struggles between a mother and daughter. But now, with the benefit of hindsight, he began to read more into Sarah's words.

Mother has decided I devote entirely too much time to my watercolors. She says all the time I spend in the garden will freckle my skin and make me unfit for a proper suitor. Sam, you are so lucky to be a man. No one cares whether or not you have freckles. The world we live in is so superficial. I will never understand why status and station are so important, while the condition of someone's heart seems to matter not a whit.

He and Sarah had had many conversations about status and how unimportant it was in the grand scheme of life. At first read, he'd thought that was all there was to it. But now, he wondered: Had all those hours in the garden been not just for Sarah to paint the beauty of nature but to spend time with the gardener, a man who, though below her station, she saw as having a good heart? And had their mother recognized that? Was that why she'd tried to restrict Sarah's painting time?

Sam frowned as he folded the thin piece of vellum and slid it back in the envelope. If that was true, it opened the door for other troubling thoughts. Before he could dwell on them, he moved to the next piece of correspondence.

The next few letters were unremarkable. Sarah continued to mention her artwork and her mother's dislike of it, but she didn't talk about her time in the garden. Then, in a letter dated five months before her death, a passage jumped out at Sam.

I've decided that, no matter what Mother says, I must live my life as I see fit. Painting fills an emptiness in my heart, and I refuse to give it up. The garden inspires me, so I have taken to visiting it in the evenings. Unless I fall prey to moon burn, my skin is in no danger whatsoever.

A kind of code was beginning to emerge, although he was sure Sarah had never meant for it to be deciphered. When she spoke of painting, she meant her romantic relationship. And when she spoke of the garden, she really meant the gardener.

If he was interpreting it correctly, then her last letter—the one in which she spoke of a scheme, the details of which she would not disclose—finally became clear. She had fallen in love with a common gardener and planned to run away with him.

Sam shook his head sharply. No. None of it made sense. If Sarah had arranged a rendezvous with Grant Diamond that night, intending to leave with him, then why would he kill her? On the other hand, if she met with him to say that she'd changed her mind, he could have been so outraged by her betrayal that he choked the life from her. The authorities hadn't reported finding any luggage, which implied she'd had no intention of going anywhere. But Diamond claimed he'd tripped over her bag when he found her, already dead. There was only one reason Sam would consider believing anything Diamond had to say.

Because Emily Forbes believed it to be true.

He carefully stacked the letters, retied the ribbon around them, and placed them back in the box. All the while he muttered under his breath. Like it or not, he would have to make a trip to the family estate. Or he might never sleep again.

⌐

"We should spend some time this evening on the phrasing in the rondo *finale*." Miss Clara adjusted her bonnet as they stepped out of the theater and into the warm evening air.

Emily nodded. After endless hours in the dry, stale atmosphere of the theater, she'd been looking forward to getting outside. But as she took in a deep breath, the smells of the city, mixed with the heavy moisture in the air, seemed to lodge in her throat.

As if sensing her discomfort, Miss Clara threaded her hand through the crook of Emily's arm and patted her shoulder. "You save your voice, dear. When we return to the room, I'll fix you a nice cup of tea with honey. That will soothe your throat and help you relax."

Miss Clara let Emily set the pace as they strolled down the street to their hotel. All around them, the city bustled. Emily had spent a good deal of her life in cities, but nothing had prepared her for New York. It seemed she found a surprise around every corner.

As they neared the hotel, another surprise greeted Emily. Sam DeKlerk stood with his back against the brick wall, his eyes trained in her direction, making it obvious he'd been waiting for her.

"Dr. DeKlerk," Miss Clara said brightly. "To what do we owe this pleasure? Is our little songbird due for a check?"

Sam stepped away from the wall and shook his head. "No. I believe Miss Forbes's leg is sufficiently healed. Unless a new injury occurs, my services are no longer needed in that regard." He turned to Emily and spoke directly to her. "I was hoping you might have a moment to talk?"

Emily blushed as Miss Clara looked from her to Sam, a sly smile quirking her lips. "Certainly. There's a sitting area off the lobby. We could talk there. If my chaperone approves, of course."

Miss Clara waved her hand at the notion. "If I can't trust you in the company of the good doctor, then who can I trust you with?"

Having overheard the entire conversation, the doorman took his cue and held the door open. Sam motioned for the ladies to enter, then followed them inside.

"I'll wait for you in our suite." Miss Clara patted Emily's cheek. "Remember, you need to rest your voice, so don't talk too much."

Emily nodded in agreement.

"A good evening to you, Doctor." Giving a fluttery wave of her hand, Miss Clara hurried down the hall and out of view.

With his hand lightly on Emily's elbow, Sam led the way to an ornately detailed settee situated against a wall between two ornamental palms. As she sat, Emily noted that the location, although still public, did offer a modicum of privacy. Still, she made a point to keep her voice low.

"Did you think about what I said?" she asked. "About Sarah?"

"I did." He didn't look at her as he spoke. Instead, he kept his back straight, his hands tightly clasped in his lap, and stared across the lobby at the registration desk. It was as though he was weighing how much to say. Finally, he took in a long, deep breath and turned his whole body to face her. "Sarah wrote to me when I was away at university, for two years, before her death. I reread her letters last night."

Emily leaned closer. "Did you discover anything?"

"Yes. Maybe. Honestly, I don't know." He pinched his chin with his thumb and forefinger, tugging on his whiskers. "It was enough for me to doubt what I've believed all these years."

"I see." What else was there to say? Emily was filled to the brim with questions, but she didn't want to push him. Thankfully, it appeared he wanted to talk through it with someone, and she was there to listen.

"She wrote things in her letters about spending time in the garden to paint, how she loved it, but how Mother thought it was unbecoming for a young lady of her status." Sam snorted. "Sarah didn't care at all about status. The more I thought about it, the more I realized it's not such a huge leap to believe that she visited the garden for the love of a man, not her love of painting plants, and that that was the real reason Mother was upset."

"Have your parents ever mentioned Sarah being in love?"

Sam jerked his head hard to the side. "Never. My father was so adamant that the gardener was the culprit, I never imagined he and Sarah could have been on intimate terms. Especially since she was engaged to Robert." His eyes opened a bit wider, as if it was the first time this thought had occurred to him.

"Well." Emily looked down at her hands. She took a deep breath, examined the palm beside her, then slowly let the breath out. This was awkward.

"You were right." Sam spoke so softly, she almost didn't hear him. "I need to talk to my parents. Which is why I came to see you."

He smiled, as though it all made perfect sense. It didn't. At her confused look, he continued.

"I wanted you to know that I am taking this step. It will likely be upsetting to them. I needed to see you. To—I need to know that this is not some sort of game you are playing."

His eyes were warm but searching as they examined her. A little wave of shame lapped at her heart. In a way, she had been treating this as a game. His obvious concern made her realize that digging into the past was going to affect people here and now, and not just the killer.

She was convinced that Grant Diamond was innocent, and that the real murderer was still out there somewhere, but she needed to approach this undertaking with the gravitas it deserved.

Emily swallowed hard and reached to touch the doctor's hand. "When you put it like that, I feel a great weight of responsibility." She met his eyes. "I promise you that I am sincere. I am not just seeking a thrill or the challenge of a puzzle."

He nodded once. "All right, then. I will go to them."

"Thank you, Doctor. I hadn't considered this before, but I think it's very brave of you to be willing to search for the truth."

He lifted his eyebrows in an exaggerated fashion. "Did you just give me a compliment?" Clutching his chest, he sagged against the back of the settee. "I don't know if my heart can take the shock."

Emily laughed, and a moment later, his deep-throated chuckle joined in. It was good to know that not only did Sam DeKlerk have a heart; he had a sense of humor. The deeper he delved into the circumstances surrounding his sister's death, the more he was likely to need it.

Chapter 15

Sam stood just outside the gate of his family's estate. Now that he looked at that disapproving façade, with its curtained windows looking like heavily lidded eyes, he regretted that he hadn't sent news of his arrival in advance. Mother and Father both would be pressing him to stay for an extended time.

The front door swung open, and the butler stepped onto the porch. "Master DeKlerk, it is good to see you." His smile was broad enough to make the tufts of white hair around his ears bob up and down.

Sam clapped the old fellow on the shoulder. "Mr. Milo, it's likewise good to see you. I trust your family is well?"

"Yessir. Mrs. Milo is still ruling the kitchen with an iron fist, as she always has. And our eldest girl, Jane, has married and is running a kitchen of her own."

"A fine tradition to carry on."

"Yessir. Thank you, sir. Your mother is waiting for you in the morning room."

"How does she know I'm here?"

Old Milo glanced to one side and then the other, then leaned closer. "She was upstairs when she saw your carriage pull in, and she hurried there, deeming it the proper place to receive you."

"Then I mustn't keep her waiting any longer." Sam would have preferred to stay chatting with Milo, but there was no use delaying the inevitable.

As promised, Sam found his mother sitting in the morning room. She held an open book in her hands, but her eyes were on the door, not on the pages. A smile creased her lips at his appearance.

"Samuel, this is an unexpected pleasure."

He approached and planted a kiss on her cheek, finding it cool, despite the summer warmth. The smell of her, all rose water, powder, and starch, cast him back to his childhood, and he felt like he was in short pants again. "Mother, you are looking well."

"I'm quite fit for my age. A good thing, since my physician son lives so far away." She patted his arm, then left her hand resting lightly there, pinning him in place.

He would not be drawn into a wrangle. "And how is Father?"

"Working, as usual. Why he wants to spend all his time in a dreary old office, even at his age, I don't know."

"He enjoys the business, I think. He always has."

"As would you, if you would simply give it a try."

Sam gently freed his arm from her hand. "Mother, I did try it, and it was not at all to my taste. I couldn't summon up enough interest to last a week, much less a lifetime."

"But it would make him so happy if you would join him in the business."

"I know it would, but not for long. He'd only be disappointed when he found I had no knack for it." The argument was so old and well-worn that the fire and bite had long ago left the words. At this point, it was merely a ritual, like haggling with a shop owner over the price of wares.

"Well." She sighed. "I know you always say that, but, just the same, I think you don't give yourself enough credit. You could do anything you set your mind to; it's simply that you have decided you don't wish to continue your family's heritage."

"That is correct, Mother. Nor do I think you wish it of me. Have you forgotten that your great-grandfather was a pirate who plundered up and down the coast? I suppose you would prefer I took up his trade, since it is part of my heritage, than practice the shameful profession of doctoring."

"Oh, rubbish, Samuel." She flapped a hand at him. "Those were only vicious rumors. And really, it isn't the fact that you are a physician that I object to, but that you live in that wretched neighborhood in New York and treat those filthy vagabonds you dote upon."

"Those vagabonds were soldiers who fought gallantly for the Union."

A heavy sigh. As usual, he had managed to irritate her with his recalcitrance. "I suppose you will do as you wish, just as usual, so I shall stop trying to get you to see sense."

A maid came in, bearing a tray of tea things, and there was a pause in the proceedings as the niceties were observed.

The worst of it was out of the way, at least for the moment. Sam relaxed back against the seat cushions. "Tell me how your committee work is going."

"Well enough." Mother closed her book and set it on a side table that was already loaded with an array of trinkets, knick-knacks, and *objets d'art*.

Sam thought for a moment that she was going to make the conversation hard work indeed. But an instant later, she launched into a tale about a power struggle between herself and an upstart rival whose family had only owned a home on Fifth Avenue for a single generation. By the time she had finished relating the story, with a relish that would have done her buccaneer ancestor proud, she was in a good humor.

She frequently reached over and patted his arm, as if to reassure herself that he was actually there. Finally she put down her teacup with the silence one would expect of well-bred hands, and eyed him shrewdly. "Now, out with it. Why are you here? And don't tell me it is because you wished to hear about my doings with that dreadful Lois Callister, because I won't believe it."

Sam was a little taken aback. His mother was not normally so direct. He decided to respond in kind. "To be honest, I have been thinking of Sarah a great deal lately."

His mother's cheeks grew a shade paler. "Sarah? Why—"

"Do you really believe that the gardener killed her?"

She drew back. "Who else could it have been? Really, Samuel, you are acting so odd today. Surely, you didn't come all this way to start an argument?"

"No." Sam smacked his teacup down in the saucer, almost hard enough to chip the delicate porcelain. "I came to ask a question."

His mother's gray eyes were remote as a winter sky. She raised her chin and then, with deliberate grace, picked up her own teacup and saucer. "Then ask and be done."

She knew precisely how to drive him right past annoyance to exasperation. He spoke with more force than he might have otherwise. "Sarah was planning to elope with the gardener, wasn't she?"

The teacup and saucer tumbled from his mother's hands. Steaming tea cascaded down the silk of her skirts. The dishes landed on the ground, but the thick woolen rug kept them from smashing to bits.

Sam jumped to his feet. "Mother!"

She didn't respond.

⌒

Emily sipped her punch delicately. It was tart and crisp, and tasted better than she'd expected. She let it linger on her tongue for a moment.

Miss Farthington approached, her hair in perfect ringlets, her gown dripping with lace, her smile dripping with sweetness. "Dear Miss Forbes, we are so glad to have you with us this evening." She linked her arm through Emily's and drew her along.

Emily forced a smile of her own. "I do appreciate the invitation. It's a lovely garden party."

"Aren't you sweet. I knew we were going to be good friends the minute I saw you."

Emily got the impression that Miss Farthington's simper was practice for more worthwhile prey. Nevertheless, she smiled broadly. "Did you organize the evening?"

"No, that was Mama. But, of course, if I'd left it all up to her, it would have been dreadfully dull."

Emily didn't know quite how to respond. "Oh?"

"Yes. I had to insist that she invite some more interesting guests, such as yourself."

Emily practiced a simper of her own. She cast a glance about, searching for a way to escape. Among the strangers all around, she saw a single familiar face. "Is that Mr. Romijn I see?"

"Oh, yes. Another one of my invitees. He is rather dashing, don't you think?"

"He is, indeed. Dashing and handsome both."

Miss Farthington shook her head. "He has the most tragic past, but I think it gives him a romantic air."

Emily's ears tingled. "Tragic? Oh, you mean the war."

Another coy shake of Miss Farthington's head. "Not the war. Seems everyone was touched by that tragedy. No, he's tragic in love." The girl looked both ways and then pulled Emily into an alcove away from the other guests. "He was engaged to a young woman who was murdered."

Emily endeavored to react with suitable astonishment.

"And not only that, but the other girl he was in love with became ill and had to be sent to a sanitarium. I hear that she is still there, wasting away, and that's why he hasn't married."

Emily no longer had to manufacture an expression of surprise. "Was this someone he fell in love with after his fiancée passed away?"

"No." The curve of Miss Farthington's lips showed how much she was relishing passing on the old gossip. "He was in love with them both at the same time. Some say that Sarah DeKlerk wasn't murdered at all. They say that when she found out about Alice, she killed herself."

"That's awful." Emily had progressed from surprise to shock.

Miss Farthington nodded knowingly, her lips pursed. "Isn't it, though?"

As Emily processed this new information, a thought occurred to her. "You said the other woman's name was Alice?"

"Yes, Alice Geddes."

The woman Emily had assumed had been a friend of Sarah's. She eyed Robert Romijn speculatively as he bent over the dainty hand of a lovely young debutante. The gossip about Sarah committing suicide couldn't be right. No one would kill herself over the demise of a relationship she had intended to end anyway.

But could the wagging tongues be right that Romijn had been pursuing another lady—Sarah's friend, at that? Perhaps Sarah had found out about his infidelity and they had quarreled. Though, if she was being courted by the gardener at the same time....

Emily took another sip of her punch while Miss Farthington continued to prattle. She knew Mr. Romijn was one of Sam's oldest friends, and it was doubtful that the doctor would be willing to consider him as a possible suspect. But the doctor wasn't there.

Emily drained her glass with one final, unladylike gulp. Miss Farthington's eyes opened wide. "Goodness, all that singing must leave one parched."

"Indeed it does," Emily agreed with a coy smile. "And this punch is delicious. If you'll excuse me, I believe I'd enjoy another glass."

Without waiting for the young debutante to reply, Emily made her way across the room to a waiter holding a silver tray laden with full crystal glasses. He also happened to be standing quite close to Mr. Romijn. And this time, Sam DeKlerk wasn't around to interrupt their conversation.

Chapter 16

Tea seeped through the knee of Sam's trousers as he knelt in front of his mother. He was used to her theatrics, but this was something more. The mention of Sarah eloping with the gardener had rendered her nearly apoplectic.

"Mother." He held her hands tightly in his. "Mother, look at me."

Slowly, she lowered her chin, but her eyes remained unfocused, staring through Sam. He'd seen that look before, on the faces of family members who had just been informed that a loved one had died on the battlefield. It was a mixture of denial—a refusal to believe the truth—and pain, because, deep down, there was no way not to believe it.

"Sarah's been gone for ten years." Sam kept his voice low and gentle. "Why does the mention of her upset you so?"

His mother blinked, then closed her eyes for a moment. When she opened them again, she was back from whatever place her mind had retreated to. "How could you say such a thing?"

For the first time ever, he found his mother's righteous indignation encouraging. She was her normal self again. "It seems I've hit upon something, Mother, or it wouldn't have elicited such a severe reaction."

She pursed her lips tightly, as though she'd been forced to bite into a lemon.

Sam gave her hands another squeeze, then stood up. After pulling the wet fabric away from his knee, he retrieved the cup and saucer from the floor, set them on the table, and settled back in his chair. "You knew she planned to elope with Diamond, didn't you?"

At the mention of his name, she snorted with derision. "A common gardener. After all we'd done for her. How could she?"

That was as good as an admission. "If she fell in love, it wouldn't have mattered whether he was a landowner or a land tender. Sarah never cared about class and status."

His mother shook her head. "I tried to tell her it would come to no good. There's a reason the classes are separate. If she hadn't been involved with that…that…man, she'd still be alive today."

"That might be true, but not for the reason everyone has thought all these years."

"What are you talking about?"

Sam took in a deep breath, not at all wanting to answer her question. "I have begun to doubt that Diamond killed her."

"Have you lost your senses?" Her voice was hard and thin, and she clenched her hands into fists in her lap. "Of course he killed her. It's the only thing that makes sense."

"No, Mother. It makes no sense whatsoever." Frustration propelled Sam from the chair, and he began to pace. "Haven't you wondered why Sarah was in the garden that night? It's because she planned to elope with Diamond. Which means he would have had no reason to kill her."

"A man like that doesn't need a reason."

The vitriol in his mother's voice stopped Sam cold in his tracks. "A man like what? How much time did you spend with Diamond?"

"None. Why would I have?"

"My point exactly. You have no idea what kind of man he is."

She turned her head away. "Neither do you."

"True. But I knew Sarah, very well. And I trusted her judgment. If she fell in love with that man, he must have had some truly admirable qualities."

"No." A whimper escaped her trembling lips. "It had to be him."

Sam heard what she didn't dare say: *If it wasn't the gardener, then who?* "What happened to the suitcase?"

Her eyes snapped to meet his so quickly, there was no way she could deny it. "How did you know?"

"I've recently learned that Diamond has always insisted he tripped over Sarah's suitcase that night, which proves that she went there to run away with him, not to spurn him." Sam sighed and rubbed his face with his hand. "Who hid it? You, or Father?"

"Your father. I begged him to. I didn't want anyone to know." She looked at him with eyes that pleaded for understanding. "I had to protect your sister's reputation."

And in so doing, she had not only sullied the reputation of an innocent man; she'd sent a Pinkerton on a cross-country wild goose chase while the real killer went free. Was there any way to make this right?

"What did Father do with the suitcase?"

He expected her to say it had been disposed of—buried, burned, or tossed in a lake. But his mother glanced up at the ceiling.

"He hid it. In the attic."

Sam nodded, stood, and walked from the room.

As he made his way upstairs, kerosene lamp in hand, he thought of Emily Forbes and how she had set this whole thing in motion. What was she doing now? Rehearsing? More likely, she was back in her room, resting. At least, he hoped she was. They would have a lot to talk about once he returned home.

⌒

"Mr. Romijn. How nice to see you."

Emily felt a tinge of guilt for pulling his attention away from the young woman he was speaking to, but if her suspicion panned out, then she was really doing her a favor. So, she ignored the girl's frown when Mr. Romijn turned away from her.

"Miss Forbes. You are lovely, as always."

Doing her best imitation of Miss Farthington, Emily fluttered her lashes and grinned in a way she knew made her dimples show. "You flatter me, sir."

Mr. Romijn glanced around quickly. "I was looking for Samuel earlier, but I haven't seen him."

"Really? I hadn't noticed." Which was true, since she hadn't been looking for him. But there was no reason for her to say where he really was.

Mr. Romijn smiled broadly. "Perhaps you and I can finally have a conversation without fear of interruption."

He took a step closer, requiring Emily to make a conscious effort not to back away. "Perhaps we can. I would love to hear more about the museum."

The mention of his work sparked a different kind of light in his eyes. As he spoke about the new exhibit he was putting together, she saw something in him she hadn't seen before: enthusiasm. From what she'd observed, he usually put up a front, a façade, to hide behind. But his interest in his work was 100 percent genuine, just as Emily had hoped.

As they continued talking, Emily waited for an opening so she could steer the conversation. It came when he mentioned his idea for an exhibit based on great couples in literature.

"What a fabulous idea!" Emily leaned forward so fast, she nearly lost her balance. "Will you focus on world literature or limit the focus to American?"

Mr. Romijn folded his arms and looked down at her. "I've been pondering that very question myself. Both approaches have merit, but I haven't made a decision. Do you have an opinion on the matter?"

Emily tapped her finger against her closed lips as she considered her next words. "The average patron might have more of an affinity for American literature, but then, you'd be denying him the truly heartrending, tragic romances."

His forehead wrinkled in a frown. "That could be a good thing."

Pretending not to notice his discomfort, Emily pressed on. "Isn't it odd how so many of the great love stories end in tragedy? You would expect love to be simple and bring nothing but happiness."

"You've never been in love, have you, Miss Forbes?"

His words were cold and brittle, encased in a thin layer of ice. All Emily could do was shake her head.

"Then it's no wonder the complexities escape you. Love is many things, but simple is not one of them."

For a moment, he looked so stricken that Emily regretted her clumsy attempt at detective work. "I'm very sorry, Mr. Romijn. I spoke out of turn."

His lips twisted into a smirk, and he regained his devil-may-care demeanor. "No need to apologize. I have loved, and I have lost, and in the process, I've given the town gossips enough fodder to fill volumes. Now, if you'll excuse me, I really should chat with Miss Farthington before she hurts herself trying to get my attention."

He bowed ever so slightly, then walked away. Sure enough, the young woman he approached was simpering and fluttering her eyelashes with such vigor, she almost looked as if she had been brought to tears from chopping raw onion. Emily continued to watch as he took her hand and barely brushed his lips across the top of her gloved knuckles. The torrent of giggles this elicited was far more than the act deserved. Biting her lip to hold back her own laughter, Emily moved into the thickest crush of partygoers. Behind the amorous couple, she'd spied Mr. Kerns, the former police commissioner, and she had a few questions for him.

His smile was tepid. "Miss Forbes," He inclined his head in her direction. "How are you on this beautiful afternoon?"

Emily swished her fan languidly. "I'm curious." She smiled and made her tone light. "It's a family failing. I take after my brother in that respect. And, speaking of siblings. I've been discussing Sarah's case with her brother, Dr. DeKlerk. I believe there are some…discrepancies in what the police reported and what actually happened that night."

Mr. Kerns' face froze, except for a muscle at the corner of his jaw that ticked alarmingly. The man obviously did not like having his department's competency questioned. "That was a long time ago. After all this time, who can really say what happened?"

Emily refused to be dismissed so easily. "I was hoping to see the original police report, but when I inquired at the station, I was turned away."

"And very rightly. Police reports can't be handed out willy-nilly; they often contain information of a highly personal or confidential nature."

"But surely, at this late date, there can be no danger of that. Particularly when everyone is so convinced that the murderer was Grant Diamond."

"Diamond was the murderer. And there is absolutely no value in raking up the old tragedy." He spoke in a soft, singsong manner, as though she was dull-witted and unlikely to comprehend him. "Police work is complex. You'd do well to leave it to those capable of understanding it."

And now he had called her stupid. Emily bristled. "See here—"

"Miss Forbes." He cut her off smoothly, his palm in her face. "I would never attempt to sing an aria. It would be a disaster. Let us agree to keep to our own professions, shall we?"

Another nod, and he turned on his heel and melted into the crowd.

What an insufferable man. Emily forced herself to take a deep breath and relax the muscles that had tightened throughout her body. If she was going to learn anything from the police department, it wouldn't be through Commissioner Kerns.

Emily walked slowly around the perimeter of the room, watching the dancers but pondering the events of the evening. Kerns was right about one thing: As a detective, she hadn't done much of a job. Carter definitely had nothing to worry about in that department. But she had learned a few things. Robert Romijn was aware of the gossip surrounding his love life, yet he hadn't denied it or made any effort to defend himself. And now, Emily knew about Alice Geddes. Had he really been in love with this other girl while he was engaged to Sarah? Or was the timing something that had been exaggerated as the story spread from one set of lips to the next?

She would have to ask Sam about Miss Geddes. Maybe he knew what illness she had. It could be the coughing sickness, or some kind of cancer that did not allow her to be cared for at home.

A disturbing thought came to Emily: Did Sam even know about this other woman? If not, how would he react when he learned his best friend might have been deceiving his sister? She'd hoped to have news to share with Sam when he returned from visiting his family home. She just wished it wasn't this particular news.

Chapter 17

Sam stared at the accumulation of debris that littered the attic: a hobbyhorse with a ravaged tail and paint nearly worn away from overuse; an elaborate dollhouse; a jumble of piled hatboxes and old lampshades; and more boxes, bags, and trunks than he could count. The organization of the attic was obviously not high on anyone's list of priorities.

He hadn't even started digging and he was already sweating. With a sigh, he took off his coat, rolled up his sleeves, and pried open the two small dormer windows.

Sarah had been fairly practical. She wouldn't have carried a bag that was too large for her to manage, but she was also sentimental and would have crammed it full of things that had meaning to her.

Sam set about his task methodically. He opened each bag he found and rummaged through it. Possible candidates he set aside for further examination. The others he stacked in orderly fashion in a corner.

It was hot, dusty, dirty work, and he muttered mild imprecations under his breath. How could his parents have been so deluded as to deliberately conceal crucial evidence? A small portion of him insisted that the murderer was still likely Grant Diamond, but it was growing increasingly difficult to heed. Too many things didn't make sense now. Sam wanted to kick himself for not paying close attention to the details sooner. He'd left it to others to do the thinking and hadn't taken enough of an interest in

115

his sister's murder to do anything but mope awhile and then head back to school. He hadn't felt this useless since the war, when he was faced with hundreds of wounded men he couldn't save.

He swiped at the sweat trickling down his forehead and doggedly picked up the next bag and then the next. His sister's suitcase was here somewhere, and he meant to find it. He was late in seeking justice for Sarah, but now that he knew there was more to the story, he wasn't going to stop until he found the answer.

Dust tickled his nose and the back of his throat, and he sneezed half a dozen times. The light of the setting sun began to slant in through the window with the mellow, golden glow of a summer evening. The dinner gong sounded. His stomach grumbled, and his mouth felt like sandpaper, but he didn't stop. He'd stay up here all night if that was what it took.

Some forty minutes later, he spotted it—a medium-sized carpetbag with a needlepoint pattern of soft pink cabbage roses. It managed to look at once both substantial and feminine.

He reached for it with hands that had gone suddenly damp. For a long moment, he stared at the brass clasp. He was being ridiculous, thinking that the bag would hold the answer to the question of who had killed Sarah. But it might hold a key to who had not.

He closed his eyes and uttered a brief prayer, then nudged the clasp with his thumb. It slid grudgingly, and he pulled the bag open. A whiff of Sarah's sweet, flowery perfume assaulted his senses, and it felt like someone had punched him. He snapped the bag closed. He would examine the contents more thoroughly later. For now, it seemed clear that he had found what he needed. He would wait and go through it with Emily. She would certainly appreciate the consideration, and her practicality would help him to distance himself from the contents.

Sam put his jacket on. Clutching the handles of the bag in a tight fist, he headed downstairs. He didn't stop to say good-bye to his mother. He couldn't, not when he was still so angry. At the base of the last flight of stairs, he shifted directions and headed for the back of the house rather than the front, then made his way onto the terrace and struck out into the garden.

Twilight had stolen in, bringing with it a refreshing hint of coolness. Sam raised his face to the faint breath of air, wishing it was a torrential rain or a scouring wind—something to wash away the disappointment and fury tormenting him.

The garden was large, laid out in an English style, with grassy, twisting paths and natural-looking beds that could fool the uninitiated into thinking the plants had just happened to grow in such a way. Certainly few people would think they were very near the heart of New York in this oasis. It was an easy place to wander, and it held a sense of openness compared with the stodginess of the house. Even without the attraction of a handsome gardener, it was no wonder Sarah had preferred spending her time out here.

It didn't take him long to find the place he was looking for. Nothing marked the spot now, but all those years ago, he had asked and been shown where her body had been found.

A white gazebo stood nearby, presiding over a stream that didn't so much ripple as trickle in the late summer heat. Sam surveyed the area around him, noting the details with a fresh eye. Trying to think like a detective.

The grassy paths meant that the murderer easily could have snuck up on Sarah without her hearing. Sam turned in a slow circle. Large, spreading trees dotted the flower beds and would have provided easy concealment, especially in the dark.

He could see the rear of the house, but, at this distance, he wouldn't be able to hear any sounds coming from there, short of a gunshot. Nor could anyone in the house hear something happening this far into the garden. So why had the hue and cry been raised the night of Sarah's murder? As far as Sam knew, no one had been in the habit of checking to make sure that she was in bed.

What could possibly have alerted someone to activity in the garden? Surely, Sarah wouldn't have been thoughtless enough to carry a lamp.

No one had ever mentioned a lamp, in any event.

He turned another thirty degrees and could see the garden shed and small greenhouse. They weren't far away, though the winding paths would make them farther to reach than if one cut straight through the beds.

There was a rustle behind him, and Sam whirled around.

His father stood some twenty feet away. "I see you found the bag." His voice sounded rusty, unused.

Sam tightened his grip on the handles. "You hid evidence and pointed the investigation toward an innocent man. How could you do such a thing?"

Father scrubbed a hand across his face. He looked old—far older than Sam remembered, and shrunken in a way that made him look ill.

"I'm sorry, Samuel. I was trying to protect the family."

"Protect the family? Your daughter was dead, and all you were concerned about was your reputation!"

"Watch your tone, young man. I was thinking of her reputation, as well." Father's face grew a mottled red as his voice rose. "I couldn't bring her back! All I could do was keep the damage from spreading. You wouldn't understand, because you've never taken responsibility for anything or anyone but yourself."

"I'm a doctor. I take responsibility for others on a daily basis."

"But you don't have to think of them after they leave your office. You treat their illnesses, and then you're finished. But I'm a father." He slapped the flat of his hand over his heart. "My responsibility for my children never ends. Not even after death."

Sam shook his head. There was no getting through to the man. He would not—could not—see his own folly. Arguing was pointless. He turned his back on his father, contemplating the gazebo.

With effort, he modulated his voice. "Did you find a lamp out here with her?"

"What?"

"Did she have a lamp with her?"

Father sighed heavily. "No, she didn't have a lamp. She didn't need one. It was a bright, moonlit night."

His voice was closer, but Sam didn't turn to look at him; he simply nodded, to show he had heard.

"Samuel, I came out here to ask you to stop this madness. Your mother is so distraught, she's taken to her bed in tears. There is nothing to be gained by raking this all up again."

Sam whirled to face him. They were a mere eighteen inches apart, and Sam realized for the first time that he had grown taller than his father. He looked down at him and shook his head. "Nothing, Father? How about clearing the name of a man who is innocent of a murder for which he has been hounded for years? How about restoring the reputation of a Pinkerton agent who didn't apprehend the supposed murderer you sent him after? How about finding real justice for your dead daughter? You see, the problem with your project of self-preservation is that it has injured so many others."

He stalked away, back straight, pulse pounding in his temples. He couldn't remember ever having been so angry, and if he didn't leave now, he might very well do something he would regret, like strike his own father.

As he marched past the house, he caught a glimpse of a figure watching from one of the upper windows. Mother, no doubt. He didn't break stride. Didn't raise a hand. Didn't acknowledge her presence. He simply kept going. Back to the clinic. Back to Emily. Back to the place where the insane didn't make him insane, too.

Chapter 18

Despite her discouraging conversation with Commissioner Kerns, Emily was convinced she wouldn't get much farther without the assistance of someone on the police force. So, the next morning, she waited for the beat cop who patrolled the Adelphia's strip of New York.

The portly gentleman stopped short as she all but leaped to ambush him. He was no taller than she, and she reached a hand to steady him as he reared back.

"Morning, miss. You gave me a fright." He tipped his cap, his red face broad and slightly startled.

"I'm sorry. I didn't mean to startle you."

"No harm done, then. A pleasant day to you." He touched the brim of his cap and took a step away.

"Officer, wait, please." Emily smiled as the man turned back to her, expectation raising his bushy eyebrows. "I was hoping you could help me."

"Of course, miss." Now his brows pulled together, and his voice lowered with concern. "Have you been the victim of a crime?"

Emily put her hand to her chest. "Oh, no. But I was wondering how one would go about getting a copy of a police report. They are accessible to the public, aren't they?"

He rubbed his jaw as though his teeth had suddenly begun to ache. "Well, yes, sometimes they are, but they're usually only requested by lawyers or reporters."

Unlike the dear Commissioner, the officer did not imply that she was too stupid to understand the report, a fact she greatly appreciated. "I understand that, Officer...?"

"Drake," he filled in.

"Officer Drake." Emily resisted the urge to simper and bat her eyelashes, no matter how well it seemed to work for the debutantes in town. "I know it may be an unusual request, but it's an old case that has been closed for years. It couldn't possibly be important to anyone, really, except—"

"Insurance, eh?" Officer Drake nodded knowingly.

Taken aback at the immediate conclusion to which he'd jumped, Emily stopped with her mouth open. She really should correct him, but her carefully concocted explanation had fled, and trying would only confuse the matter more. "How do I go about making my request?"

"Normally, you would need to go to the station. But that's no place for a lady such as yourself. It's a bit of a puzzle, I'll tell you. I'm sure your companion wouldn't like it if you was to go there." His nose wrinkled.

Emily pulled back slightly, examining Officer Drake's homely features afresh. He was observant and, more than that, shrewd.

"Of course, I'm there regular as clockwork," he continued. "Morning and night."

"Yes." Emily was wary. "I imagine it would be quite easy for you to pull the file."

"I don't know about 'easy.' Pulling it unauthorized could land me in a passel of trouble." He hung his head. "But I could possibly try. If it was worth the risk."

Now they had reached the nub. Emily straightened. "Two dollars."

"Seven."

"Five, and not a penny more."

He nodded. "Five it is. Now, tell me the name of the victim and the approximate date of the crime. I'll locate the file and bring it here tonight for you to read."

Officer Drake was all business now. After she'd given him the information and agreed on a meeting time, he gave a two-fingered salute from the brim of his hat, then walked down the street.

Now that Emily no longer needed to visit the police department, she reentered the Adelphia. If she hurried, she could slip back into the room before Miss Clara noticed she was gone.

⌒

Sam stared at the bag in his lap. It was moderately heavy, but it felt like the weight of the world. Sarah had packed this bag thinking it contained her future and her dreams. How could he even consider opening it and analyzing its contents? It was a gross impertinence. He sighed and turned his attention out the cab window to the staunch, stodgy buildings of Manhattan, which had replaced the garden freshness he had so recently turned his back on.

Disembarking from the cab, he paid the cabbie, then stood and stared at the façade of the building that housed his practice and his home. He needed to open this bag, but he couldn't do it alone. He needed Emily.

He swerved away, turning instead toward the Academy of Music.

A figure moved toward him from the shadows of a nearby alley. Sam spun to face the form, lowering his center of gravity and automatically assuming a fighting stance.

The man pulled back. "Sorry, sir. I didn't mean to startle you none."

Sam straightened. "I know you, don't I?"

"Yessir." The man snatched off his hat and started revolving it between grubby hands as he glanced down the street both ways. Then he drew back into the shadows. "You tended my boy."

"That's right. Is he doing well?"

"Gettin' stronger every day." A slight smile quirked the man's lips, but it disappeared again before it could make any real impression on his features. "It's on account o' that I come to warn you."

"Warn me?"

"Be careful, sir. You're in someone's bad books, for true."

"What? Whose?"

The man was again searching the street with his eyes, and Sam followed the movement of his head, trying to figure out what he was looking at or for.

"Just be careful, sir. That's all." With that, the fellow scuttled away.

By the time they had completed their second rehearsal of the entire opera, Emily's stomach growled almost as loud as the final crescendo. She'd had no lunch and only a light breakfast of tea and toast. Now all her thoughts were consumed with getting something to eat. Soon.

Instead, the opera house's costumer presented her with what looked like a plaid wedding cake, with tiers and ruffles and—were those feathers? She put the costume on and examined herself in the glass. A hysterical laugh welled up in her throat. It was awful. Viewed from the audience, she would be little more than a mountain of plaid moving across the stage. An enormous swath of singing fabric.

Miss Clara met her eye and gave a minute shake of her head. Then, with a smile, she turned to the man and escorted him out, ostensibly so that Emily could change. "You made some very interesting choices, Mr. Fabrini. Can you—" The door shut, cutting off the rest of the conversation. Emily sighed. Miss Clara would handle the fellow.

She stared at herself critically in the mirror, trying to find something positive about the gown. Perhaps if she wore it longer… no. She shook her head. She could wear the costume every day for a year and never come to consider it appealing.

A knock sounded at the door, and Emily darted to it, thinking Miss Clara had managed to sway Mr. Fabrini, and they were returning to discuss changes to the dress. She yanked open the door. "I'm glad I wai—"

Sam stood on the other side, a carpetbag clutched in both hands. At the sight of her, he blinked and stepped back.

"It's a costume." Her shoulders jerked in a weak shrug. "It needs some work."

He hesitated, as if choosing his words with care, and then a bemused smile slanted the corner of his mouth. "What are you supposed to be?"

"The lady of—oh, never mind." She flapped her hand, wishing she could erase the image of herself in the plaid nightmare from his mind. "Miss Clara will fix it, even if she has to break out needle and thread herself. What are you doing here?"

He glanced up and down the hall, tension returning to his demeanor in a rush. "I need your help." His anxiety communicated itself through the stiff way he held his body and the tight grip he held on the carpetbag.

Frowning, she stepped out of the room and pulled the door closed behind her. "What's wrong?"

He lowered his voice. "Is there someplace we can go?"

"This way." Emily led him out into the stands. "No one will be able to eavesdrop without us seeing."

"Good." He sat with the bag perched on his knees, both hands holding the handles.

The silence lengthened until Emily reached a finger to trace the tapestry covering of the bag. "What's this?"

"You were right that Sarah had a bag. This is it. My parents had it all along."

Emily jerked her hand away, as if the fabric had suddenly caught fire. "I can hardly believe they would keep such a thing. I never dreamed…. What's inside?" Her fingers itched to open the latch, but the pain in his eyes stayed her hand.

"I don't know."

Another surprise. "You haven't looked?"

"I couldn't." The admission was timid, as if he were a small boy ashamed of a weakness.

Her heart ached, and she recalled anew how personal this was for him. He had loved Sarah deeply. She touched his arm tentatively. "What would help?"

"I don't know. I...." He looked away, took in a few deep breaths, then turned back to Emily. "It feels like such an intrusion—as if I'd be looking into something private she never meant for anyone to see."

It would have been easy to contradict him, to tell him there was no reason to feel awkward, but with his solemn gaze pinning her to the plush red velvet of the seat, she knew she had to be honest. "I suppose, in a way, it is. But surely there is justification in the fact that we aren't doing it to be nosy. We want to give her justice at last." She squeezed his arm. "And I think if she knew that it might clear Mr. Diamond, she would tell us to do whatever was necessary."

Sam nodded. "Yes." He sighed. And then, as if the handles were as heavy as a ship's anchor, he opened the clasp and pulled them apart.

Emily bent forward to see inside. On the top were a few envelopes. Sam lifted them out, handed her a couple, and kept a couple for himself.

She opened the first, a letter of apology and explanation from Sarah to her parents. It gave no details of her plans, other than that, by the time they read it, she would be married, and that she would contact them to let them know when she was settled.

The second was addressed to Sam. Emily started to open it but then stopped. "This is yours." She handed it to him and gently took the two letters he had in his hand.

Careful not to look at him, she busied herself with these two missives in order to give him privacy. The first was addressed to Robert Romijn.

Emily tore it open.

Dearest Robert,

I suppose that by the time you read this, you will have already found out what I have done. I am so very sorry for having hurt you in any way. But you know, as well as I do, that we'd never suit. Even though you have every right to be angry with me, I hope that you will look on my actions as a sort of gift. I've freed you as much as I have myself. You are a dear man. I wish you every happiness, and I hope that one day, you will find it in your heart to forgive me.

Interesting. This made it sound as if Sarah had known Robert wasn't really in love with her. Could she have been aware of his affections for another lady? Perhaps she'd merely suspected them?

The second letter was addressed to Alice Geddes.

Sweet Alice,

You've been my dearest friend since those dreadful dance lessons when we were ten. It grieves me that a distance has sprung up between us over the past few months. Though you may not care for me as you once did, I couldn't bear not saying farewell. I am throwing away all my prospects. I know you will scorn me for it, and I don't blame you a bit. I hope that one day, you, too, will find a love for which you're willing to do anything. But, in your case, I hope that it doesn't require anything but that you be happy with your beloved.

Emily lowered the paper and stared out over the stage. What had Sarah and Alice quarreled about? Had Alice disapproved of Sarah's relationship with Grant Diamond? Or had the argument been over Robert?

Emily sighed. She was reading too much into the few words on these pages. She glanced over at Sam. He was staring into the middle distance, fingers absently caressing the pages before him.

"Are you all right?"

"Yes." He started as if she had awakened him from a dream. "It hurts to think that she died believing I would be ashamed of her."

Emily handed him the letters to Robert and Alice and waited while he read them. When he looked up at last, she said, as neutrally as possible, "I understand that Robert Romijn may have been interested in another young lady at the same time he was courting Sarah."

"Robert wouldn't—" Vertical lines appeared between Sam's eyes as he frowned and looked back down at the letter. "I guess I can't say that. It would have been in keeping with his character. At least, as it was back then." The tension had returned to his bearing. "Who was the young lady?"

"Alice Geddes." Emily nodded at the papers in Sam's hands.

Sam shuffled back to his letter. "Listen to this: 'A part of me feels as if I am letting everyone down. But I've never been able to do anything but disappoint Mother and Father, anyway. Other than you, the only person who might have truly cared is Alice, but I have done something to alienate her, as well. She hasn't spoken to me in months. So there is really nothing restraining me. If it weren't for my worry over what you will think, I would be perfectly happy.'"

"Do you think she and Alice were at odds over Robert?" Emily ventured.

"I don't think Sarah knew why they were at odds."

Emily took the letter from him, folded it neatly, and slid it back in its envelope, as she had done with the others. "I propose we find out."

"How?"

"Simple. We shall talk to Alice's mother."

Sam shook his head. "If memory serves, Alice contracted tuberculosis. She's in a sanitarium, if she still lives."

"That's why we need to talk to her mother. Then we will find out where Alice is."

"You propose calling upon a woman you've never met and demanding to know to which sanitarium she sent her only child?"

"Of course not." Emily handed him the neat stack of envelopes. "I propose that you do."

His eyebrows shot up. "Me?"

She pulled the carpetbag closer and began taking out other objects. "Yes. I would encourage a more subtle approach, myself, but you are acquainted with her. She will be much more likely to speak with you about her daughter. Especially if you express admiration for the girl."

Sam stared at her as if she'd spoken in a foreign language. "What possible excuse could I have for calling on her out of the blue?"

"I said nothing about calling on her."

"You most certainly did—"

"I suggested talking to her. She moves in the same social circles as your family. I'm sure you can find a way to procure an invitation."

She sorted carefully through Sarah's things, being as respectful as she could while still being thorough. The rest of the contents appeared to be just what one would expect from a young woman eloping with her love. Emily's cheeks flushed as her fingers brushed against some fine lace edging a white, gauzy fabric. There was no need to look any further.

Snapping the satchel closed, she glanced back up at Sam. If this hadn't been such a serious task, she would have laughed out loud at the look of consternation on his face. As it was, she had to clear her throat before speaking.

"Now let me tell you about my interactions with the police over the last few days."

❧

Sam didn't like it, not one bit. Perhaps, where Emily came from, the police were trustworthy; but in New York, everyone did his best to avoid them, even law-abiding citizens. When she'd told him that she'd spoken not merely to an officer but to Kerns, his stomach had clenched. The last thing one wanted to do was openly question the workings of the New York Police Department.

He had tried to talk her out of the meeting that night, but she'd been adamant. Officer Drake was expecting her, and she would not go back on her word. Which left Sam standing in the shadows of the Adelphia, pretending to look bored, while Emily waited beneath the glow of the gas lamps, looking up and down the sidewalk.

Out of habit, Sam pulled his watch from his pocket and flipped it open. Of course, it was impossible to see the position of the hands, so he snapped it shut and tucked it away. Surely the meeting time had come and gone. He should escort Emily back inside. But then, a police officer approached. He was not a tall man, and he filled out his jacket so completely that it resembled a sausage casing. From what Emily had told Sam, this must be Officer Drake.

When the man reached her, Emily smiled. "Officer. It's a pleasure to see you again."

From where he stood, Sam could see the officer's back and Emily's face. Thankfully, he could also hear most of what they said.

Officer Drake scratched the back of his head. "You may not be so pleased when I tell you what I found out."

"What did you find?"

"Nothing."

Emily frowned. "Nothing? That can't be. There must be something."

"There isn't." Drake jerked his head from one side to the other, looking quickly over each shoulder. Sam had to strain to hear what he said next. "There *should* be something. There should be a report, but there's nothing."

"Do you think—"

"I don't think anything, miss. People who think too much tend to be…dealt with." He took a step backward. "I'm sorry I couldn't help you."

Emily was crestfallen, the disappointment clear on her face. It nearly broke Sam's heart; and, apparently, it had a similar effect on Drake. He sighed, he shoulders slumping, and took two steps toward her, so he was standing closer than was proper.

"I was on the force when that woman was killed. I didn't work the case, but I know who did. Marty Reed took the lead. Talk to him, and you might find your answers. Whatever you do, keep my name out of it."

"Of course." Emily nodded. "Thank you."

With that, Officer Drake walked away, his determined stride making it clear he wouldn't be turning around again.

Chapter 20

Sam tugged at his collar. He'd been at more social functions in the past few weeks than he had in the last six years. At least this was an "intimate" dinner party, with only twenty-five or so guests.

He had been quite proud of his maneuvering to get on Mrs. Geddes' guest list, until he had sent a note to Emily, to which she had responded saying she and Miss Clara would be there, as well. He hadn't bothered to ask how she'd managed it. For all her self-conscious fears of clumsiness, she navigated the social world far more gracefully than he ever would.

He watched her covertly as she conversed with the gentleman on her right and then with the fellow on her left. The pink flush in her cheeks was heightened by the rosy hue of her gown. It was relatively simple, lacking the lace and ruffles that bedecked most of the ladies, but cut just right to accentuate her charms without being immodest.

Mrs. Geddes was seated to Sam's right, and she turned at that moment, catching his scrutiny of Emily. "She is a lovely young woman, isn't she? And very talented, from what I hear."

"Very." Sam couldn't help the fierce blush that scorched his cheeks. "How have you been, Mrs. Geddes? I haven't seen you in a long while."

She was a handsome woman, her dark hair just beginning to show streaks of silver at the temples, her posture straight as a plumb line. "I'm very well, thank you. And you? I understand you've opened a clinic of some sort."

"It's not much, but I'm doing what I can."

"I'm sure you're helping your patients very much. Is it for veterans?"

"Largely. Many of them have been wounded far beyond their physical injuries." Sam warmed to his subject. "Their minds have been scarred by the things they have seen and done. There is a whole new field of science emerging...." He trailed off when he noticed that his hostess had gone green around the gills. "Are you all right?"

"I'm fine." She reached for her glass and took a large gulp.

"I tend to take off at a gallop when anyone asks me about my work." He smiled. He needed to remember why he was here. It wouldn't help to ramble on about the clinic to anyone who would listen. "How is Miss Geddes faring? I do hope she is able to keep in touch with you."

Mrs. Geddes' complexion grew even more ashen, and she put a hand to her breast. "Excuse me, please." She pushed back from the table and stood so abruptly that her chair toppled over with a resounding crash. She didn't even look back as she hurried from the room.

Sam also stood, and found that all eyes had turned to him. "Mrs. Geddes seems to have become unwell."

Her husband got to his feet. "Will you excuse me?" He followed his wife.

Sam returned to his seat. Gradually the flow of conversation around the table resumed. Sam kept glancing over his shoulder at the door. Should he offer his services?

A quarter of an hour passed before Mr. Geddes came back. He assured them all that his wife was fine but was resting.

The dinner party broke up quickly after that, the guests sensitive to their hostess's absence.

Sam caught up with Emily and Miss Clara on the sidewalk. "May I escort you ladies back to the Adelphia?"

"That's kind of you, Dr. DeKlerk." Miss Clara was all smiles. She gestured for him to take Emily's arm and then hung back a couple of steps as they began to stroll.

Emily's smile was more wolfish than grateful. "What did you say to her?"

"Who?"

"Mrs. Geddes, of course."

"I only asked her how her daughter was doing."

"That's all?"

"Well, I rambled on a bit about my clinic and my patients," he admitted sheepishly.

Emily nodded. "Mm-hmm. That was it. Poor woman. It must have been an unpleasant blow."

Sam stopped short. "What are you talking about?"

She looked like the cat that ate the canary. "The combination."

"Must you talk in riddles?"

She sighed. "Alice isn't in a sanitarium. She's in a lunatic asylum."

"What? How do you know this?"

She gave another smug smile. "I talked to the servants."

"Surely, they wouldn't share such gossip with a stranger."

"I have my methods," she said, looking mysterious.

"Your methods," grumbled Sam. "I'll have you know that there's—"

A crash split the nighttime quiet. Emily staggered against Sam, knocking him off his feet. They sprawled on the ground in a tangle of limbs. From somewhere above him, the high-pitched scream of a woman went on and on.

⤵

Emily struggled to breathe against the weight pressing on her chest. What in the world?

"Are you all right?"

She looked up into Sam's concerned eyes. At least now she knew what—or who—had fallen on her. "What happened?"

Behind them, Miss Clara had stopped screaming and was now shouting for help. All the commotion had caught the attention of a police officer, who ran to their aid.

"Get off her, you rascal." The officer grabbed Sam by the back of his jacket collar and yanked him up with such force, he resembled a jack-in-the-box.

Apparently, the officer had misread the situation and believed Sam had accosted Emily. It didn't help that Miss Clara had dropped to her knees beside Emily, completely ignoring Sam's plight, and begun fawning over her.

"You have it all wrong." Sam tried to pull away from the man's grip, but he held firm.

With Miss Clara's help, Emily sat up. As she struggled to regain her breath, she held a hand out toward the officer. "Please, sir, unhand Dr. DeKlerk. He did nothing wrong."

"It's true," Miss Clara spoke up, suddenly aware of the need for clarification. "The three of us were walking, and there was a tremendous crash. It knocked these two off their feet."

The policeman looked from one woman to the other, as if weighing the truth in their statements. Then he released Sam's collar and took a step back. "Apologies for the misunderstanding, sir. Can't be too careful when a woman's virtue is in question."

"No, you can't." Sam straightened his jacket as he moved back to Emily. Hunkering down beside her, he took her hand. "Let Miss Clara and me help you up."

Gratitude washed over Emily. Because of her artificial limb, it would be much easier, and she would appear more graceful, if both of them assisted her. She nodded her assent, and a moment later, she was on her feet.

Sam pointed at a pile of shattered granite less than a foot from Emily. "I believe this was the cause of the trouble."

The policeman surveyed the damage, nudging one of the larger pieces with the toe of his boot. As his eyes moved upward, they all inclined their heads, their gazes ascending the three stories of the brick-fronted building to the roof. Perched on the edge was a row of statues, their hulking figures looming over the street below. Judging from an obvious gap, the trio had once been a quartet.

Miss Clara gasped. "You could have been killed—both of you!"

Emily turned to Miss Clara to calm her, but as she did, a piece of the destroyed statue dislodged from her skirt and fell to the ground. The statue hadn't crushed her, but the impact had been great enough to knock her off her feet and shower her with debris. Another few inches…. The shaking started in her knees, then moved up her spine and into her shoulders. For the first time, her wooden leg felt like the only stable part of her body.

Sam slipped a steadying arm around her waist. "If you'll excuse us, Officer, I need to see these ladies home."

The policeman waved them on, muttering something about strange accidents. Emily was vaguely aware of being helped into a hansom cab. As it bounced down the street, through ruts and over bumps, the shaking in her extremities worsened. Her fingers were useless, cold to the point of numbness. But one thought played over and over in her mind.

What if it hadn't been an accident?

⌒

Despite Miss Clara's assurance that she and Emily would be fine once they reached the Adelphia, Sam insisted on staying with them until he was certain Emily was all right. He'd seen this kind of reaction before. He'd even experienced it himself on the battle-field. She was in shock.

Most doctors would note her lack of physical injury as an indi-cation that she was perfectly sound. But Sam knew better. How many soldiers had been sent home with a clean bill of health, when, inside, they were broken almost beyond repair? Emily would undoubtedly have nightmares that evening, but Sam wouldn't leave her until they'd had a chance to talk about what had happened.

Once at the hotel, he helped the women from the cab, then escorted them inside. He nodded pleasantly to the doorman and the bell captain, politely ignoring their inquisitive looks.

Inside the suite, Sam waited by the door as Miss Clara helped Emily settle into a chair beside the window. He needed to talk to her, but it would be much better without Miss Clara's well-intentioned hovering.

He moved farther into the room and touched Miss Clara's elbow. "I think some hot tea might help."

Miss Clara's brows drew together, creating deep creases across her forehead. She was likely weighing the propriety of leaving him alone in the room with Emily.

Sam smiled. "I'm asking as Miss Forbes's doctor."

The reminder that he was indeed a physician wiped the worry from her face. "Of course. I'll hurry."

Sam dragged a chair over from the other side of the window and positioned it so he could sit directly in front of Emily. As he heard the door click shut, he leaned forward and spoke softly. "Emily. Talk to me."

She looked straight ahead, eyes focused on nothing in particular. He took her hands in his and squeezed her trembling, icy fingers.

"Emily." His voice was more forceful now, commanding. "If you don't speak, I shall have to inform Mr. Jerome that you're not fit to perform."

Her eyelids drifted closed, then opened, then blinked rapidly. He had her attention now. "What did you say?"

He chuckled. "Nothing of any importance." He rubbed his thumbs across her knuckles, trying to warm them. "We need to talk about what just happened."

She drew in a breath, but it stuttered as she fought to hold back tears. "We could have been killed."

"But we weren't. Other than the possibility of a few bruises, we're both fine."

She nodded. Then she opened her mouth to speak but quickly snapped it shut again, as if afraid to utter the words.

"Tell me what you're thinking," Sam encouraged her.

"It could have been an accident, but…." She swallowed hard, then continued. "What if it wasn't?" When he didn't answer, her eyes grew wide. "You don't think it was an accident, do you?"

"I must admit, the timing is a bit coincidental. We start asking questions about Sarah, and then something like this happens."

He watched Emily closely. Acknowledging that someone may have intentionally tried to harm them might agitate her further. Thankfully, it had the effect he'd hoped for. Now that she'd stated her fear, and he hadn't dismissed it, she seemed more focused. Better yet, her tremors had stopped.

He gave her hands one more squeeze before letting go and sitting back in his chair. "I hate to think someone would do anything so vile, but the possibility certainly exists. Which means there's only one thing to do."

"Keep digging," Emily said, at the very same time that Sam said, just as emphatically, "Stop searching."

"What do you mean?" Emily asked. "We can't stop now."

"Well, we certainly can't keep on, not if your safety's at stake."

A glint of determination sparked in her eyes. "That's exactly the point. If tonight wasn't an accident, then we've made someone nervous. Even if we don't ask another question, that person may try something else. The only way to make sure either one of us is safe is to figure out who killed your sister and bring him to justice."

Sam shook his head. "You are a unique woman, Emily Forbes."

She finally offered him the tiniest smile. "I'll take that as a compliment."

"As it was meant. And, though I wish it weren't the case, I do see the logic in your thinking. Not only do we need to find Sarah's killer; we also need to stop whoever may have tried to attack us tonight."

"The hunt continues, then?"

Slowly, he nodded, hoping he wouldn't regret his decision. "It does indeed."

"Where does it continue?"

Sam looked deep into her eyes. The answer was simple, and it was the only possible option. "We find Alice Geddes."

Chapter 21

Emily put her ear to the door. Not a sound. *Good.* It had been two days since she had last spoken to Sam, and when his note had arrived the previous evening, it had been all she could do not to head straight out into the night to wring more information from him.

Luckily, today was Saturday, and she did not have to go to the theater. She had prepared the way with Miss Clara—having breakfasted and done her scales, she had announced her desire for a quiet day of catching up on her correspondence and resting her leg in her room. Alone.

Surely, the reply she had smuggled to Sam via a friendly bell-boy counted as correspondence, and she would be very careful not to overtax her leg. Now she just had to make her escape cleanly. Emily sighed. Getting out wasn't the most difficult thing; it was getting back in unobserved. But she'd worry about that later. After one last check to make sure her hat was securely affixed, she took a deep breath and cracked open the door.

Careful not to make a sound, she closed the door behind her. Soon she was in a cab on her way to Sam's clinic. He would no doubt have called for her, but then Miss Clara would have wanted to know where they were going and would have insisted on accompanying them. In fact, more likely, she would have ruled the expedition out of the question and forbidden Emily to go.

There was no other way.

Having adequately justified her behavior to herself, Emily allowed her mind to examine the idea of visiting a lunatic asylum.

A frisson of unease scurried up her spine. Would Alice Geddes even be able to converse? Would she be coherent? Sam would probably know.

He was waiting outside the clinic when the cab pulled up. The moment she saw him, Emily's heartbeat accelerated, and a lovely warmth spread through her chest. Her lips began to slide up into a smile, but then she stopped herself. Her reaction was totally inappropriate. The happiness she felt upon spotting him was akin to what she would feel upon seeing a suitor, and Sam was most definitely not that. This wasn't an opera, where love, be it tragic or not, was almost always a certainty. This was real life, and in real life, men like Samuel DeKlerk didn't fall in love with women like Emily Forbes. She had to keep her mind on the task at hand.

The instant he stepped into the cab, she began peppering him with questions. He settled himself in the seat and adjusted his top hat, which had gone askew while he'd climbed in, then put up his hand. "Hold on, there." He rapped his knuckles on the roof of the cab, signaling to the driver that they were ready to go.

As they pulled into the flow of early-morning traffic, Emily squeezed her hands together in her lap, determined to ignore the feel of his shoulder brushing against hers in the confines of the cab. "Forgive me, Sam. I'm a bit nervous about the idea of visiting an asylum."

"There's nothing to forgive. To tell you the truth, I'm nervous, too."

"You are?"

He nodded gravely. "An asylum is an unsettling place, even for those accustomed to working with the mentally unbalanced."

"Is it dangerous?" The question came out of Emily in a high-pitched squeak.

"As a rule, no." A bit of a smile appeared on his lips, and she was sure it was more for her benefit than from actual emotion. "The physician treating Miss Geddes is Dr. Hughes. He pulled her file for me. He wasn't in charge of her care at the time of her admission, but it appears the initial diagnosis was hysteria. She was frantic for several weeks and tried to escape more than once. Since that time, she has settled into a state of persistent melancholy."

Emily bit her lip to keep from interrupting him with questions.

"She speaks little. They have done everything possible to remove her from the vicinity of stimulants that could upset her. They make sure her food is bland, and she isn't allowed to read anything of a challenging nature. They keep her to a strict routine, and she is permitted few visitors. Dr. Hughes was most reluctant to allow our visit, but I convinced him of the gravity of the situation and assured him that we have no intention of upsetting his patient."

"Is he concerned she might attack us?"

"No. She was fairly violent when she first arrived, but since then, it seems she has been a danger only to herself. She has attempted suicide twice."

Emily's mouth dropped open. "She tried to kill herself?"

Sam nodded.

"Why would she do that?"

"I don't know." His eyes brimmed with compassion. "She must have a great deal of mental pain."

"How did you find her, anyway?"

His smile still held a tinge of sadness, but he appeared ready to be diverted. "I asked around among my colleagues. There aren't that many places in the city to treat such patients."

"We're lucky they didn't send her farther away."

He shrugged. "After talking with Dr. Hughes, I'm not certain we're going to find out anything from Miss Geddes. She may not even speak to us."

"You mean, she won't receive us?"

"No, we'll get the opportunity to see her. But she may not respond to anything we say."

"Why would she be so rude to visitors?"

"She wouldn't act intentionally rude. It's difficult to explain, but mental patients are sometimes locked inside themselves. Their real self—their personality and their essence—is stifled and suppressed under the disease from which they suffer."

Emily thought about this. "So, she doesn't know she's being rude?"

"She might not, or she might know but be unable to choose a different way of behaving."

"I see." Emily tried to digest this information. She sometimes felt like a prisoner to her lost limb. Trapped and powerless. How much worse would it be if the issue was with her mind? "And she's been in the asylum for ten years. She must feel very isolated."

Once again, that bittersweet expression settled on Sam's features. "That's why I want so much to help. I believe that knowing they are not alone, that someone cares, could begin the healing process for a great number of such people."

The hansom lurched and slowed.

"We're almost there," Sam said.

Emily had been so caught up in his revelations, she hadn't noticed the scenery changing around them. The area was practically rural, with fields and trees; the road was no more than a wide dirt track. "Are we still in Manhattan?"

He nodded. "Morningside Heights, to be precise. There are a couple of plateaus, and the asylum is at the top."

Emily peered up the hill. "It doesn't seem that intimidating."

"In truth, it shouldn't be. They're just people like you and me. People with problems."

At last, they crested the hill, and soon the grounds came into view. The wide road split and went around either side of the asylum's broad brick face.

Sam clambered out first. After paying the driver and asking him to wait, he handed Emily out of the carriage. He tucked her hand into the crook of his arm, and they swept up the front stairs.

Inside they were met by an attendant who identified herself as Mrs. Ingleside. She was a large woman with broad hips. And while she wore a plain, dark dress, her hair was pinned up in an elaborate coiffure complete with braids and ringlets. Dr. Hughes wasn't in, but, luckily for them, he had left instructions that they were to be allowed to see Miss Geddes.

Mrs. Ingleside led them up a series of stairs, the keys at her belt jangling as she walked. "Her room is on the third floor." She showed remarkably little interest in the visitors.

"Would it be possible to see her out in the gardens? I've often found that—"

Sam's request was interrupted by a snort and a shake of Mrs. Ingleside's head. "'Fraid not. The gardens agitate her. I've never seen the like. But every time we try to take her out there, she grows weepy and begins to shake."

"That's odd." A deep *v* creased Sam's brow. "Is she frightened to be outside in general, or is it something about the gardens?"

"That I don't know. Not sure if she knows, to come down to it."

Mrs. Ingleside stopped at an anonymous wooden door about halfway down a long passageway of other anonymous wooden doors. "Here we are." She pulled the keys from her waist and began to sort through them.

From somewhere down the hall, someone started moaning. At the sound, someone else gave a high-pitched cackle of laughter that went on and on. A chill lanced through Emily.

"Why is she locked in?" Emily asked.

Mrs. Ingleside looked at her as if she should be a candidate for admission. "They're all locked in, sweetie. Otherwise they'd sneak out and wreak havoc all over the countryside. That'd be a fine kettle of fish."

"Oh." Chastened, Emily lapsed into silence.

Sam wasn't so easily cowed. "Is Miss Geddes prone to wreak havoc?"

"She's tried to escape, if that's what you mean. When she first arrived, she was wild as they come."

"You were here, then? What was she like?"

Another indelicate snort. "Wild, like I said. She was raving and tried every which way she could think of to escape. Even made it as far as the front door one time before she was stopped."

"What did she say?"

"Oh, the usual. Something about a man." She sighed. "Every woman in this place is here because of some man." She clicked her tongue against her teeth. "Aha, here it is." She held up a metal key darkened with age.

"Do you recall exactly what she said?" Sam persisted.

"Nah. Just that she wanted to get to some man or other. Said he needed her." Mrs. Ingleside tapped her lip with the key. "What was it? He needed her because he was going to be sad, but she could make it better…something like that. Unless it's one of these others we've got in here that I'm thinking of."

Mrs. Ingleside scraped the key into the lock and turned it. Emily braced herself for what was coming, but when the door swung inward, she saw only a small room with bare walls. A woman stood with her back to them, staring fixedly out the barred window, which let in a bit of light and provided a view of the drive in front of the building. The only pieces of furniture were a narrow cot, a fragile-looking bedside table that held a single book, and a straight-backed chair.

Mrs. Ingleside waved them inside. "Ring when you're done, and someone will come let you out." She pointed to a sturdy leather bell pull beside the door.

Sam nodded, and she departed, locking them in with Miss Geddes. Emily fought down a swell of irrational, choking fear.

"Miss Geddes?" Sam's voice was low and soothing. "It's a pleasure to see you again. I know you and your family."

"I have no family." Alice's voice was pleasant, not at all like the rusty hinge squeak Emily had half expected. At last, she turned from the window and regarded them. She was attractive—tall, with a frame that must have once been statuesque but now appeared diminished somehow. Still, she held her head high, and there was no gleam of madness that Emily could detect.

Emily looked at Sam. He didn't challenge the assertion. "Why do you say that?"

"Because they forgot about me." She walked toward them, her eyes fixed on Emily.

Swallowing hard, Emily held her ground and managed not to flinch as Alice drew within a couple of feet of her, then reached out a finger and touched Emily's hat—fashionable and blue, with a sweep of peacock feathers that framed her face. "This is very pretty. Is it the style now?"

Throat dry as chalk dust, Emily could do no more than nod.

"I don't know what's in fashion anymore." Alice turned, paced the few steps to her cot, and lay down. "Who are you? Why are you here?"

"I'm Sam DeKlerk. You knew my—"

She sat bolt upright. "You're Sarah's brother."

"Yes."

Her face grew pale. "What do you want with me?"

"Just to ask you a few questions. Would that be all right?"

She huddled back into the corner, tucking her knees up so they were near her chin. "I don't want to talk to you." She started shaking her head violently.

"All right," Sam soothed, "all right. Why don't you talk to Miss Forbes, instead? You like her hat, don't you?"

Emily almost dropped her purse. What was he thinking?

Alice stopped shaking her head, but Emily started shaking hers, in a desperate bid to get Sam's attention, to let him know she was incapable of this. He ignored her.

Alice stared at her for a long moment, and Emily gave up trying to signal Sam.

Finally, Alice unwound herself and stood again. A cunning glint shone in her eye. "I'll talk to you if you give me your hat." She spoke to Emily as if Sam were no longer there.

"My hat? But you don't even go outside."

"I might if I had a pretty hat."

Emily examined her with narrowed eyes. "If I give you my hat, you'll answer all my questions?"

Alice nodded.

"You'll get the hat when I'm done asking questions."

"No. The hat now, or I won't answer any questions at all."

Emily glanced at Sam. He gave a slight shrug. Sighing, she unpinned her hat, a twinge of regret making her movements slow. It was her favorite hat, after all, and she'd have to explain its loss to Miss Clara somehow. But if that's what it took to loosen Alice's lips, then it was worth it.

Alice all but snatched the hat from her when she held it out. She immediately put it on and walked to the window, moving her head this way and that, as if she were trying to see her reflection in the glass.

"What do you think?" she asked.

"Very becoming," said Emily, though it was disconcerting to see it worn with Alice's shapeless, smock-like dress, which looked like nothing so much as a nightgown.

"I was the most sought-after debutante of them all, the year I came out."

Sam made a rolling motion with his hands, which Emily took as encouragement to continue with that line of inquiry. She remembered his open-ended style of questions that invited people to keep talking.

"Tell me about that."

A nod from Sam.

Alice continued to seek her reflection. "It was wonderful, of course. I was the queen of New York, I had beautiful gowns, and all the boys wanted to marry me." Her voice lilted with the remembrance of past glories.

Trying to keep in mind their reason for coming, Emily attempted something more pointed. "Who did *you* want to marry?"

"Robert, of course."

"Robert Romijn?"

"My Robert."

"Did he propose?"

Alice didn't respond. She continued to stare at the window, preening and adjusting the feathers so they lay at a more flattering angle.

Emily let the silence extend before trying again. "Alice, you promised to answer my questions. Did Robert propose to you?"

Alice breathed out a heavy sigh of annoyance. "He would have."

"What does that mean?"

"It means he would have; he just didn't have time."

"Time before what?"

"Before they brought me here." Alice was growing agitated, as if the questions were pointless because all of this was self-evident.

"When did they bring you here?"

"I don't know. It's been a while, I think."

Sam shook his head, then motioned with his chin.

Emily had no idea what he wanted, but she went back to less concrete matters. "How did you know Robert was going to propose?"

Sam nodded his approbation.

"I made it so he could." Alice looked coquettishly over her shoulder, a small smile lifting the corners of her lips.

This was worse than pulling teeth. Emily tamped down her impatience. "How did you do that?"

Alice began shaking her head again. "I don't want to talk about that."

"You promised to answer my questions."

"I'm done now. I'm tired. I don't want to talk anymore."

Emily wasn't exactly surprised. Alice needed something more to encourage her to continue. Emily opened the drawstrings of her purse and pulled out a compact mirror. "You would like to see yourself in that hat, wouldn't you?"

Alice turned around. Her gaze lowered to Emily's hands. "What's that?"

"It's a mirror. Would you like it?"

Alice opened her palm.

Emily shook her head. "You have to answer my questions first." She didn't give Alice a chance to argue. "Robert was engaged to Sarah. How did you make it so that Robert could marry you?"

Alice's gaze was fixed on the mirror. "We loved each other." She bit her lip so hard that a trickle of blood began creeping down from the edge of her mouth. Still she did not move. Did not stir. Her eyes did not waver from the mirror in Emily's hand.

The thought that dawned on Emily made her insides quiver, but she held herself steady and asked another question. "Alice, did you do something to Sarah?"

Tears welled up in the girl's eyes, and when she opened her mouth again, a thin, high-pitched wail came from her, piercing and eerie.

Calmly, with a measured gesture, Sam reached for the bell pull.

Emily walked to Alice and handed her the mirror. Alice grabbed for it, and the wailing quieted. She climbed back into her cot with her back to them and began to preen, gazing at her reflection. Smiling, she turned her face to see it at every angle.

She glanced over her shoulder. "Do you think Robert will like my new hat? He always liked me in blue."

Emily shuddered, wanting nothing more than to be out of the cell.

Chapter 22

When Mrs. Ingleside unlocked the door, she took one look at the bright hat perched on Alice's head and frowned in disapproval.

"Alice." She spoke from the doorway, not putting even a toe across the threshold. "Give this woman back her hat."

Alice looked over her shoulder, her lower lip sticking out in the pout of a petulant child. "It's mine. She gave it to me."

Mrs. Ingleside turned her sour expression on Emily.

"It's true," Emily said in a rush. "She liked it, and I gave it to her. As a gift."

She would have continued to ramble, if not for Sam's light touch on her back. He then turned his attention back to the woman on the cot.

"Good-bye, Alice. Thank you for receiving us."

"Give my love to Robert." She had turned to face the corner again, but her voice was dreamy, as though she saw something other than a cracked plaster wall in this dark, dim place.

Sam and Emily turned to leave, but then they heard something that stopped them dead in their tracks.

Alice was singing.

She was a beauteous flower,
*   Just blushing into day,*
And nought in field or bower,
*   Could e'er such charms display....*

Alice rocked faster as she sang, her voice becoming louder and shriller with each word.

> *But, blight o'ertook her early bloom*
> *Ere dawn of summertide,*
> *And we laid her in the lonely tomb,*
> *Earth's young and spotless bride.*

A chill skittered up Emily's spine. Alice was clearly agitated now, rocking with such vigor that the peacock feathers on the hat flapped as if trying to take flight. The song died on Alice's lips and became a sharp, keening wail. Sam stepped forward but was immediately stopped by Mrs. Ingleside. If her grip on Sam's arm was anything like the clutch she had on Emily's, then her fingers dug into his flesh with surprising force.

"You two have to leave now." She pulled them into the hall, then hurried to shut and lock the door, as if afraid Alice might try to run for freedom.

As they walked down the hall, Emily glanced back at the row of closed doors behind them. Alice's wail had been joined by the voices of others on that floor, creating a dissonant cacophony. "Aren't you going to help her?"

Mrs. Ingleside scoffed. "By doing what? Anything I do now will only agitate her more. If she doesn't settle down on her own, I'll get a doctor to help." She shook her head. "Never should have let you two in. I knew it would come to no good. Now I've got a whole ward of 'em worked up."

Emily looked at Sam, intending to ask if there was anything he could do, but the set of his jaw made her think better of it. Instead, they walked in silence to the front door, not even speaking when Mrs. Ingleside showed them out.

Once they boarded the waiting hansom cab and were out of sight of the institution, Emily couldn't stay quiet any longer. She laid her hand gently on Sam's wrist. "Are you all right?"

"No, I don't think I am."

Sam seemed to deflate before her eyes. His shoulders sagged, and his head dropped forward into his hands. He scrubbed his face with his palms, then looked up and turned to Emily. "Could it be true?"

She had been wondering the same thing. Could it be that Alice, in a fit of blind jealousy, had killed Sarah?

"It could be." Emily spoke slowly and carefully, weighing each word. "The way she talked, and then that song...she's clearly tormented by the memory of something."

"Something too painful to face. But we have no proof. We have conjecture, that's all."

Sam turned his head toward the side window, as though the proof they needed might flash by outside the cab. Emily's eyes followed his gaze. They certainly were moving at a leisurely pace. The driver was probably being cautious because of the sharp turns ahead, but at this rate, it would take them all day to get back to the city. Just as she was about to mention it to Sam, she heard a thudding sound, like boots hitting hard-packed dirt, followed by the crack of a whip and a cry of "Yah!"

The horse let out a frantic whinny, then the cab surged forward with such force, Emily and Sam were pushed back against their seats.

"What's going on?"

"I'm not positive," Sam said, struggling not to bounce off the seat, "but I think our driver has left us."

⌒

Actually, Sam was quite sure their driver had left them. He'd seen the figure of a man, clad in black, running away from the carriage just as it accelerated. But he hoped his feigned uncertainty might soften the news.

Emily was having none of it. Clutching the seat with white-knuckled fingers, she motioned ahead with her chin. "We have to stop the horse before the road gets bad."

"*We* aren't going to do anything. You are going to hang on and say a prayer, and I'm going to stop the horse."

For a moment, he thought she might argue, but she obviously realized that, with her long skirts and artificial limb, there was nothing she could do. "I will pray without ceasing, Sam."

This should be simple, Sam thought. The reins went over their heads and through eyelets on the roof of the cab, then back to the driver's seat. All he had to do was reach up, grab the reins, and pull. Except the reins weren't there. They were still threaded through the collar around the horse's neck, but from there, they hung loose, flapping and bouncing and dragging through the dirt. There was only one way to stop the cab.

Sam swung open the low doors that hemmed the passengers in, then clambered over the piece of wood that separated the horse's hindquarters and the passengers' legs. The distance between him and the broad, brown back was small, but he froze at the sight of the bouncing tail and the way its hard, black hooves pounded the ground, sending up clods of dirt. Behind him, Emily's voice grew louder, and he heard a snippet of her prayer.

"Hold him in Your hands, sure and steady, Father."

Sure and steady. Sam inhaled deeply, then jumped.

He didn't intend to yell as he jumped, but he did. Whether shocked from his scream or from something landing hard on its back, he didn't know, but the horse whinnied again and jerked to one side. Sam's arms shot out, fingers grasping for anything. One hand found a strap; the other wrapped around the trace. His forehead hit another piece of the harness, and he bounced against the rough leather as the horse ran.

"Hurry, Sam!"

At Emily's call, Sam looked up. They were dangerously close to some treacherous curves. Summoning all the strength and courage he possessed, he pulled himself forward until both of his hands touched the collar. A second later, he had the reins. Gripping the horse's sides tightly with his thighs, he sat up and pulled back with all his might. The horse screamed in protest and shook its head against the bit. Sam pulled harder, silently apologizing for any pain he caused the innocent animal.

The horse slowed, but the momentum of the carriage pushed against it. It jumped sideways, sending the right wheel into a rut. The leather reins, dry and cracked from exposure to the elements, dug into Sam's skin, but he held on. The other wheel hit a rock, sending the cab bouncing out of the rut and nearly tipping in the opposite direction. Emily shrieked and then called out the name of Jesus, over and over again.

Then, as suddenly as their harrowing ride had begun, it was over. The horse slowed, almost tiptoeing to a stop. Sam fell forward and wrapped his arms around the animal's hot, sweaty neck. Behind him, Emily was speaking, but he couldn't make sense of her words.

The cab swayed. A moment later, gentle hands touched his arms and pried them apart. He looked up into Emily's eyes. So warm, so full of concern, and of something else. Gratitude? Something more, perhaps? Whatever it was, it would have to wait.

Emily grabbed either side of the horse's bridle, holding it still while Sam slid off its back. His legs felt about as solid as his mother's Christmas pudding. "I think we can safely come to one conclusion: This was no accident."

"I agree." Emily let go of the bridle and wiped her palms on the sides of her skirt. "Which means the mysterious, broken gargoyle wasn't an accident, either."

Sam looked for any sign of the shock Emily had experienced the first time she'd considered the possibility of someone's having deliberately tried to hurt them. But her face was a study in determination.

"We've made someone very unhappy by investigating Sarah's murder," Sam conceded.

Emily nodded. "But it doesn't make sense. If Alice killed Sarah, she would have the most to lose by our uncovering the truth. But there's no way she could have been behind what happened today, or the narrow escape the other evening. Whoever it is most likely has ties to the Geddes family."

Sam sighed. He'd hoped that speaking to Alice would shed some light on Sarah's murder, but instead, it had created more questions. Yet there was one thing that was definitely not in question anymore: As long as they continued on this path, Emily would be in danger. Commanding her to give up the quest would be useless—he knew that without a doubt. So it was up to him to protect her, just like he should have protected Sarah.

No matter what it took.

Emily patted the horse's velvet muzzle and peered up the road the way they had come. It was better than looking down the hill at what would have been if Sam had not acted so quickly.

Sam stood, bent double, hands on his knees, and panting as if he had run after the cab. She wished she could help him the way he had helped her the other night. But, unlike him, she didn't know what to do, what to say. Instead, she focused her compassion on the horse, soothing and clucking, until the animal's eyes stopped rolling and it nudged Emily's hands with its nose in a gesture of apparent gratitude.

Emily offered her own murmured thanks to God for His protection.

Sam straightened. "We'd better get back up to the asylum."

"Do you mind driving, or shall we walk?"

"It'll be faster if we drive."

"You fear for the driver?"

He merely nodded.

Emily handed him the reins and clambered into the cab. It was no time to be concerned about her personal dignity. She glanced anxiously back up the hill. No matter the provocation, no cabbie would destroy his livelihood by sending his horse and cab careening off a cliff. That meant someone else must have done so. Which, in turn, meant that something had happened to the cabbie.

A chill seized her heart. If someone had harmed the driver, the purpose was to get at her and Sam. Someone had followed them to this place and was determined that they should tell no one what they had learned.

"The question is, does someone fear we'll discover that Alice killed Sarah, and thus is trying to protect her name—or the Geddes name—or is the real murderer simply concerned that we're investigating at all?" She mused out loud, trusting him to follow her train of thought.

Sam held the reins loosely, his hands shaking ever so slightly. "That's *a* question. *The* question is, how did this person know we were investigating at all?"

Emily shook her head and leaned back in the seat, biting her lower lip. "All we have are questions."

From somewhere, he summoned a smile for her. "Let's start finding some answers."

It was all Sam could do to minimize the shaking in his hands. Dread sat on his shoulder like a carrion bird waiting to pounce. All the way back to the asylum, he waited on guard for someone to attack. What would the faux driver do when he realized his plan hadn't worked? Would he try again? Had he even stayed around to watch the results of his handiwork? As soon as they drove up in front of the building, Sam pulled them to a halt and jumped down. The driver had to be around somewhere.

Tall shrubs lined the front of the building, and he pushed his way into them, calling as he went, "Sir? Are you here? Sir?" Sam shook his head at his own ineffectualness. He was searching for a man, not a lost cat.

He looked up at the sound of another voice. Emily had approached the shrubbery on the other side of the door and was poking it with her parasol. He had wanted her to stay in the carriage, where it would be marginally safer, though he hadn't said anything, since he knew she wouldn't listen.

In spite of the situation, he couldn't help a brief smile. The woman did everything wholeheartedly. She straightened abruptly and caught him staring.

She waved him over. "I've found him."

Heart in his throat, Sam ran to her side. He fell to his knees by the driver's body and huffed out a breath of relief when the man groaned. "Thank the Lord," he murmured.

A nasty cut marred the man's head, the blood pooling on the ground. Sam probed the edges of the wound carefully. The skull didn't feel fractured. He sat back on his haunches. "Can you fetch help? We need to get him inside. This cut requires stitches."

"Will he be all right?"

Sam looked up into her concerned eyes. "Yes. He'll likely have a concussion and a headache that may make him wish they'd finished the job. But I think he's going to live."

Relief sparked in Emily's eyes. She turned and hurried into the asylum.

Sam put his ear close to the man's chest and noted unlabored breathing. A quick examination revealed no other injuries. Some of his guilt eased. He hadn't anticipated this, but a part of him felt that he should have.

The jangle of keys announced the arrival of Mrs. Ingleside. Two orderlies followed her, and Emily completed the procession.

"What is he doing over there?" Mrs. Ingleside's querulous voice was shrill enough to wrest another groan from the driver.

"We don't know," Emily said, her voice placating. "As I said, we believe he was attacked. Is there any chance a patient got loose?"

"Don't be ridiculous," Mrs. Ingleside snapped sharply, but then she jerked her head at one of the orderlies, and he headed back to the building. Sam suspected there would be a count of the patients.

With the help of the other orderly, Sam got the driver transferred to a stretcher, and they soon had him inside.

The sharp scent of antiseptic in the surgery wing stung Sam's nose and took him straight back to the battlefield, as it always did. He forced away the memories that threatened to flood his senses.

Laid out on the examination table, the poor fellow's color was awful. How much blood had he lost? Head wounds bled copiously, but this one didn't seem that large. Still, Sam had no idea when the man had been knocked unconscious or how long he'd lain bleeding in the bushes.

Mrs. Ingleside brought smelling salts and waved them under the man's nose. He coughed and gagged, then rolled to his side and threw up over the edge of the table.

Standing beside Sam, Emily didn't flinch. Instead, she patted the fellow's shoulder and murmured the same meaningless reassurances that she'd used on the horse. They seemed to work just as well with the driver. After a moment, he rolled onto his back.

"Don't worry." Emily's voice was soft and sweet. "The doctor, here, will help you feel better soon."

Sam lowered the surgical needle he was threading and offered what he hoped was a kindly smile.

The man blinked up at them. "Nellie?"

"No, my name is Emily. But we can fetch Nellie for you, if you'd like. Can you tell me where she is?"

He furrowed his brow and winced. Then he blinked. "I dunno. I think somebody stole her." A tear trickled down his grizzled cheek. "Stole my cab, too."

"Oh, Nellie is your horse." Emily patted his hand. "She's outside, safe and sound. As is your cab."

This seemed too much for the fellow. "He didn't get away with her?"

Sam leaned over his patient. The skin was beginning to swell, and the poor fellow was going to have a goose egg the size of an actual goose's egg. "What's your name, sir?"

"John Feeney. My head hurts."

"I know, Mr. Feeney. I'm going to try to help with that. Can you tell me what happened?"

"I dunno. Fellow came up to me and asked the way to some farm. I told him I didn't know. Not from these parts. Then he swung a whopping cane straight at my head." The shock of the sudden violence was echoed in the disbelief that tinged his voice.

"Did you notice anything about him? Anything memorable?"

"Nah." He tried to shake his head but apparently thought better of it. He gave a groan.

Sam turned to Mrs. Ingleside. "I need some ether, Madam."

"I don't know that Dr. Hughes would approve of using our patients' supplies on a vagabond from the street."

Sam's patience was running thin. "This poor man is no vagabond, and what's more, he was attacked on asylum grounds." Time to throw the card Emily had supplied him earlier. Clever minx. "For all we know, his attacker was an escaped patient, which means this facility is liable for the injuries. I suggest you cooperate."

The old gorgon whirled around, unlocked a cabinet, and retrieved a small brown bottle. Grudgingly she handed it to him. Sam wet a cloth with the ether and placed it over Mr. Feeney's mouth and nose. In seconds, his eyes drifted shut, and he began snoring slightly.

Sam washed out the wound and then, with a half dozen quick, neat stitches, closed it up. Emily acted as his assistant. Mrs. Ingleside stood stiffly off to the side, refusing to budge.

By the time the patient started coming around, Sam was done. He gave him a dose of laudanum to help with the pain. He would have preferred to have him taken to a room where he could spend the night, but he could imagine the amount of fuss Ingleside would put up at that. He elected instead to have Emily help him get the fellow back outside.

Mr. Feeney cheered up markedly at the sight of his horse. They got the poor fellow settled between them, and as they took the road away from the asylum, more decorously than their earlier attempted departure, he fell asleep with his head resting against Emily's shoulder.

"Shove him over here," Sam said.

She shook her head. "You have to drive. And besides, that would be where his wound is."

Sam shrugged. "Suit yourself." Silence fell for a long moment. "So, what do you think?"

"I've been wracking my brain, trying to come up with something I noticed about the fake driver. I think his coat was green."

At the same time, Sam said, "Gray."

They looked at each other over Mr. Feeney's shaggy head.

"Grayish green?" she ventured.

"Brown hat?"

"Yes, I think so." She grimaced. "I wasn't really paying any attention."

"Neither was I."

"Oh, wait. There was something." Excitement lit up her features. "When he opened the door, his cuff pulled back. I think I saw the beginnings of a tattoo, about here." She held out her arm and indicated a place about an inch above the wrist.

"A tattoo?" That could be significant. "Maybe he's a sailor. What did it look like?"

"Nothing, really…I think it was the edge of a larger picture. It was a sort of faded blue in color." Her forehead was wrinkled with thought lines. "I don't think it was a particularly good tattoo. The lines were a bit blurry."

Sam smiled ruefully. "So far, our answers aren't any more enlightening than our questions."

She grinned back. "You know, there is a lead we haven't pursued yet."

Sam lifted his eyebrows in an unasked question.

"Officer Drake told me the name of the officer in charge of Sarah's case. I believe it's time I looked up Marty Reed."

"Over my dead body."

Emily's eyes widened in surprise, and Sam immediately regretted his sharp remark.

"And why shouldn't I speak to him?" Emily spoke in the measured tone of a woman fighting to keep her temper at bay.

"Because dealing with the police force is a tricky proposition." He didn't want to tell her about the people who had "disappeared" after crossing the police. "Besides, it's highly unlikely they would share information with you, since you have no direct connection to the case."

He could tell from the begrudging acceptance on her face that he had made a good point. "But you do." She nodded. "You're right; you need to be the one to make contact."

Thank heaven she hadn't chosen to argue the point. It was probably only because she was as emotionally exhausted as he was, but he was thankful nonetheless.

The rest of the trip passed in silence. Yes, Sam would find out what he could from Officer Reed. But first, he had someone else to meet with. And right now, that was all he could think about.

Chapter 24

Sam's footsteps echoed in the cavernous entrance of the New-York Historical Society. He'd purposely come at a time when he knew he could speak to Robert alone, before patrons began arriving. Emily would undoubtedly be miffed when she found he had gone without her, but after the censure Miss Clara had given them upon their return from the asylum, he'd thought it prudent to make this trip on his own.

As he headed toward the back of the large, open room, a man came around a corner straight ahead.

"Sam!" Robert's expression shifted from concern to pleasure. "I heard footsteps and was afraid we were being visited by Lincoln's ghost. What a relief to find you instead."

Sam grasped Robert's hand and pumped it. "I hope you still feel that way after we've talked."

"Sounds serious." Robert frowned, but his voice still held a joking lilt. "We'd best go to my office, then."

The heels of Robert's highly polished boots clicked sharply against the tile floor as he led the way. Following him, Sam glanced down at his own boots. Even though he kept them clean, no amount of polish could conceal the well-worn condition of the leather. There was a time in his life when he wouldn't have dreamed of wearing anything less than the finest shoes. Like Robert, Sam had been raised with more than he needed. It hadn't been until his wartime service, when he'd seen soldiers straggling into camp, their feet bare and bleeding, that he'd begun changing his opinions about what was really important.

Once in the office, Robert went straight to a side table against the wall and pulled the stopper from an intricately cut crystal decanter. He held it up and looked over his shoulder. "Care for a glass?"

Sam shook his head. "No, thank you."

"Suit yourself." Robert poured a splash into a short, fat tumbler, then tipped his head back and finished it in one swallow. Smacking his lips together, he put down the glass and motioned Sam to the sitting area. Rather than join him, Robert remained standing within reach of the liquor.

"It's a little early to be imbibing, don't you think?" Sam asked.

"All depends on your perspective. Someone, somewhere in the world, is having a brandy. I drink to him!" Robert pivoted on his heel, poured himself another glass, and turned back to Sam, the drink raised to his lips.

Concern niggled at Sam. He'd seen Robert drink too much at parties, but he hadn't been aware of his friend imbibing this early in the day.

Robert leaned his shoulder lazily against the wall. "So then, what is this serious matter you need to discuss with me?"

"It's about Sarah." Sam watched Robert closely, to gauge his reaction.

Robert dropped all pretense of pleasantness. "What about her?"

Sam's throat was so dry, he almost changed his mind about that drink. "I've been thinking about Sarah lately. About how she died."

"What's there to think about? She was murdered by that gardener." Robert's voice was flat and cold.

"Not according to the Pinkerton agent assigned to the case."

This was apparently new information to Robert. His spine stiffened, and he pushed away from the wall, eyes snapping. "Does the Pink have evidence to the contrary?"

Sam didn't want to say too much, so he tiptoed around the question. "The gardener, Grant Diamond, has been cleared of all charges. So, naturally, it's gotten me to thinking about who the real culprit could be."

"And your thoughts led you here?" As Robert spoke, he turned slightly and filled his glass again.

"Yes. But first they led me to Alice."

The glass slipped from Robert's fingers, landing on the floor and shattering, but he paid it no mind. Instead, he whirled around and faced Sam. "You stay away from Alice."

"I'm afraid it's too late for that. I paid her a visit at the asylum."

"You *what?*" Robert spit out a curse one might expect to hear at the docks, not in the New-York Historical Society. "You had no right!"

"I only wanted to speak to her." Sam jumped to his feet and approached Robert, who had begun pacing the floor, grinding glass beneath his boots.

"You don't understand. Alice is fragile. She's already been through enough."

"You're right; I don't understand. What has she been through, Robert? What put her in the asylum in the first place?"

Robert shook his head sharply. "I can't talk to you about this." He attempted to storm to the office door, but Sam grabbed his arm as he passed.

"Why not? You were engaged to my sister, but you were really in love with Alice, weren't you? Don't I deserve the truth after all these years?"

"The truth is not as black-and-white as you think." He yanked his arm free of Sam's grasp.

"And it's not as complicated as you think. Did you love my sister?"

Robert closed his eyes, and his face softened, the corners of his mouth lifting ever so slightly, as if he was reliving a pleasant memory. "Oh yes, I loved her." When he opened his eyes, the pain and regret in his soul shone through. "But it was a safe, familiar love. We were the best of friends."

Sam drew in a slow breath. "And Alice?"

"Alice took me by surprise."

Now that Robert had begun talking, the fight seemed to have drained out of him. He moved slowly to the desk with measured steps, then settled carefully into his chair.

"I'd never met a girl like Alice. She was full of fire and life. There was a spark between us, a palpable energy. Sarah saw it. That's why she broke off our engagement."

"She broke it off?" Sam leaned forward with his hands on the edge of the desk. "I never knew that."

"Neither of us wanted to deal with being badgered by our mothers, so we agreed to keep it quiet."

The explanation made perfect sense. Both Robert's mother and Sam's would have been more concerned with how a union between their children would strengthen their social status than whether that union were based on mutual affection.

"What happened with Alice?" Sam asked gently.

Robert propped his elbows on the table and rested his forehead against the knuckles of his clasped fingers. "I don't know. She was always mercurial. It was one of the things that attracted me. But after Sarah's death, it became worse. She would sink into bouts of depression that lasted for days. No one could pull her out of them. Then her emotions would soar, and she'd be nearly euphoric."

The behavior he described was consistent with what Sam had witnessed for himself at the asylum. "It sounds as though she suffered a great trauma to her psyche."

"The physician who treated her said she was in the grip of hysteria." Robert kept his eyes on the desktop, rolling his head from side to side. "I just wish I knew what she saw."

Sam recalled the melancholy tone of the song Alice had sung, and the wail of despair that had followed. "Or what she did."

Robert's head snapped up, and his eyes locked onto Sam. "What are you implying?"

"Nothing." He stepped backward, hands up, palms open, in what he hoped was a calming gesture. "I'm asking...is it possible Alice had something to do with Sarah's death?"

"No!" The word thundered through the office. Robert shot to his feet, pushing the chair back with such force that it rammed into the windowsill behind it. "No, it isn't remotely possible. I'd like you to leave now."

With a silent nod, Sam walked to the door. Before exiting, he looked over his shoulder. Robert moved to the little side table, kicking bits of broken glass out of his way as he went. He grabbed another tumbler and the decanter, then glared at Sam.

"Good day, sir." The cold, low tone of Robert's voice was somehow more menacing than his earlier shouts.

"Good day." Sam pulled the door shut behind him.

People coped with trauma in different ways. Alice dealt with it by retreating into a world where her mind protected her from reality. And Robert, who had quite obviously suffered a trauma of his own, dealt with it by numbing his emotions with alcohol. Despite his protestations, Sam was now surer than ever that Alice had been involved in Sarah's demise. And now, it seemed possible Robert had been involved, too. But how?

As he exited the museum, Sam wondered what to do next. To the right was his office, where he could employ his own coping mechanism of burying himself in his work. To the left was the Academy of Music, and Emily, who would challenge him and make him face the truth, no matter how painful it was.

How had he come to this? Before he'd met Emily Forbes, his life had been somewhat boring and predictable, but it had made sense. Now, nothing felt right anymore, except the times he was with her.

With a sigh, he turned to his left and strode down the street.

Chapter 25

Emily closed the door of her dressing room on the chaos behind the stage and leaned against it. Days like this made her question why she'd ever had any interest in performing. A week to go before the opera's debut, and the whole show seemed mired in pandemonium.

A knock on the door made her sigh. Ten minutes of quiet. Was that too much to ask?

She turned and opened it reluctantly. Sam stood on the other side, hat in hand. His expression was morose—the kind of look a dog wears when it's been kicked.

She shifted immediately from the guarded stance she'd adopted. "What's wrong?"

He scraped his fingers agitatedly through his hair. "I'm not sure I want to know who killed Sarah."

Emily took him by the hand and drew him inside the dressing room, then shut the door. He gave her a panicked look, as if she might bite him. She gestured to the settee, and he sat down hesitantly. "Why do you say that?"

He answered her question with one of his own: "What good will it do?"

Emily examined his face for a long moment, then looked at his hands, crushing the felt of his hat; at the rigid cast of his shoulders. She sat in the chair across from him. "We talked about that before, about what good would come from solving the case. But we never stopped to ask ourselves what harm it could do, did we?"

He huffed a breath out through his nose. "Emily Forbes, sometimes you can be amazingly perceptive. That's it, precisely. I'm starting to believe that searching for the truth could hurt a number of people."

"Who are you thinking of at the moment?"

"Robert." Again, that miserable expression.

"Robert? I thought our suspicions lay with Alice at the moment."

As Sam recounted his conversation of that morning, Emily listened carefully, setting aside her annoyance that he'd gone without her. She had to admit that Robert was likelier to be forthcoming with Sam alone than in her presence.

The door burst open, and a bug-eyed Miss Clara stormed inside. Her face was a shade of crimson Emily had never seen it before. She and Sam both jumped to their feet.

"This is the last straw!" Rather than yell, Miss Clara hissed out the words, and they were all the more awe-inspiring because of it. "I am ashamed of you, Emily Forbes, entertaining a gentleman in your dressing room without a chaperone."

"But—"

"Oh, no." Miss Clara cut her off with the sweep of her hand and a wave of her finger, mere inches from Emily's nose. "I've abided your questionable behavior up to this point because Dr. DeKlerk is a physician. But your wounds are long healed. The two of you have no business carrying on in such a way."

"I assure you, nothing untoward is going on between Miss Forbes and me." Sam took a step forward, but he, too, was stopped by Miss Clara's waving finger.

"You had best leave now, Doctor. And you!" She turned to Emily, her cheeks stained scarlet. "I shall be writing your brother about this, and then we will be going home."

"What? You can't do that!" This couldn't be happening. How could Miss Clara be so cavalier about killing her dream? Especially when she had done nothing wrong.

"I most certainly can."

"I won't go." Emily blurted out her refusal without reasoning.

Miss Clara stood her ground. "I may not be strong enough to force the issue, but Carter is. He'll come here and drag you home, if need be."

"Is this how you treated Juliet?" Emily cried. Her sister-in-law had once been Miss Clara's charge, too, but she had failed to mention how unreasonable the older woman could be.

"Juliet gave me no reason to distrust her. Besides that, she was a grown woman when I came to live with her."

"As am I."

"You most certainly are not, as evidenced by this behavior."

Sam cut off Emily's next volley with a hand on her arm. "I think it's best if we tell her."

Miss Clara's glare was hot enough to scald, and Emily couldn't help but wonder why Sam would draw the attention back to himself at that moment. The older woman stepped closer to him, hands on her ample hips, neck jutting out so that she was nearly nose to nose with him. "I want you out. Be gone! I don't care what kind of doctor you are. As a physician, aren't you supposed to take some kind of oath not to harm? Don't you know what you've done by sullying her reputation this way?"

Sam remained calm in the face of her fury. "Miss Clara, I assure you, Emily's honor is in no danger with me. I intend to marry her."

Miss Clara froze as if she had sighted Medusa. "What?"

Sam reached for Emily's hand, which had turned cold and tingly. "We are going to marry."

Miss Clara turned back to Emily, her gaze searching.

Emily bit her lip and then nodded. And a not-so-small portion of her heart ached for the admission to be real—for Sam to have proposed to her. And she marveled at her own feelings. He could be so stiff and formal, no one would ever have matched the two of them. And yet, now that she had come to know him, she knew he wasn't really stiff; he was shy. And he was kind and gentle, and strong in a way that few men were. Her heart gave a pang of longing.

An instant later, she was enveloped in a suffocating hug. "Oh, my darling." Miss Clara had tears in her eyes. She took Emily's shoulders and held her at arm's length. "Why didn't you say something, you silly thing? Folks are getting the wrong idea about what kind of girl you are."

Again Sam intervened. "We thought it best to keep it quiet because I haven't had a chance to speak to Mr. Forbes yet. He doesn't know me or my—"

"Oh, pish!" Now Miss Clara's waving hand was accompanied by an enormous grin. "You write a nice letter, and we'll post it, and that will be all there is to the matter."

Emily wasn't so sanguine. Carter would probably launch a comprehensive investigation, backed by the entire Pinkerton force, into any man who asked for her hand. She gave herself a little shake, as if waking from a dream. This wasn't real. If she wasn't careful, she'd begin to fall for the story, too, and wind up like poor Alice.

"Do you approve, Miss Clara?" Sam asked humbly.

"Do I—? Do *I*? Of course I do! I think it's a fine match. Emily hasn't talked about a soul but you since we've arrived in New York. I had to start wondering."

Emily's cheeks stung as if Miss Clara had slapped her.

"In that case, may I take my fiancée for a drive? I promise not to keep her out late."

"I suppose that would be all right." Miss Clara fluttered about them like a moth, plucking at Emily's skirts to straighten them, then passing her a bonnet and a parasol. "A bit of sun would do her good. She's been shut up in this musty old place all day."

"Thank you, Miss Clara. I shall deliver her to the Adelphia in plenty of time for dinner."

"See that you do, young man. Until the ink is dry on the marriage certificate, she is still my responsibility."

Laughing, Sam swept Emily from the room, his arm around her shoulder, as if she really were his betrothed. Her heart ached.

Outside, he hailed a hansom and handed Emily up with a flourish. Now that they'd left the dimly lit theater for the full summer sun, she could see that his ears were tipped cherry red.

She opened her mouth to speak, but he beat her to it. "I completely understand if you're angry. I thought that if we were going to have freedom to continue to investigate, she needed to hear something that would reassure her. You can throw me over at any time."

"What excuse will I give?"

He looked at her as if she were being difficult. "Any you like. Though I would prefer we come up with one that will preserve both of our dignities."

Emily couldn't quite bring herself to voice the question that burned most in her mind: *What if I don't want to throw you over?*

Sam was having trouble swallowing. He couldn't believe what he'd done. It was unthinkable. And yet...and yet, it felt right and natural. He had no desire to take back the words; though, if he'd given it more foresight, he would have gone about things a little differently. For instance, he would have asked Emily if she would marry him before he announced their engagement.

What must she think of him?

He glanced sideways at her and found her looking at him in a studious fashion. He resisted the urge to swipe at his face, as if some stain lurked there. "Are you angry?"

She shook her head. "No." She did not sound angry.

Sam relaxed a little. It was time to bring their focus back to the investigation. "We need to speak with Kerns as soon as possible."

"Kerns?" Emily wrinkled her nose as if something putrid had fallen into her lap. "I thought you were going to speak with Officer Reed."

"Yes, that was the plan. And after I spoke to Robert, I went to the police station to do just that." What he'd discovered was more than a little disturbing, and he wished he could keep it to himself. But Emily would never let him get away with that. "As it turns out, Marty Reed disappeared a few years back."

Emily's eyes narrowed. "What do you mean, 'disappeared'?"

"From what I'm told, he left the station on a Monday night, presumably for home, but didn't show up for work on Tuesday. Or any day after that."

"I see." She threaded her fingers together and pressed them tightly against her stomach. "When did this happen, exactly?"

Sam didn't answer right away, but when he did, he felt the gravity of every word. "Two weeks after Sarah died."

Emily put a fist to her mouth and turned away from him. When she regarded him again, her eyes were red, but there were no tears. "So," she said slowly, "the police report is missing, as is the officer in charge of the investigation."

"Yes."

"No wonder Officer Drake asked me to keep his name out of it." She shook her head. "But are you sure about Kerns? The man was horrid to me when I brought up Sarah's case. I can't imagine he'll be any help at all."

Sam nodded. "You may be right about that, but I still think it's worth a try. At the very least, he's the lesser of multiple evils."

"What do you mean?"

"You may not be aware of it, but the New York police do not have a sterling reputation for honesty and impartiality. Right now, I don't know that we can trust anyone in law enforcement."

Emily met his gaze. "So, you're saying that if the culprit is someone like Robert or Alice, they could have paid to have the evidence suppressed."

Sam nodded. "They or their families. Exactly."

"Still...Kerns."

"I may have a little leverage with the man. The rumors I'm hearing are that he's chummy with Tammany Hall. Very chummy."

"Tammany Hall?"

"*The* political power in New York City, all run by a fellow named Boss Tweed. He's turned graft and corruption into an art form."

"And Kerns is one of them."

"Right in the thick of it. Mayor Hoffman is expected to be elected governor in November. And when his position is vacated, the rumor is that Tammany Hall will fill that vacant position with Alderman Kerns."

Emily was regarding him with wide eyes. "How do you know all this?"

"Mostly from patients of mine."

He noticed her slight recoil, and laughed. "They're not all as destitute as the poor patient you saw at my clinic. Most of them are finding ways to cope with their various traumas, and some of them are rather well connected."

Emily's brow furrowed as she absorbed the information he had provided. "But how does that give you leverage?"

"When it comes to politicians, they always want to be well connected. The DeKlerk name carries weight. I doubt Kerns will want to disappoint me, and have the news get back to Father and his cronies."

"I see." Her eyes sparkled with understanding. "How wonderful that your social status can serve a useful purpose."

It was exactly the kind of thing Sarah would have said, and the thought brought a smile to Sam's face. It crossed his mind that, whenever Emily really fell in love and promised herself to another, she would be a helpmeet, in the true sense of the word, to whatever man was lucky enough to marry her.

⌒

At the Kerns residence, Sam passed his card over to the butler. The home was a decent brownstone, stately and well-appointed, but nothing like the mansions being erected in New York by the city's new business moguls. The style was just right for a potential mayor. There was wealth here, but not ostentation. Though, Sam realized, it was a bit more than one would expect from a man who had worked for years as a policeman and, before that, had been so poor, it was rumored he'd joined the force in order to get the uniform, as his clothes were falling apart at the seams.

A man capable of working his way up through the ranks of the police force and on to even greater success must know the nature of men. That was what Sam was counting on. If there was anything on Reed or the other police detectives, Mr. Kerns would know it. The question was, would he share his knowledge?

Mr. Kerns was just as Emily remembered, and then some. As he entered the parlor where she and Sam stood waiting, he seemed to fill the room with his presence. He went straight to Emily.

"Miss Forbes, it's a pleasure to see you again."

"Likewise."

She held out her hand, and he went through the standard greeting, bowing over her and kissing the air above her knuckles. Then he turned to Sam.

"Mr. Kerns." Sam extended his hand.

"Dr. DeKlerk." As they shook, Emily watched Kerns closely for any sign of irritation or anger at their visit, but she saw nothing of the sort. Either Kerns was a very good actor, or he had completely forgotten his earlier conversations with Emily.

"I'm afraid that I cannot obtain any police reports for you, Miss Forbes. Even if I wanted to, I am no longer commissioner, and it would be inappropriate for me to try to use political pressure to wrangle favors from the police. I'm sure you can understand." With his lips pulled back in a smile that was mildly predatory, he turned to Sam. "Both of you."

"I do understand." Emily had known Sam long enough to be able to decipher his body language, and the stiff way he pulled his shoulders back, plus the small lines around his pursed lips, told her he didn't appreciate Kerns' condescension any more than she did.

"Excellent." Kerns rubbed his hands together. "I would invite you to sit, but I'm on my way out to an important meeting, so this will have to be brief."

"In that case, let me be direct." Sam looked Kerns square in the eye. "It has come to my attention that all the evidence from the night my sister died might not have been recorded in the police report. Are you aware of any officers who might have been...persuaded...to look the other way?"

"Dr. DeKlerk, I'm well aware of the rumors about the New York Police Department, but I don't like what you're implying." Kerns kept his voice even and pleasant, but from where she was standing, Emily caught how the skin behind his ears flushed red.

"I mean no disrespect," Sam replied, "but an innocent man was targeted as the one and only suspect, while important information was completely ignored. Doesn't that seem odd to you?"

"Indeed it would, if it were true." Kerns ran his fingertips over the top of one ear, as if smoothing back an errant strand of hair on his meticulously coiffed head. "All the evidence pointed to the gardener. And, may I remind you, he's a fugitive. He ran. Innocent men don't run."

Emily could stay silent no longer. "They may when they're being made a scapegoat."

Sam looked at her with a combination of surprise and pride.

When Kerns turned his attention to her, his glare could have bored a hole through a brick wall. "Remember your place, Miss Forbes. Proper young ladies do themselves no favors by speaking out of turn."

Lifting her chin, Emily put aside the fear that told her to be quiet, and continued. "I have every right to express my opinions. But, in this case, I am sharing fact. Mr. Diamond was cleared of all charges."

Kerns sneered. "By your brother, no doubt. Had it not been for that Pink's incompetence, this case would be closed."

Emily was about to rush to Carter's defense, but a sharp look from Sam stopped her short. They were here to get information about Sarah's case, not to stand up for her brother.

Once again, Kerns turned his back on Emily and addressed Sam. "May I remind you that spreading vicious lies about peace officers is libel, a crime for which you can be prosecuted? Tread lightly before you step in the middle of something you can't control."

Before Sam could say another word, Kerns pulled a watch from his pocket and flipped open the cover. "I must be going."

Without so much as a good-bye, Kerns slid from the room. He was immediately replaced by the butler, who motioned silently to the doorway. A moment later, Sam and Emily stood on the front step, and the heavy door swung closed, shutting them out of the house.

As they moved down the walkway to the street, Sam offered the crook of his elbow, and Emily put her hand in it. The gesture was so natural, but when she realized what she'd done, it flustered her.

"Why didn't you mention the missing report and the officer's disappearance?" Maybe, if she returned their attention to the investigation, the awkward feeling would vanish.

"It wouldn't have done any good." Sam shook his head. "The way he reacted to our questions, even if he knew about the disappearances, he wouldn't have admitted it."

"He did react strongly, almost as if he took it personally."

"The mystery deepens." Sam patted the top of her hand. "He's protecting someone, but who?"

A plan was taking form in Emily's mind, but it was so outlandish, she was afraid to speak it aloud. She was still busy untangling the threads of ideas in her head when they reached the waiting hansom cab. They both looked up at the driver, to verify he was indeed the same one who had driven them here. As she slid her hand into Sam's and allowed him to help her up to the seat, Emily realized she was going to need something in order to make her plan work.

An engagement ring.

~

Sam fought the urge to pinch himself. If he did, the result would be no different from the other two times he'd tried it. There was no dream to wake from, no delusion of the mind. He really was standing beside the lovely Emily Forbes, her right arm entwined in his, while she held out her left hand, so the young women surrounding her could ooh and aah over her ring. And he really was grinning like a fool, as though the engagement party were real and not an elaborate ruse.

Why had he let her talk him into this? Telling Miss Clara they were engaged to throw her off track was one thing, but announcing it to the entire community, and celebrating with a party at his family home...well, that was entirely different. What would they do when it was time to call off the charade? Nothing good could come of this. Nothing.

Yet it had taken Emily hardly any effort to convince him to go through with it. Her smile had melted him, leaving him as malleable putty in her hands. Even now, when common sense should take over, he was still charmed by the warmth of her hand on his arm, and the lilting music of her laughter.

Emily shifted beside him, and he felt a slight change to the pressure on his arm. He looked down at her with concern. They'd been standing a very long time. "Are you all right?"

"It would be nice to sit for a moment."

He frowned. "You should have said something sooner."

With a laugh, Emily batted her eyelashes demurely. "I will endeavor to do better in the future, dear."

She was teasing—part of the charade, for the sake of anyone who might be listening to them. He knew that. Still, his heart swelled in his chest at the sound of the endearment. Sam shook his head as he led the way to a pair of empty chairs near the huge picture window on the west wall. He was in deep, deep trouble.

As soon as they were settled, a smartly dressed waiter approached with a tray of punch. Sam took two glasses and offered one to Emily.

"Mmm. Delicious." She'd smiled the moment the sweet liquid had touched her lips. "This whole party is marvelous."

"If there's one thing my mother loves, it's a good party. She can put one together better than anyone I know."

"Oh yes, that too. But I meant the guests." She scanned the room. "I believe everyone we hoped would come, did."

Emily's plan had been simple: Hold a grand party to announce their engagement. Considering the social standing of the DeKlerk family, anybody who was anybody had been invited. These were the people who had known Sarah and had been part of the DeKlerks' life. Amongst them were many familiar faces—Robert Romijn, Mr. Kerns, Mr. and Mrs. Geddes—as well as some who weren't familiar. Any one of them could be the killer.

"I wish we could have figured out a way to get Alice here," Sam said under his breath.

"So do I, but that would have given us away, for sure." Emily patted his knee. "But I believe we'll be able to make her presence known. Shall we?"

Sam pulled in a deep breath, then helped Emily to her feet. This was the part that worried him. If they were wrong, it would simply be an anecdote for their guests to share about the Forbes/DeKlerk engagement party. But if they were right—if the person they sought was in the room—they could very well be putting themselves in danger.

Sam led Emily to the small platform where a string trio was set up. He motioned for the musicians to stop playing, then turned to the crowd, gesturing with his hands for them to quiet down.

"Thank you all for coming tonight to share in our joy." He put his arm around Emily's waist and hugged her to his side. "I have been blessed with a woman who has the voice of an angel, and now we would like to share something else with you."

Sam took a step backward, then took Emily's hand and raised it to his lips. *Please let this work*, he prayed. *And please keep her safe.*

Polite applause followed. Emily tipped her head to Sam as he stepped down from the platform.

She faced the crowd again. "Thank you so much. I hope you enjoy this song. It's one that has recently come to mean a lot to Sam and me."

The musicians began to play the simple notes of a popular tune, and then Emily began to sing the words she'd heard from Alice.

> *She was a beauteous flower,*
> *Just blushing into day,*
> *And nought in field or bower,*
> *Could e'er such charms display.*

Emily had barely made it to the end of the first verse when a crash and a scream brought her performance to an end.

Mrs. Geddes had fainted, and she'd taken a waiter down with her.

Chapter 27

Agasp went up from the crowd, and there was a push forward as everyone tried to get a good look, but no one was doing anything to help. Sam forced his way to the front of this encircling mass, Emily following closely in his wake. He stooped by the prone woman and took her limp wrist in his hand. With his other hand, he pulled out his pocket watch.

Emily peered over his shoulder at Mrs. Geddes. Had she simply reacted to a song she'd heard her demented daughter sing, or did her swoon indicate some guilty knowledge? All of a sudden, her brilliant scheme didn't seem quite so brilliant.

Sam looked up at Mr. Geddes, hovering on the edge of the onlookers. "Mr. Geddes, would you help me get your wife up to a room? I believe she is going to be fine, but we should make her comfortable."

There was a collective exhalation, and then the assemblage began murmuring. The two men managed to carry Mrs. Geddes between them and carefully maneuvered the stairs. Emily followed. "Sam, is there anything you need?"

"My medical bag is in the study."

Emily went to fetch it, then hurried upstairs, nodding and smiling at her guests all the while but refusing to be drawn into conversation. She pulled the smelling salts from the bag and handed them to Sam. He waved them below the lady's nose, while her husband clung to her hand. The woman snorted and turned away from the offensive stench.

Emily let out a relieved sigh. Mrs. Geddes would be all right. Thinking of what else she could do to be useful, Emily moved to light the gas lamps.

As she did so, she watched the crumpled figure laid out on the bed. The woman looked shriveled somehow. As she came to, she began to sob and hiccup. Her husband patted her hand but looked at a loss.

It took a moment before Emily could make out the words.

"Alice's song," Mrs. Geddes muttered. "It was her song. She sang Alice's song."

"There, there. It will be all right."

"No." She jerked her hand free of her husband's caress. "Nothing will ever be right again."

Sam again pinched her wrist between his thumb and forefinger and pulled out his pocket watch. "Mrs. Geddes, I need you to try to be calm. Your pulse is racing. It's not healthy."

The woman inhaled a shaky breath, but it seemed to do little to calm her agitation.

Emily stepped to the foot of the bed. "I'm sorry the song choice upset you so."

Mrs. Geddes shook her head back and forth, her lips pressed tight together.

A maidservant entered, carrying a tray with a pitcher of water, a spoon, and a tumbler. Sam accepted the items and poured Mrs. Geddes a drink. He then rummaged in his case until he found a small paper packet. He unfolded it, dumped the powdery gray contents into the water, and mixed it thoroughly with the spoon. "Drink this, Mrs. Geddes."

She accepted the glass obediently and took a sip. She grimaced at the taste but then took a second, larger sip, and then a third.

"What's that you're giving her?" Mr. Geddes asked.

"A mild sedative. She's overwrought." Sam looked the man in the eye. "Why did that song upset her?"

Mr. Geddes straightened his cuffs. "You heard what she said. It reminded her of Alice. As you know, our sweet girl contracted tuberculosis, and we had to put her in a sanatorium. It is terribly painful for my wife to think about."

Sam's next question was quiet but clearly audible in the small space. "As painful as thinking of her in a lunatic asylum?"

Mrs. Geddes dropped the glass in her lap and covered her face. The water spilled unheeded across the silk and lace of her evening gown.

Her husband's eyes were wide, and two spots of color burned high in his cheekbones. "Where did you hear such tales? I hope you're not spreading rumors. That would be grounds for a defamation suit."

Sam didn't flinch. If anything, his face became harder, like granite in the flickering light. "Truth is a defense to a claim of defamation, Mr. Geddes. Now, no more games. I intend to find out who murdered my sister. I already know that Alice—"

Mrs. Geddes grabbed at Sam's sleeve. "Dr. DeKlerk, she didn't know what she was doing. She didn't want to harm Sarah. She loved Sarah. She couldn't have known."

Emily froze, afraid to even breathe, for fear of shattering the tension in the room. Had that been an admission?

All of the banty-rooster fight drained from Mr. Geddes as he plopped down on the bed. "Oh, Patricia." Those two little words held a world of despair.

Deliberately, Sam drew a chair over to the bedside and then motioned for Emily to take the seat. He stood at her side, hand resting lightly on a shoulder bared by her ball gown. His hand was warm, but it was trembling ever so slightly. Emily reached up to cover it with her own, as if she could protect him from any hint of vulnerability before these people.

"Tell us everything, right from the beginning." Sam's command was quiet but irresistible.

Mr. Geddes sighed. His eyes were rimmed with red, and he looked immeasurably tired. "Alice was in love with young Robert Romijn. I think…I think maybe she had been for years. When it—when he proposed to Sarah, I…I don't know what happened, but it was like a lever had been pulled inside Alice. She changed." He rubbed at his eyes. "She wouldn't go out into society anymore. She was worst of all with Sarah, but, up until then, they had been best of friends. We didn't know what was wrong, at the time. We thought perhaps she was jealous that Sarah had a beau when she did not, but we didn't know that she wanted Sarah's beau, in particular."

Silence descended on the room as his words staggered to a halt under the weight of his own guilt and sorrow.

Emily reached forward and touched the man's hand. It was cold. "Mr. Geddes, we know you couldn't have anticipated what happened."

He shook his head. "We never dreamed."

"Our Alice." Mrs. Geddes buried her face in her hands, a broken woman with a broken heart.

Mr. Geddes put his arm around his wife's shoulders. He breathed in deeply. "The entire day before Sarah was killed, Alice was frantic. I didn't, and still don't, know what got into her."

"She heard from Maura Chester that Sarah was eloping with Robert." Mrs. Geddes' voice was tentative.

Mr. Geddes raised his eyebrows. "Why would they elope? They were already engaged, and the wedding date was set."

Mrs. Geddes shook her head, at a loss.

Obviously still trying to work out this conundrum, Mr. Geddes continued. "Alice became so agitated that I had to lock her in her room. Late that night, she wandered into the parlor, where we were sitting. She was wet and covered in mud. There were scratches on her face and cuts on her hands. She was crooning that song. I was angry that she'd managed to sneak out of the house, so I demanded to know where she had been. But she didn't seem to hear me. She started babbling about how she and Robert could be together now."

His words came faster and faster, as if he were verbally sprinting for a finish line he alone could see. "When her mother asked her what had happened, Alice started raging. I thought she was going to attack Patricia. We managed to calm her down and called the doctor. The next day, when we heard the news about Sarah, we knew what she'd done. That's when we took her to the asylum...a place where she would be cared for and couldn't harm anyone else."

Sam's fingers tightened slightly on Emily's shoulder. "Why didn't you tell the police what really happened?"

Mr. Geddes looked at him as if he were a simpleton. "What would that have accomplished? There was no use in sullying our name and Alice's reputation. We couldn't bring Sarah back, and Alice could never have stood up to a hearing and jail time. No, this was better for everyone."

"Everyone except the innocent man who was accused of the crime." Sam's voice was devoid of the compassion Emily felt for this couple. They were obviously far, far out of their depth.

"That man ran away," Mr. Geddes said. "We believed he must have been guilty of some crime. If he'd been caught, we would have cleared the record somehow."

Emily glanced up at Sam and found him shaking his head. "You've kept this secret for ten years. It must have seemed important for no one to ever learn the truth."

Mr. Geddes looked slightly confused. "You're right. We didn't want anyone to know."

"How did you learn that Emily and I were investigating?"

"What?" Mr. Geddes looked briefly at his wife, as if she could shed light on Sam's question. "You were investigating? Why would you start investigating now?"

Emily started to answer but stopped herself. "Which one of you pushed over the statue or followed us to the asylum and knocked out our driver? It had to have been you, Mr. Geddes. Mrs. Geddes couldn't have leapt off the back of the hansom while it was in motion."

They were both shaking their heads. Mr. Geddes raised his hands. "I don't know what you're talking about. We haven't had anything to do with any hansom cabs or statues. I don't even know what that means."

Emily looked up at Sam again. He looked down at her. Could it be that neither Mr. nor Mr. Geddes had been behind the attacks? It did seem unlikely for this couple, who had been shaken to their core by a mere song, to have the presence of mind or the fortitude to plot a series of vicious physical assaults. But if not them, then who? Who else would have a motive to protect Alice Geddes?

The door burst open, and Robert Romijn stood silhouetted in the frame. He held a pistol in one hand and a glass in the other. "Samuel DeKlerk, I challenge you to a duel."

Sam glared at Robert. His friend was drunk as a lord. He could hardly stand straight, much less shoot straight. "Robert, don't be a dolt."

"I'm not a dolt. I'm serious as a judge." He raised the gun to his mouth, gave it a surprised look, and then raised the glass instead.

"I am not going to duel with you."

"Then everyone will know you for the coward you are." Robert's voice had risen to a shout, and the murmur of voices below the stairs quieted.

"You're making a scene," Sam gritted out through clenched teeth.

"I don't care. I have to avenge her honor. You must fight me."

"I don't want to fight you, Robbie." The childhood nickname came out without any thought—perhaps because he was acting childish, or perhaps because Sam was beginning to understand his friend's pain. "I have no quarrel with you. Nor you with me, which you will realize when you sober up. Why don't we get you home? We can talk later. I think we need to clear the air between us—"

"No! All you ever want to do is talk. Like talking ever solved anything. This is between you and me. And we're going to duel it out like gentlemen of honor."

Sam sighed. Robert was the most stubborn person alive when he was in his cups. "Okay, Robbie. Okay. I'll duel you tomorrow at dawn. That's the hour for duels, isn't it?"

"I'll have satisfaction tonight, sir. The dishonor may not stand. First, your insinuations at the museum, and then having Miss Forbes sing that song."

"What do you know about the song?"

"It was one of Alice's favorites. You had her sing it to taunt me, didn't you?"

"Why should it be a taunt?" Sam asked.

Robert's face twisted with pain and anger. "Because she sang it that night!"

Sam glanced briefly at Emily. What did Robert know about that night? Had he been there?

"Did you see Alice in the garden?" Emily seemed to take Robert by surprise. His eyes widened, and he peered into the room, as if just noticing he and Sam were not alone.

"I was too late. I couldn't help them. Couldn't help either one." Twin tears tracked down his cheeks. "But I'll help Alice tonight. I'm not going to have him going around dredging it all up again. I won't let him hurt her."

Once again, Sam shook his head. "I don't want to duel with you, Robbie."

"You don't have a choice—unless you don't have any honor."

"What is honorable about fighting?"

"Now you disparage all our brave soldiers!" Robert brandished the pistol, waving it awkwardly from side to side. "You don't know what bravery is. You never entered into the fighting. You didn't even carry a gun. All you did was wipe up blood and put on bandages."

A red fury clouded Sam's eyes as memories bombarded him: soldiers begging him to save limbs that were beyond hope. Screams during amputations when the ether had run out. Standing in puddles of blood so deep that it pooled around his ankles. Robert had no idea what he was talking about.

"If you were sober, I would lay you down where you stand. But you are drunk and far out of your senses. I will not fight you."

Robert's voice rose to a howl. "If you won't duel honorably, then I will shoot you here." He pointed the pistol at Sam.

Beneath his hand, Emily's shoulder began to shake. Besides the normal amount of fear that came with staring down the barrel of a gun, the experience no doubt took her right back to the time when her parents were killed and her leg was destroyed.

And now, Sam had no choice. The way the muzzle of the pistol bobbed, the chances were very good Robert would shoot one of the other three people in the room. The only way Sam could think to appease him was to give him what he wanted. Once they were out in the open, there was no way Robert would be able to hit the broad side of a coal barge, let alone a person at twenty paces. When the time came to shoot, Sam would simply aim into the air. Then they would be done with the whole thing, and he could get Robert home to bed, where he belonged.

"If I duel you, will you be satisfied?"

"Yes."

"Sam, no!" Emily grabbed his wrist.

He looked down at her and brushed a light kiss on her forehead. "Don't worry, love. I know what I'm doing."

She didn't look convinced.

He turned his attention back to Robert. "When the duel is over, will you go home?"

"Yes?" He sounded suspicious.

"Your word of honor, now."

"Yes, I'll go home after we duel. My word of honor."

"All right, then. I'll have to find another pistol."

Robert set down his drink and pulled a pistol from his waistband. "I have an extra." He sounded as proud as a schoolboy exhibiting his best penmanship.

Sam refrained from rolling his eyes. "We have to go out in the grounds, where no one else can get hurt."

"Of course." Now he sounded disdainful, as if he couldn't believe that Sam would state something so obvious.

"Well, let's go, then."

Emily jumped up and grabbed his sleeve. "You're not going to really duel with him."

"He won't stop until I do. Don't worry, though; I'll aim at the sky."

She followed him. "I'm coming, too."

"I'd prefer you stay out of the path of danger."

She raised a single eyebrow in a look chock-full of irony.

"Fine," he said. "Do as you like."

"I shall." She hurried alongside him, keeping pace, though he could see it was hurting her leg. He slowed slightly.

"Aren't you at least going to check to see if that gun is loaded?"

"Why? I don't really intend to try to shoot him. What do I care if it's loaded or not?"

The moon hung low in the sky, its light filtering through the avenue of trees lining the drive, in ghostly beams that shifted and swayed like souls in torment. The screech of an owl sounded, and there was a flap of wings, followed by an abrupt end to a tiny rustling in the underbrush.

Sam and Robert stood back-to-back. Robert had pressed Mr. Geddes into service, and he counted out twenty paces.

Shadowy figures came nearer, and Sam sighed. The guests were getting far more entertainment tonight than they had bargained for. He ought to shoot Robert just for being so pigheaded. This would be talked about for years. He could only guess at what story was already going around about the reason for the duel, and what his parents thought about it all.

The word came to turn and fire.

Sam turned around, aimed straight over his head, and pulled the trigger. An instant later, he heard the sound of Robbie's shot, and an instant after that, searing pain blossomed in his chest. The pistol fell from his hand as his legs buckled, and he fell to his knees. All around him were screams and shouts, but they quickly became indistinct sounds, as though he was deep beneath the surface of a lake. He fell forward. He turned his head and saw the moon was full and bright. The stars twinkled and blinked. Then a thick fog rolled in. He strained to see through it, desperate not to lose the stars, but it was no use. A moment later, the stars were gone, and the fog had swallowed him.

Chapter 28

For once, Emily gave no consideration to looking graceful. She ran full tilt, stumbling over the uneven ground at the edge of the lane, and managed to make it to Sam's side. She fell to her knees, heedless of the fine silk of her gown. All of her attention was on the hideous red stain spreading across the white of his shirt.

"Sam!" She pressed her hand against the wound, desperate to stop the seeping blood.

The guests who had filtered down from the house gathered in. Emily couldn't make out their faces through her tears. She swiped angrily at her eyes with the back of one hand. Why were all these sheep just standing there, looking at him?

She motioned at the nearest young man, a fellow in a ridiculously bright green bowtie. "Get a blanket. We need to carry him back to the house."

The fellow jumped, as if he'd been stung, but then hurried away obediently. Someone handed Emily a handkerchief, and she pressed it to the wound, praying it would do more good than her bare hand.

"What have I done?" Wild-eyed and red-faced, Robert pushed through the crowd. "Sam! Sam, I'm sorry. I wish I'd shot myself instead." He lit up, as if this was a brilliant idea, then looked around, as if in search of a gun.

Harrison Kerns stepped up beside Robert. "Mr. Romijn, I've sent for the police. I'm going to have to ask you to surrender yourself to me while we wait for their arrival." He took hold of Robert's shoulder, in case he should try to run, but Emily knew there was no chance of that. She had never seen anyone so defeated.

"Yes," Robert mumbled. "That's a good idea. I should be locked up."

Sam groaned, immediately drawing Emily's attention to his face, which was creased in pain.

Now that the first, panicked shock had subsided, she realized that his wound was high up and on the right, far from his heart. There just wasn't enough light out here to get a good look at it.

Sam's father collapsed to his knees next to Emily. He kept blinking, as if unable to believe the evidence before his eyes. Emily's heart cracked for him. It was the second time he'd found one of his children violently struck down.

She reached out and touched his arm. "I believe he will be all right, sir."

He looked at her, but his features registered no comprehension.

The fellow in the green tie returned, and Sam was carefully maneuvered onto the blanket. Then several men took hold of the edges and lifted, staggering slightly, and carried him into the house.

Emily followed in their wake, half supporting, half being supported by, Mr. DeKlerk. Her fingers alternately curled into fists and uncurled, as a prayer unspooled in her mind. *Dear God, please let him be all right. Don't take him from his family and his patients. Or from me.*

The DeKlerk family physician had arrived by the time they lowered Sam onto the bed. The doctor shooed everyone from the room, including Emily, but allowed Sam's parents to remain. As his injury was tended, Emily paced outside the door, heedless of Miss Clara's attempts to draw her away.

It seemed hours—three? twelve?—before the doctor reappeared. He closed the door behind him and removed his spectacles.

Emily wrung her hands, barely feeling the warmth of Miss Clara's arm encircling her shoulders. She opened her mouth, but the question that every nerve cried out to have answered was lodged in her throat.

The doctor polished his lenses on his waistcoat, then put them to his eyes and blinked owlishly at her. "Ah, Miss Forbes." He sounded mildly surprised to find her standing there.

Emily wanted to scream at him. Instead, she managed at last to voice her question. "How bad is it?"

He began a rambling explanation, full of long words that Emily barely heard, much less understood.

Miss Clara stopped him in full stream. "Doctor! Will he live?"

"I…uh, why, yes. I believe so. Barring infection, of course. Or a virulent fever."

Emily exhaled the breath she hadn't even realized she'd been holding. "May I see him?"

"Yes, of course. It's a flesh wound. Two ribs nicked, but I don't believe they were broken. He'll be deuced sore for a while, but he should recover quite nicely."

Emily didn't wait to hear more. She brushed past the doctor and opened the door, with Miss Clara right on her heels.

Emily took a few steps into the room, then drew to a halt. The gas lamps were turned low, leaving shadows pooling in the corners and hunched beneath the furniture. In the dimness of the sickroom, Sam lay eerily still. The coverlet had been pulled over most of his chest, but a spray of dark, coarse hair peeped out from beneath, and his shoulders were bare.

His mother, who had not been shooed away, as Emily had, sat in a straight-backed chair at his bedside. The woman turned to give Emily a hard stare, then turned back to face Sam. "Is it true that Romijn and my son were dueling over you?"

Emily gasped. "Me? No, Mrs. DeKlerk. Absolutely not."

"You deny it, then? What other young woman could they have been fighting over? I had a bad feeling about this match, an opera sing—"

"Mother." Sam groaned. To Emily's ear, he was more annoyed than pained. Whatever the emotion, the sound of his voice was the most beautiful thing she'd ever heard.

"Samuel?" His mother leaned forward and reached for his right hand.

Emily hurried to the other side of the bed to stand beside him.

"Leave Emily alone," he said. "It's not her fault."

"I'm sorry, Samuel, but when two men fight over a young woman's attentions, she can't be held entirely blameless."

"We weren't fighting over her."

His mother snorted. "Then what, Samuel? What could cause you to fall out with your best friend?"

"Sarah."

Mrs. DeKlerk released his hand and sat back abruptly in her seat.

Emily stepped closer. Uncaring about propriety, she placed her hand on Sam's bare shoulder, relishing the firm, warm, *alive* feel of his skin. "Sam, are you all right? The doctor said it was a grazing wound."

"I'll be fine. Don't fuss. How is Robert?"

Emily straightened. "He didn't get shot, if that's what you mean."

"You must let go of this morbid obsession," Mrs. DeKlerk inserted.

Sam looked unutterably weary. "I can't, Mother."

"You can. You just don't wish to." She stood and swept from the room without a backward glance.

Sam sighed and tried to move, but he was trapped beneath the tightly tucked coverlet. "Emily, would you please help free my arms?"

Without a second thought, she carefully pulled back the bedspread and positioned it beneath his left arm. Then she went around the bed and did the same thing on the right side. Then she froze. *Oh, my.* The blanket was lower now, and Emily saw even more hair matting his chest. She averted her gaze, but it fell on

Sam's arms, which were corded with muscles. His body was not at all the kind you'd expect of a doctor. Not that she'd spent time thinking about his body. Not at all.

Oh, my.

A weak chuckle drew her eyes to his face. He'd caught her staring and was apparently quite humored by it. "Sit down, dear Emily."

Emily assumed the unoccupied chair. "You scared me to death, Samuel DeKlerk."

He quirked an eyebrow. "Uh-oh. It's never good when a woman uses the entire name."

"I'd use your middle name, too, if I knew what it was." Despite her teasing, the worry still sat heavily on her chest. "Maybe your mother is right. Maybe we should stop." The thought of someone causing him graver injury than he'd sustained that night, or actually killing him, made her feel nauseated.

"Don't you start. I thought we were in agreement."

Emily could not quite put her fear into words.

Gingerly, he raised one arm and laid it over his eyes. "I'll not hold you to continuing with the investigation. In fact, I'd prefer that you stay out of it."

Temper turned her cheeks hot. "I'm getting in the way, am I?"

He lowered his arm. "No. I don't want to see you get hurt. Besides"—he looked at her with serious eyes and dropped his voice—"we confirmed tonight what really happened. Alice killed Sarah. The investigation is over." Sam started to roll to his side, moving as if he intended to get up.

"What are you doing?"

"I need to talk to Robert."

"You can't."

"Yes, I can. It's just a flesh wound and some dented ribs."

Emily had heard that doctors made the worst patients, a point Sam was proving true. "No. You *can't*. He's been taken to prison."

"What? Why?"

"What do you mean, why? He shot you. He's been arrested for dueling and nearly killing you."

"I have to bail him out."

"You can't." Emily barely managed to keep from sounding like an army sergeant.

Sam glared, making his feelings clear without words.

Emily sighed. "You could be arrested for dueling, too. Kerns said something about it as they were taking Robert away. But if you stay here in bed, they'll likely leave you alone. Now, if you refuse to be still, the doctor will have to dose you with something to make you sleep."

"Have it your way." Sam sank back against his pillows with a grimace. "You certainly can be a bossy thing."

"You'd do well not to forget it."

"That's exactly the kind of woman he needs." A rotund servant with gray hair and apple-red cheeks bustled into the room. She carried a basin of water with both hands, and a clean towel was draped over her arm. "The DeKlerk men have a stubborn streak that only a good woman can temper. Now"—she set the basin on the bedside table—"the doctor said to make sure your wound stays clean."

Emily moved to withdraw. As she stood and turned, she realized Miss Clara had been standing off to the side of the doorway the whole time. The older woman had remained silent, blending into the background.

Lips pursed, Miss Clara cocked an eyebrow at her.

Emily closed the door gently behind them. "Goodness, but I'm tired. Let me gather our things, and we can get back to the Adelphia." But Miss Clara's pointed gaze pinned her where she stood like a butterfly to velvet.

"Investigation?"

Emily's heart plummeted to her toes. This did not bode well.

Chapter 29

Morning light filtered through gauzy curtains the next morning as Emily applied salve to her stump and then strapped on her wooden leg. All the excitement of the previous evening had worn her out, and she'd fallen asleep almost as soon as her head had settled on the pillow.

There was also the relief of no longer keeping secrets from Miss Clara. She'd insisted on being told everything, but she had taken the news of Emily's involvement in a murder investigation in stride. She'd shaken her head and muttered something about "Juliet's influence" and "Carter's blood." All in all, she'd seemed most put out that they hadn't included her from the beginning.

A tap sounded at her door. "Are you ready, Emily?"

"Just a moment, Miss Clara."

"All right, dear. I'll have them flag us a cab."

Emily completed her toilet in a rush. It seemed the only negative consequence of Miss Clara's involvement was not that she would keep Emily from the investigation but that she would be too eager to lend a hand.

Forty minutes later, they stood staring up at the unprepossessing façade of the police station nearest the DeKlerk home.

Emily glanced at Miss Clara.

The older woman beamed, as if she'd always wanted to visit such a place. "Nothing ventured, nothing gained."

Or lost, thought Emily. But she kept the sentiment to herself and followed Miss Clara up the stairs.

The officer they came upon first, in a long blue jacket with a double row of brass buttons and a gleaming badge pinned to his chest, looked very official indeed. He did not seem to intimidate Miss Clara, however. She marched up to him, parasol swinging jauntily from her arm. "Good morning, sir. We are here to speak to one of your prisoners, Mr. Robert Romijn."

"Y' are, are ya?"

Miss Clara smiled brightly but forbore commenting further.

"Are ya related?"

"No, not to Mr. Romijn, but this is Dr. DeKlerk's fiancée, and she has a message from him for Mr. Romijn."

At the DeKlerk name, the fellow straightened. "DeKlerk, eh? Well, give me the message, and I'll see he gets it."

Emily offered him her sweetest smile. "It's not written down. I have to tell him directly."

After several more moments of bluster, the officer had them take a seat. A frustrating hour later, they were called and told to follow another officer. They descended into what would have been a cellar in a normal building. But this one was lined with steel cages.

Prisoners leered at them from both sides. Some hooted. One reached out through the bars, grabbing for Emily. She shied away, and the guard smacked his billy club against the bars, narrowly missing the man's fingers.

This had been a bad, bad idea.

"Isn't there somewhere else we could have met Mr. Romijn?"

"Sorry, miss; the holding pens are a rough place. I wouldn't have brought you down here, but Sarge said you could only see him in one of the interrogation rooms."

He held open a metal door for them, and they entered a windowless box of a room that contained nothing but two chairs. One of them was occupied by Robert Romijn, who sported an enormous black eye and a split lip.

"Robert!" Emily rushed to his side and knelt there, lifting his face so she could get a better look at it. "What happened?"

"I ran afoul of my cell mates. Doesn't matter." He pulled free of her grasp. "How's Sam?"

"He'll be fine."

Robert crumpled and buried his face in his hands. "Thank God. Oh, thank God. I never would have tried to hurt him if I'd been in my right mind. I don't know what I was thinking."

Emily put a hand on his shoulder. "Robert, Miss Clara and I are here to bail you out."

He looked up then, panic dilating his eyes and stretching the planes of his face taut. "No. You can't."

"Why not?"

"I deserve to be here. I deserve to hang."

"Don't be absurd. Sam will be all right, I promise, and he doesn't bear any grudge. He's the one who provided your bail money."

Robert moaned and squeezed his eyes tightly shut as he rocked back and forth in his chair. "I don't want his money."

"Robert, what did you do?" Emily had made her voice sharp.

He winced. "I…I murdered Sarah."

The admission would have shocked her, had it come a day before. But after what had happened with Mrs. Geddes, and the state she'd seen Robert in, Emily had a suspicion she knew what had really happened. "You did not hurt Sarah."

"I did. I went there that night and I murdered her. I must have."

Emily narrowed her eyes. "Why would you have done such a thing?"

"She wasn't really going to let me go. She wanted to get married, after all."

"Robert, I've seen letters written in her own hand. Letters she wrote the same day she was murdered. They were packed in her bag to mail. She hadn't changed her mind."

He shook his head. "Yes, she did. She changed her mind."

"Then what happened to Alice?"

"She…she saw me, and her mind rebelled at what I'd done. I lost her, too." Tears streamed down his face.

Emily stared at him for a long moment as the pieces began to slip into place. "Robbie, I simply don't believe it."

"It's true."

She waited, watching him all the while.

"Why won't you believe me?"

"Because of the way you reacted with Sam. If you had really killed Sarah, even if you'd been drunk as a fish when it happened, you couldn't have kept silent about it for ten years. Especially not when Alice's parents believed her to be the murderer." She put her hand on his. "After all this time, you still love Alice, and you're trying to protect her."

He sighed. "It was worth a try."

"I don't think Sam has any interest in pursuing some sort of conviction against Alice, if that's your concern. He merely wants to know the truth—and there may be more to the story. There have been some…incidents."

Robert raised his head to look at her, but it seemed to take a great effort for him to hold it up. "What kind of incidents?"

Emily smiled. He was interested, which was some progress.

"You let us bail you out, and I'll tell you all about it on the way home."

⌒

Sam grunted as he pulled on his frock coat. By the time it was properly in place, he was sweating. It was dashed hard to do, with his ribs in the shape they were in. The mere act of breathing was a chore, so getting dressed felt like riotous activity. Breathing heavily, he sat on the edge of the bed and stared at his shoes. If he plotted carefully, he should be able to manage them.

Ten minutes later, having decided to forgo a tie, he opened the bedroom door. With any luck, he could sneak out with no one the wiser. At this point, he just wanted to be home. His patients would be wondering where he was, and he needed to check on Robert. The idea of his friend in prison made his chest ache worse than the bullet wound.

He made it as far as the stairs before he was cornered. His mother stood on the second-floor landing, looking up expectantly. She'd probably been waiting and wondering what was taking him so long. "I knew you wouldn't heed the physician's orders."

"I am a physician, Mother. If anyone knows which orders do and don't have to be heeded, I do."

"One might think so, but I know you too well. You are too stubborn for your own good."

"I wonder where I learned that trait."

"Your father, no doubt." A hint of a smile quirked her lips. "Samuel, I'm worried about you. Please stay and rest."

Drat. As long as she maintained her icy hauteur, he could resist her, but when she warmed, he struggled. "Lying in bed isn't going to help matters, just as being up and about isn't going to hurt anything. The wound is no worse than a cut; it's just the cause that has made everyone so squeamish." He took her hand in his. "If I promise not to overexert myself, will you be satisfied?"

"No, but it will have to do, I suppose."

He dropped a kiss on her cool cheek and then made his way out the door. It seemed to take an inordinate amount of time to walk a single block. At the corner, he paused, wiping the sweat from his forehead with a handkerchief. Maybe he should break down and flag a cab. At the rate he was going, it would be the only way to make it home before nightfall.

At that moment, a hansom pulled to the curb just a few feet from him, and Emily's face appeared in the window. "Aren't you supposed to be in bed?"

"Aren't you supposed to be at the opera house?"

She shrugged in a casual way that endeared her to him. "I fixed it with Mr. Jerome. I've brought you a present."

She opened the door, and Sam could see, in the dim interior of the cab, a battered and bruised Robert seated next to Miss Clara.

"Hop in," said Emily. "We're taking Mr. Romijn home. He needs rest, even if you do not."

Robert looked utterly forlorn. "I'll understand if you don't wish to ride with me. I can walk from here."

Sam shook his head. "Do shut up, Robbie." Grunting at the effort, he pulled himself up into the cab.

Emily knocked on the roof, and they were off.

"You look worse for wear." Sam tried to shift into a comfortable position but quickly discovered there wasn't one.

"You're not looking so rosy, yourself."

Sam suppressed a grin. "I did get shot yesterday."

Robert flashed a smile in response. "Just a flesh wound, from what I understand, while I was knocked about quite viciously for my wallet, and have a wicked headache, to boot."

"I guess I must concede that your injuries are greater than mine." Sam leaned forward, and they clasped arms.

"I'm sorry, Sam. I'm glad you're all right."

"No more regrets, my friend. It is over, so far as I'm concerned. But don't expect me to duel you again."

"Not ever." Robert met his eye and held it steadily.

Sam nodded and sat back in the seat.

A moment later, they pulled up in front of Robert's apartment. Sam climbed slowly down and waited on the walk as the others alighted.

As he handed Emily down, despite her protests, he noticed a carriage draped in black parked at the curb. When Robert stepped from the hansom, a footman hopped down from the other carriage.

He approached and tipped his hat, then handed Robert a letter. "No response is required, sir. Mr. Geddes said to tell you that Mrs. Geddes is unwell, and they are going away for a while for a rest cure."

With furrowed brow, Robert accepted the letter. "Thank you."

The footman tipped his hat again, then departed.

Robert stared at the envelope, and then, with shaking fingers, opened it. A moment later, a moan came from somewhere so deep inside him, it didn't even sound human. His face blanched, and he fell to his knees, the letter crumpled in his hands.

Chapter 30

Emily's heart constricted and sank right to the pit of her stomach. She could think of only one piece of news that might affect Robert in such a way. Sam waved over the doorman from the apartment building, and between the two of them, they managed to get Robert upstairs.

Once inside, Miss Clara immediately set about making tea, while Emily drew the curtains in the living room and generally tidied up. She didn't pay much mind to what she was doing; she simply needed to stay busy. By tacit agreement, they left Robert for Sam to deal with.

It was a long while before Sam emerged from the bedroom. When he did, his face was gray with fatigue, and sweat covered his forehead. Miss Clara immediately shooed him into a seat and handed him a cup of strong, sweet tea. "Drink that up, and you'll feel better in a moment."

Obediently he drank, but without any noticeable pleasure.

There were a few moments of silence, and then Emily could stand it no longer. "Alice?"

Sam nodded. "Dead. Suicide, they think."

Emily's hand flew to her heart. "How is he?"

"About as one would expect." He rubbed his temple. "After I read the letter, I thought for sure he'd blame me for her passing. But it was worse. He's blaming himself for not doing more to help her."

"What could he have done?"

"Nothing, really. Unfortunately, we have very few ways to treat the mind, much less to attempt healing it."

"The poor man." Miss Clara folded her hands and bowed her head in a posture of prayer.

Emily let out a ragged sigh. "This morning, he tried to convince us that it was he who murdered Sarah. I think that if I hadn't called him on his ridiculous claims, he would have gone to the gallows rather than let Alice be tried for the crime."

Sam straightened slightly at this. "I'm not a monster. I wouldn't have tried to prosecute that poor woman. She was already incarcerated."

"How long had it been since her last suicide attempt?" Miss Clara asked.

"Several years, by all accounts," Sam said.

Emily set aside her teacup. "But then we arrived and stirred up all those memories. We upset her. Perhaps Robert *ought* to be blaming us for her suicide."

Sam frowned and let his head fall back against the chair. "Unless it wasn't suicide."

"You're thinking murder." Emily stood and began to pace. She waved Sam back down when he made to stand, as well. "I need to think, and pacing helps."

He didn't argue but returned to the main point. "Is it really so unbelievable? People and evidence surrounding this case continue to come up missing. Someone has tried to kill the two of us at least twice, but we have proved to be surprisingly durable. Perhaps they thought that if Alice died, we would be satisfied with the answers we'd already found and would stop digging into the matter."

Miss Clara leaned forward, looking eager to add her thoughts. "Or perhaps they were worried she could tell you something more."

"How can we find out one way or the other?" Emily asked.

Sam rubbed his palms on his pants. "I'll request an autopsy."

Emily gasped. "An autopsy? Isn't that rather extreme?"

"It's the only way I can think of to ascertain the cause of her death. That, and we'll have to go back to the asylum and ask some more questions."

Emily's stomach twisted at the thought of returning to that place, but Sam was right. If they wanted to know what had happened to Alice, they had to investigate. Just as they had done with Sarah. And their prying was likely to make the same person unhappy, which meant they'd have to be on the lookout for falling statuary and runaway horses.

The drive to the asylum the next afternoon passed largely in silence. Even Miss Clara's usual volubility had been flattened. For his part, Sam was struggling just to maintain an air of collected calm. Between his wound and the weight of Robert's grief, Sam felt worse than he had the day before. He had stayed the night with Robert, to make sure that he didn't drown his sorrow in a bottle, and also to keep him from doing anything ridiculous—say, coming to the asylum and demanding to interview someone.

He sighed and rubbed the back of his neck. What hubris possessed him? To think that he had not only the ability, but the right, to see justice done. As if there were any such thing. The war ought to have taught him that much, at least.

When they reached the asylum, a burly orderly opened the door and instructed them in no uncertain terms to remain in the foyer while he fetched Mrs. Ingleside. When the dour woman saw them, she looked even more pinched than usual. "I suppose you haven't heard."

Sam stepped forward and inclined his head. "About Miss Geddes' death? We did. That's why we're here."

"Well, what can you possibly want now?" She sounded exasperated.

"We have a few questions."

"Wait a minute." She pointed an accusing finger from one to the other. "Are you the ones behind the autopsy request?"

"It was an unexpected death," Sam replied. "The coroner is obligated to investigate."

She snorted. "That's exactly what happens all the time around here."

"Miss Geddes' family is quite well connected."

"And I'm sure they wanted to have their daughter carved up on a slab instead of decently buried. She's already an embarrassment."

Emily stepped slightly in front of Sam, drawing Mrs. Ingleside's gaze. "How did poor Alice die?"

"Slit her wrists. In fact, she broke that mirror you gave her, and used the shards. We wouldn't have given her something sharp like that."

Sam met Emily's eyes, doing his best to convey that Miss Ingleside's unkind comment should be ignored. Then he turned his attention on the unpleasant woman. "Had anyone come to visit her that day, or the day before?"

"No. We were getting ready for the city aldermen's inspection, which went very well, by the way. I'm certainly glad she didn't kill herself before that. I can just imagine finding her stiff as a board, with all those distinguished gentlemen in tow."

"Is her room occupied by another patient?" Emily's lips were thin, and Sam could see the effort it was costing her to maintain a pleasant tone, but she managed.

"Not yet."

"Then may we see it?" Sam put on his most ingratiating manner. "We promise not to take long."

Mrs. Ingleside sighed heavily and drew out her big ring of keys. "Suit yourselves. But I don't have time to supervise you all day. I've got work to attend to."

"Of course. We thank you for your kindness." The irony seemed lost on the woman.

Mrs. Ingleside escorted them upstairs and unlocked the heavy door. "I'm sure you can see yourselves out. The orderly will lock the door behind you." She went on her way without another word.

Miss Clara glared after the departing figure. "Such a cozy personality."

The first thing that struck Sam as he entered the room was the smell of blood. There was a pool of red beside the narrow cot. It appeared the space hadn't been cleaned since the discovery of the body. The blood had congealed completely by now, but there were numerous footprints, from where people had tracked through it while it was still wet.

That meant Alice couldn't have been dead long before she was found.

Sam knelt beside the obscene puddle and stared at it for a long moment. Then he looked at the mattress itself. Other than a few smears, there was no blood soaking its cotton surface.

Sam looked again at the stained floor.

Emily frowned. "Do you think there's enough blood?"

Sam glanced up at her. "I'm beginning to think you ought to have been the Pinkerton in your family."

At that, her cheeks flushed, right up to the tips of her ears. "Then you noticed it, too?"

"Yes, indeed. We did the right thing to make sure an autopsy was done."

They scoured the room but found nothing else of interest. There were no personal papers or other effects—not even the hat Emily had sacrificed.

Out in the hall, a young woman was scrubbing the floor with a big-bristled brush. Emily stepped hastily back to avoid treading on her. "I'm sorry. I didn't see you there."

"Oh, that's all right. I can be invisible sometimes." She sat back on her haunches. "Did you come to see Alice? She's dead, you know."

Sam crouched down until he was eye level with the young woman. "We'd heard that. Did you know Alice?"

"Not real good. She didn't come out of her room much. She's one what doesn't have to work."

"Oh?" In Sam's experience, indirect inquiry often reaped rewards where a direct question would cause a nervous patient to remain silent.

"She was out more lately, though. I think she was being good, so they would think she wasn't crazy anymore."

"Has she had visitors?" Emily asked.

"I'm not her keeper. Ask old Broadsides."

Sam smiled. "But I bet you see things. You seem to know all about what goes on here."

"I do make it a point to be well informed." The woman patted her hair back with her red, work-roughened hands. "I did happen to see a fellow go in to her room yesterday afternoon, but this was before she died."

"You are observant," Sam complimented her, knowing it would encourage her to keep talking.

She preened a bit more. "I'm not dumb, like some seem to think. I know he knew her, 'cause he said her name when he went in. And I know he had dark hair, 'cause he took his hat off."

"Was there anything else you noticed about him?"

"I bet he was rich, but stingy." She grinned like someone about to explain a riddle. "His shoes were all bright and shiny, but there was a hole in the bottom of one."

Sam was impressed. He raised his eyebrows. "Very clever. What about his face? Did you notice anything about his face?"

For the first time she looked a little downcast. "I couldn't really see his face."

"Marie!" A harsh voice rocketed down the hallway. "What are you doing?"

The woman hunched over her sudsy water again.

An orderly hustled down the hallway. "I'm sorry she was bothering you folks. She is too forward."

"I think we were bothering her. She's been nothing but kind."

Sam's response seemed to flummox the man for a moment. "Perhaps I can help you with something?"

Sam smiled. "Thank you, but we're leaving."

He ushered Emily and Miss Clara down the stairs and out the door. After checking to make sure that the driver was the same one who'd brought them there, he assisted the ladies into the carriage. Then he gave the driver Dr. Lee's office address.

"Where are we going?" asked Emily.

"To talk to the coroner about his autopsy." Sam grunted as he sat. He hated to admit it, but the wound was troubling him more than he let on.

⌇

Emily walked into Dr. Lee's office with a flutter in her stomach. She was not at all sure she wanted to do this. The first thing she noticed was that it didn't smell terrible. While she couldn't say exactly what she'd expected, it hadn't been the faint whiff of beeswax and books.

Dr. Lee welcomed Sam effusively and brought in three extra chairs. They settled in his consulting room, and once again, Emily felt obscurely relieved that it wasn't some sort of laboratory.

"Sam, you were right." The doctor linked his fingers together and lowered his fists on the desk before him.

"I was?" Sam leaned forward.

Despite his excitement, he looked haggard, with his cheekbones jutting out and his eyes bloodshot. Emily determined that as soon as the interview was over, she would make sure he went home and got some rest.

Dr. Lee pulled a paper from a sheaf on his desk. "You were, indeed. The cause of death was pulmonary congestion from a narcotic. It's the classic sign."

"You would know." Some of the fatigue briefly lifted from Sam's features.

Emily scooted in closer. Sam had told her that Dr. Lee was brilliant—one of the first to figure out how to determine cause of death by certain poisons. "Then, she was drugged?"

The good doctor nodded. "I suspect laudanum."

"And the cuts on the wrist?"

"Definitely inflicted after death. The heart had stopped pumping, so what little blood loss there was, was caused by gravity. My men said that when they picked up her body, the arm was hanging down over the edge of the bed."

"That's consistent with what we saw." Sam stood. "My thanks, Dr. Lee. If there's anything I can ever do for you—"

"Ah, Sam." Dr. Lee stood and clasped his hands. "You've already helped me more than I can say. If you hadn't been around, I don't know what we'd have done when Jim returned from the war. I think you saved his life. You certainly saved his sanity."

Sam nearly squirmed under the praise, and Emily assessed him anew. He was typically so self-contained. Criticism seemed to affect him little. But this reaction told her that wasn't true. He must have somehow perfected a way to insulate himself from critique, but praise penetrated right through his defenses.

They said their good-byes, and within a few minutes, they were on the street again. They weren't far from the Adelphia, so they chose to walk. The first hint of fall was in the air, carrying a briskness that raised Emily's spirits as she lifted her face to it.

"You know what this means." Sam wasn't asking a question.

Emily nodded. "Murder."

"Precisely."

"But why would someone murder Alice now?" Miss Clara's cheeks were pink from the breeze. "Especially if she was the one who killed Sarah?"

"Perhaps one of her parents murdered her to keep the story from coming out, hoping thereby to keep their family name unsullied," Emily mused aloud. "They did practically flee New York, after all."

Sam shook his head. "But there would have been no guarantee of that working. Besides, it would make more sense for them to attack us rather than their own daughter. That's why I suspected them in the beginning."

"The only other option I can think of is that Alice knew something—something that someone is willing to kill in order to protect. But what could be serious enough to kill over? And not only that, but why would this new murderer believe that anyone would listen to a certified lunatic?"

Miss Clara put a hand to her mouth in a pensive gesture. "It sounds like it would have to be the sort of person to whom even a hint of scandal could prove ruinous."

Sam nodded, a new gleam in his eye. "Right. Perhaps someone on the brink of something—a new career, a business deal, a marriage."

The clanging of a firehouse bell reached Emily's ears, and she, Sam, and Miss Clara stopped at the corner. The thunderous hooves of the heavy horses made the ground shake as the fire truck neared. The red-hatted firemen shouted, waving wildly for pedestrians and other carriages to move.

There was a scramble as vehicles tried to pull out of the way.

The truck began its turn past the corner where they stood, watching. As it did so, a hard shove caught Emily in the small of the back. She staggered forward into the path of the truck.

Chapter 31

The horses' metal shoes flashed. Emily splayed her hands wildly, trying to find something to stop her from sprawling beneath the crushing wheels.

An instant later, she felt briefly as if she were being cut in two. But she had stopped falling. Sam had ahold of her skirt and was hauling her back, away from the danger. He pulled her close to him, and, despite the public setting, she let her head rest against his chest as she blinked back sudden tears.

Finally, mindful of the strangers all around, she pulled herself together and looked up at him. "Thank you."

With the side of his thumb, he wiped away the only tear that had managed to escape her control. "What happened? Your leg?"

Emily swallowed hard and shook her head. "Someone pushed me."

Miss Clara was clucking nearby. She began looking around, but the crowd that had gathered briefly on the walk at the fire truck's passing had immediately dispersed once it had gone by. "This had to have been an attack of convenience."

"Which means someone is still following us." Sam sounded grim as death.

"I think you should check into the Adelphia tonight, as well." Emily's face burned at what could be taken as a somewhat scandalous suggestion. "I don't want you walking home alone, particularly since you are already injured."

He seemed to consider her suggestion. "I think I'd like to be able to keep an eye on you two, as well."

They hurried the last few blocks to the Adelphia, their conversation replaced by uneasy watchfulness.

When finally they had made it, and had confirmed there was an available room for Sam, Emily was glad to shut the door of their suite against the world. She had hid it as much as possible, but that near fall had unnerved her.

She dawdled over her routine before finally lying down. She was fairly certain her sleep would be packed with nightmares, so she was in no hurry to pursue slumber. But the next thing she knew, the sun was shining, and Miss Clara was knocking on her door.

The woman poked her head inside. "Sam is going to join us for breakfast."

Emily flung aside the blankets. "I'll be right out."

When she emerged from her room, Emily found them waiting for her over a basket of steaming muffins and an urn of coffee. The rich aroma made her salivate.

"Good morning." Sam looked much better today. Less haunted.

The sight of him brought a smile to her face. No matter what happened, meeting him had been a blessing. Because of that, she didn't regret becoming involved with the investigation.

"I was thinking we should go back to the newspaper and look through the archives again," Emily said. "With this new information, we might find something I didn't consider important the first time."

"That is not the proper response to 'Good morning.'" Miss Clara's scowl gave way to a smile. "Sit and eat, my girl. We were just discussing what we ought to do today. I think that's a fine idea, but we'll have to be quick about it. I don't want Mr. Jerome to think that we are neglecting the opera."

"There should be plenty of time for practicing. And you've certainly drilled me enough. I dream about the staging and have nightmares about my voice cracking during the duet with Malcolm."

"No fear of that. I drill you to avoid just such incidents."

Emily grinned and snatched a muffin.

⌒

As luck would have it, Miss Clara found what they were looking for at the bottom of page four in the society section. She'd called Emily and Sam over, and when they were standing on either side of her, looking over her shoulders, she tapped her finger on the newsprint.

"Look at this. It's an article about the upcoming social season, and how Miss DeKlerk and Miss Geddes will be missed."

Emily began reading out loud, but she stopped short when she neared the end. "I don't believe it," she whispered.

"What is it?" Sam leaned in closer.

Emily read the last line out loud: "While the case of Miss DeKlerk is still open, the guilty party has been identified and is the subject of a cross-country manhunt, according to Officer George Drake."

Sam made a fist and pounded the table. "That lying skunk."

"What?" Miss Clara looked to Sam, but he didn't answer, so she turned to Emily. "What's going on?"

Emily stood up straight. "Officer Drake is the one who told me Sarah's file had gone missing, and referred us to Marty Reed."

Her mouth dropped open, then she snapped it shut and shook her head. "I still don't understand the significance."

"Look at the date." Sam pointed to the top of the paper. "This is one month after the murder. Reed disappeared two weeks before this. There's a good chance that Drake was put in charge of the case."

Emily nodded. "Or, at the very least, he knows more than he told me."

"I don't understand." Miss Clara frowned at her. "If he has something to hide, why would he tell you anything?"

Good question. Emily looked to Sam.

Sam shrugged. "To throw you off the trail. To feed you false information." He paused, obviously not wanting to voice the thought that had come to his mind. "Or to get information from you that he could take back to his boss."

A shiver ran through Emily as she remembered how helpful he'd been. She'd thought she'd had him figured out, but now.... How could she trust her own judgment? Maybe she was too naive and sheltered to be able to investigate. But then again, maybe not. "Come on." She headed for the staircase, and the other two followed.

Miss Clara scurried to keep up. "Where are we going?"

Without breaking stride, Emily answered, "To speak to Officer Drake."

Emily's determination was tempered by the fact that they had no idea where George Drake lived. It seemed unlikely that anyone at the police station would help them find him. But they did know where he would be each day—walking his beat.

"We could simply invite him in for tea," Miss Clara suggested.

Sam vetoed the idea. "I want to see where and how he lives. We need to get the measure of the fellow somehow. Right now, we don't know anything about him."

They met in the lobby of the Adelphia in the late afternoon following Emily's rehearsal, and watched for Officer Drake to make his final pass in front of the hotel. They didn't have long to wait, and when he'd gone, they hurried out into the street after him.

He turned in at the police station. The minutes ticked by, while they tried to loiter inconspicuously on the street. Sam started to wonder whether Drake had gone out some back door.

He was on the verge of expressing this fear when Drake finally emerged. Sighing in relief, Sam looked at Emily and found that her expression mirrored his own. She seemed to have a knack for reading his mind, for finishing his thoughts. Considering how much space she occupied in those thoughts, perhaps he shouldn't be surprised.

Their quarry walked fast, and they picked up their pace to keep him in sight. A new fear struck Sam. What if Drake caught an omnibus? There'd be no way for them all to get on without him noticing.

But Drake continued on, giving no sign of flagging or stopping for an omnibus. On and on he led them, and gradually the neighborhood began to change. Gentility gave way to tidy, working-class neighborhoods, where the owners weren't necessarily rich but did care for their property.

They stopped at a corner, waiting for it to be clear enough to allow their crossing, and Miss Clara's panting was plain to be heard. Sam turned to her. "Are you all right?"

"Just…winded." Her words came out in gasps.

Sam glanced back toward Drake's figure, which was growing smaller in the distance.

"Go on," said Miss Clara. "You and Emily go on. I will wait for you in that little café." She pointed across the street at a well-kept eatery.

"Are you sure?" Emily's voice conveyed concern.

"You could wait with her." Sam was proud of this sudden inspiration. It would be much better if both women waited here, well away from any potential danger.

Emily seemed less enamored of the idea. "I'm fine, and I'm coming."

They left Miss Clara at the café and hurried on after Drake. He now had a lead of several blocks, and they needed to close the gap.

Despite their best efforts, they were still more than a block behind when he turned again. They had moved into the edge of the slums. Even the air here seemed to be of a poorer quality.

Practically running now, they hurried to catch sight of him again. Sam regretted not insisting that Emily stay at the café with Miss Clara. It would have been better for everyone.

Just as they rounded the corner, Sam spied Drake climbing the steps of a tenement building. They had him.

Slowing slightly, they waited for him to enter, then followed. The entryway was Spartan, a bare area with a rough wooden floor and cracked plaster walls that hadn't even been whitewashed, much less painted or papered. There were no tidy mail slots here with tenants' names in neat lettering.

Listening hard, Sam heard the sound of boots on the stairs. Surely that was Drake.

"Go!" whispered Emily. "I'll be right behind you."

It was all the encouragement he needed. He bounded up the stairs, taking them two at a time. On the fourth floor, he caught sight of a door closing down the hall.

⌒

As Emily mounted the third flight of stairs, she caught sight of Sam, bent over slightly with his hands on his waist, as he caught his breath.

"Did you see where he went?" she asked in a low voice.

"Just down the hall, there." Sam led the way and knocked on the door.

Drake answered it, wearing a threadbare shirt that was almost as snug as his uniform jacket had been.

Now, Emily took the lead. "Hello, Officer Drake."

"Miss." Recognition and shock registered on his face. "What are you doing here?"

"We've come about Sarah DeKlerk."

Drake spread his hands wide. "I told you, that file went missing. I don't know any more."

Sam stepped closer. "Oh, we think you know a lot more. You were put in charge of the investigation following Reed's disappearance, after all."

Drake tried to slam the door, but Emily had put her wooden foot over the threshold. She nearly laughed out loud at his look of surprise when the door wouldn't budge and she evinced no pain.

"Here now, I don't want any trouble."

"We don't want trouble, either, Officer." Emily was all sweetness. "But this man is Dr. DeKlerk, *brother* of the deceased, and he very much wants you to tell him the truth."

"You're not being a very good host, Drake," Sam said. "You should invite us to come in so we can have a civilized talk."

All Drake could do was shake his head. Sam pushed past him into the apartment. "Now, tell us what you know about my sister's murder."

The man spread his hands and hunched his shoulders in a shrug. "I already told the lady everything I know."

Emily followed Sam into the room. "You forgot a few details, such as the fact that you were there the night Sarah died."

She was fishing, pure and simple. But when Drake looked down at his feet rather than deny the accusation, she had her answer. Buoyed by her discovery, she pushed further.

"And you were paid money to keep quiet about certain things you saw. And did."

"Miss!" He managed to cram a boatload of outraged innocence into a single syllable.

"Don't bother acting innocent." Sam shook his head. "We know it's true."

The bluster drained from him. "There was no harm in it."

That has yet to be seen.

A low growl came from Sam's throat. "What did you see?"

Sighing, Drake dropped into a chair. Without being invited to do so, Emily also took a seat. She wanted him to know she didn't plan on going anywhere for the foreseeable future. Sam remained standing, looking down at him.

"I'm just a beat cop, mind you." His tone was wheedling, as if this fact made up for everything.

Neither Sam nor Emily said a word.

"So, I was patrolling my beat, as usual, when this girl comes flying right through the hedgerow—"

"Wait a minute," Sam interrupted. "You were there *before* the crime was reported?"

Drake nodded.

"Go on," Emily said.

"Like I said, she ran out of the bushes and practically into my arms. Scared me about out of my wits. She looked dreadful. Her dress was covered with dirt and mud, and her hair was tumbling down around her ears. And there was a cut across her palm." He shuddered. "Spookiest thing I ever saw. Because, despite the way she looked, she was smiling in this sort of far-off way and singing kind of low."

Emily glanced at Sam, and their eyes met. *Alice.*

"What did you do?" Sam asked.

"She looked a bit familiar, and I thought she might have been a guest of the DeKlerks', so I told her I'd escort her back to the house. I thought maybe she'd been playing some silly game and gotten lost. But as soon as I said that, she started crying. Said she didn't want to go there. Kept babbling and saying she wanted to go home, and she wanted some fellow—Roy, or Ronald, or something like that."

"Could it have been Robert?"

"Maybe. So then, I said I'd escort her anywhere she liked. She told me her name, and I started walking with her, trying to get her to tell me where she lived. But then I heard a commotion near the house. Sounded like someone was screaming. I told the girl to stay right there and then ran off to see what the trouble was. Before I made it to the other side of the hedgerow, she took off.

"When I found murder had been done, other officers got involved. That night, I reported what had happened with the girl to the commissioner."

Sam raised a skeptical eyebrow.

"It's true." There was a wounded note in his voice, as if he couldn't believe his word could be doubted. "The next day, I came in to the station, and he pulled me aside, told me that I didn't need to put anything about the girl in my report. Said she didn't have anything to do with the murder. Then he gave me a little bonus for all my hard work."

"What was your commissioner's name?" Emily knew already, and so did Sam, but they had to get him to say it.

He looked around, as if fearful of being overheard in the stuffy little room. "You don't understand. The man's got power. I can't cross him."

Sam shook his head. "I don't care."

"I'm telling you. He's not one to be trifled with."

"His name." Sam stood, towering above the smaller man.

"Harrison Kerns."

"And what was the girl's name?"

"I don't know."

Sam took a step forward.

"Honest. It was made very clear to me that it was something I should forget, so I did. But, really, none of this matters, 'cause they went after the gardener, or whoever it was that murdered the DeKlerk girl. I thought maybe this other girl saw something that pushed her round the bend. Or maybe she was someplace she shouldn't have been, and didn't want her nobby family to know."

"You never spoke to the girl's parents?"

"Not ever."

"Did you ever see the girl again?"

"No. Sometimes I wondered if I imagined her, like maybe she was the dead girl's ghost."

"With another girl's name?"

He shrugged.

"Have you been up to the Bloomingdale Lunatic Asylum lately?"

"The—what do you take me for? I'm not some loon." Drake stood. "I told you what you wanted to know. You get on out of here, now, and don't come back. It's harassment, and I could call the police."

Sam's smile was malevolent. "You could. But I have a great deal more money than you. I could put them all in my pocket, and then you'd have the police after you, as well. Or, I could draft a well-worded letter to Harrison Kerns, and tell him how helpful you've been at filling in the blank spots."

What little color was left in the man's pudgy cheeks drained away.

Sam moved another deliberate step toward him. "And if I find that you've lied to us, I'll do it anyway."

With that, he spun on his heel, and Emily followed him out of the room. She glanced back as she closed the door and saw Officer Drake drop heavily into a chair, his head in his hands. She almost felt sorry for him.

⌒

Sam sat on the settee in Emily's dressing room. She and Miss Clara were behind a large screen, getting her ready for a dress rehearsal.

Her voice came to him, slightly muffled by fabric. "Kerns must be behind all of it. He was probably paid off, too."

Sam agreed. "And he's about to be nominated to replace Hoffman as mayor. This is the worst possible timing for him to have any hint of scandal."

"Could he truly have been so worried about what a certified lunatic might say about him that he'd have her killed?" Emily's voice was no longer muffled but was heavy with disbelief. "It would be easy enough to wave away anything she might have claimed. After all, he left her alone for the last ten years without any apparent concern."

"No one was digging then. Nor was his career at such a critical juncture. He must have panicked when he realized we were sniffing around." Sam rubbed his temples, trying to think it all through. "What I don't understand is, why kill Alice and leave anyone else alive? The Geddeses admitted that they paid someone hush-money. It had to have been Kerns. We know that some of the money went to Drake, but I bet Kerns kept the vast majority for himself."

"And what about Officer Reed?"

Sam had been mulling that over, himself. "I think Kerns offered him a bribe to withhold evidence, and he refused. That left Kerns no choice but to get rid of him."

"Oh, dear." Emily's slender hand appeared above the top of the screen as she tossed a garment over it. "What if the same thing happened to the Geddeses? They may have left town simply because Mrs. Geddes was advised to have a rest cure, but maybe they were told to leave."

"Or maybe they were threatened and fled."

Miss Clara stepped out into the open. "Or maybe they were grieving and wanted to avoid more questions and pressure from either you or Kerns."

Surreptitiously, Sam pressed against the bandage on his wounded side. "No matter how it came about, I think their disappearance is far too handy. For Kerns, I mean. Now we can't question them any further about the bribe they paid. For all we know, they bribed others, as well."

"Maybe Kerns really wasn't concerned about them at all," Emily said. "After all, they paid to preserve their place in society. He knows they would have something to lose if the truth came out, just as he does."

"Right, but because he couldn't control Alice, he had to act."

"We can speculate endlessly, but how can we prove any of it at this point?" Miss Clara asked. "It all happened so long ago."

Emily emerged from behind the screen. She wore a long, loose-fitting white linen gown that fell all the way to the floor, with a tartan plaid draped across one shoulder. One impossibly small, bare white foot occasionally peeked out as she moved.

Sam lost his thread of the conversation, and his voice grew tight. "Is that your costume?"

She took a seat in front of the vanity and began brushing her hair. "Yes. Isn't it delightful? It's so easy to move around in, and quite authentic—what a Highland lass might have worn at the time the opera is set."

"Well...um...." Sam swallowed past the lump in his throat. "It's much better than the first costume you tried on."

"Hideous, wasn't it?" Emily wrinkled her nose and laughed.

Sam's response to the costume took him by surprise. It wasn't that it was revealing. Not at all. Perhaps it was the informal nature of the ensemble. In it, Emily was so slight, a little wisp of a thing, without the structure of her crinolines and voluminous skirts.

Emily tucked a strand of hair behind her ear and stood up.

"You'll leave your hair down for the performance, as well?"

"Yes." She glanced back at the mirror, a *v* of worry appearing between her eyebrows. "Is something wrong?"

"Not at all. This will be a very memorable performance for staid old New York."

Emily looked down at her costume and back up at him.

Miss Clara handed Emily a basket filled with heather. "Back to the original subject. About that proof?"

Sam rose to his feet. "Right. Um…well, if we suspect that Kerns took bribes, there may be records of them at his bank—say, substantial sums being deposited. I'll talk to a couple of friends and see what I can find out in that regard."

Emily rearranged the contents of the basket. "We'll start asking around about his connection to—what was the name of that political group?"

"Tammany Hall? Don't go asking about Tammany. If anything, they are even more corrupt. I don't want you poking around in Boss Tweed's hornet's nest."

Emily nodded.

Sam narrowed his eyes. "Truly, Emily. They are dangerous."

A knock sounded at the door. "You're needed on stage, Miss Forbes."

"I've got to dash, Sam. We'll see you tonight at the Adelphia."

Before Sam could say another word, she breezed through the door and was gone.

Miss Clara patted his shoulder. "Don't worry, love. She's a bright girl. She won't take unnecessary risks."

Sam raised her hand to his lips. "Miss Clara, you are ever the voice of reason." He just wished her assurances could banish the uneasy feeling in the pit of his stomach. Because, the truth was, they'd already poked the hornet's nest, and the next sting could be fatal.

By now, Emily knew her way through the opera's staging, but she still had to concentrate on keeping her movements fluid and making her performance believable. Gazing adoringly at Malcolm presented another challenge, as "he" was actually a woman playing a trouser role. Emily would never understand why Rossini had assigned the role of his story's nominal hero to a contralto.

Truth be told, though, Malcolm really wasn't the hero; it was King James, in the same way that Alice, while she might have killed Sarah, didn't seem to be the real villain of the piece. Not considering all that had gone on lately.

During a break, Emily stood chatting with Benedetta. A pace away from them, the actor who played King James, and happened to actually be named James, mentioned the upcoming election for governor.

"Do you think Mayor Hoffman will win the race?" Emily asked in her very best tourist's voice.

"I'd say he's going to walk all over Griswold, unless something big happens."

"So, what happens if he is elected? Who will be mayor?"

"One of the aldermen would be asked to fill the office until the next election."

"I see. I wonder how that person is selected."

James snorted. "Easy enough. They pick whoever Boss Tweed tells them."

"Who's Boss Tweed?" Emily didn't actually bat her eyes, but she did widen them a bit.

"He's the head of the organization over at Tammany Hall."

"I see," she said, in a tone that conveyed the opposite.

"Tammany Hall is the political power in New York City. Any candidate for office has to have their vetting if he has any hope of winning."

"But how can they have so much power if the candidates are elected?"

"Because they control the immigrants. Because they buy votes. Because they stuff the ballot boxes. There isn't an underhanded way of getting a vote that they haven't already thought up and don't employ."

Benedetta shifted, her sword clanking. "That hasn't been proven."

James barked out a laugh. "Only because no one cares enough to investigate. The people with the power to investigate were put in place by Tweed, so they certainly aren't interested in looking into the matter."

"Voluntary blindness," Emily added.

"Precisely. And the very people they take advantage of the most, the poor and the immigrants, are their power base. They are fed so many lies, and Tweed does provide some superficial services that are sometimes the only assistance they get. Combine that with the free beer that's doled out for every vote, and...well, there is no stopping them."

"It sounds like you know a lot about it."

He bowed with a bit of a flourish. "A failed career in politics landed me on the stage instead."

"Are you sure it's not just sour grapes?" Benedetta poked his shoulder.

"Sour grapes? Sour grapes! My foray into politics was so many years ago, I'm quite sure I can be unbiased at this point."

These New Yorkers certainly did take their politics seriously, which was saying a lot for a girl who came from Washington, D.C. "And now you are a king, at least temporarily." Emily smiled, hoping to lighten the suddenly tense atmosphere.

It did seem that Sam was correct, though. Tammany Hall was dangerous and powerful. She'd promised him she'd stay away from them, but she couldn't shake the beginnings of a plan that was forming in her mind.

She'd have to walk carefully.

~

Sam strolled out of the bank building wearing the broadest grin he'd managed for months. It had taken trips to three different banks, but he'd found Harrison Kerns' accounts. Being a DeKlerk had paid off handsomely, and he now knew that the former commissioner hadn't received a single payment from the Geddes. No, indeed; there had been significant deposits made every single month for the last ten years.

It appeared Kerns had required ongoing bribes. And the Geddeses weren't the only ones paying him. Others had paid various large amounts on a regular basis. It was these monies that had, in large part, funded his political aspirations to date. But now the shoe was on the other foot. Kerns was in a place where he needed to keep his personal skeletons firmly secured in the closet.

It was becoming more and more obvious that Kerns was the man they needed to bring down if Sam and Emily were to be safe going forward. Now they just had to figure out how to do it.

Chapter 33

Emily and Sam sat across from one another at a curtained table at Delmonico's. They had chosen a public meal as part of their charade of an engagement, but the privacy of the booth allowed them to plot in peace.

Emily listened, absorbed, as Sam described what he'd been able to uncover in his search. There was a great deal to consider, but the one thing she was sure of was that she was tired of reacting to what happened. She wanted to take the reins and drive events for once, and she thought she knew how to do it. Unfortunately, she had a feeling Sam would object to her plan.

Sam fingered the stem of his water glass as he continued talking. "Perhaps we can speak to some of his other victims and make them see it's in their best interest to work with us, and get him convicted of taking bribes. That would at least remove him from the political picture, and after that, we could investigate more thoroughly. For that matter, the police could get involved at that point."

"Sam, I don't think any of those people will cooperate. If they've been paying him to keep their secrets, they are likely to see us as the enemy. They may even have more to lose than Kerns and could come after us, too."

He put down his fork. "Good point."

"I did have an idea."

"Let's hear it. I'm tapped out."

"What if I contact him? Tell him I've found evidence regarding his corruption but offer to sell it to him, instead? We set up a meeting to exchange the information for pay, and I get him talking. If you, and maybe a few others, are hidden nearby, where you can overhear, then we would have all the proof we need."

Sam frowned and shook his head. "No, it's much too dangerous. For one thing, why would he believe your story?"

Emily snorted. "I'm finding that people are willing to believe almost anything about an opera singer."

"I'd be more comfortable if I was the one to propose the exchange."

It was Emily's turn to frown. "He'd never believe that you would let anyone off the hook who was involved in your sister's murder. Not after you've been so diligent in your pursuit."

"But why would he believe that you would betray me like that?" He laid his hand on top of hers and ran his fingertip across her engagement ring.

This was the worst part. Emily drew in a deep breath, then blurted it out: "We'd have to break the engagement."

⌒

Sam stared at her. It seemed for a moment that the air had been sucked out of the room.

Emily held his gaze steadily. She was serious.

His heart gave a painful thump. "Why?" It was all he could manage.

"So he will believe I'm a vengeful, scorned woman. If we break the engagement very publicly, he will be able to verify my story through his own sources."

"I don't like it. He still might not believe you. And even if he does agree to meet, it's entirely likely that he won't put himself in your power by paying you off." The progression of the thought was terrifying. "He may try to kill you instead."

"Not if it's a very public place." Emily turned her hand beneath his, so that her palm faced up, and their fingers intertwined.

"Besides, there will be no danger. You will be there and can stop him if he makes a move to hurt me. I trust you to keep me safe."

This was true. If Kerns so much as spoke too crossly to Emily, Sam would jump in to protect her. But even the best of plans could go wrong, and this plan certainly wasn't the best. It pinched and pulled like a wrong-sized shoe.

Emily smiled sweetly. "Who do you think you should ask to join you?"

She seemed to take it for granted that he would go along with her idea. And likely he would. It might be their best chance to smoke out Kerns, even if it did make his stomach roil.

Over their steak course, they drafted the note that would be sent to Kerns. Then they decided on a guest list, which included the names of the chief of police, a judge, and an attorney, all of whom Sam knew either socially or officially as a physician.

"Now we have to decide when to stage our break," Sam said.

Their waiter drew back the curtains in order to wheel in a cart carrying their desserts and coffees.

"No time like the present," Emily whispered. She stood and flung her napkin down. "I've never been so insulted, Samuel DeKlerk."

The clink of silver on china stilled; the low murmur of polite conversation quieted.

Emily continued, her voice growing progressively louder. "If you think for one minute that I'll marry you after this, then you are sorely mistaken." She managed to add a little hitch to her tone, making it sound as if she was about to break into sobs. Chin held high and back ruler-straight, she stalked out of the restaurant.

Sam stared after her, his face growing hot as the patrons watched her departure and then turned as one to gape at him.

She was a good actress. A convincing actress. He was not so theatrically gifted, but then, he didn't have to manufacture the shocked disbelief that was causing his flush. He stood, pulled some money from his wallet, and handed it to the flabbergasted waiter. Then he left as abruptly as she had. The scowl he wore was no act. Even knowing what was coming had not softened its impact.

He did not like this plan.

Chapter 34

Emily paced the South Hall of the Astor Library. It was an imposing space, with arches forming a colonnade two stories high. The area was mutely bustling with readers bending low over hefty tomes and librarians moving thick volumes from one location to another on well-oiled carts. The books here never left the building; but, as a research library it was renowned, with hundreds of patrons visiting each day to delve into its documented wisdom.

If she went to the second floor, she could see him arrive, but then she'd be out of hearing range of the listeners concealed in the stacks, where patrons were usually prohibited. The plan wouldn't work if she didn't stay near them.

The minutes ticked by, and Emily watched the door. She did not bother to hide her increasing anxiety. Kerns was no doubt delaying on purpose, in order to put her on edge and thereby give himself the upper hand. Well, they would see who had the upper hand when all was said and done.

Slowly, the sun shifted through the sky, lengthening the shadows as it poured in through the tall windows. Two hours after their scheduled appointment, Emily looked back to the stacks. Sam emerged and shrugged. The jowly lawyer and the judge with the imposing muttonchop whiskers were right behind him. Bringing up the rear was the police chief. His naturally red face was as purple as a beet and swollen with suppressed rage.

"I hope this will be a lesson to you, Samuel DeKlerk." The judge shook a finger under Sam's nose. "Pride goeth before destruction.

How you thought you could better solve a decade-old murder, I'll never know."

The police chief planted his hands on his ample hips. "And slandering a fine man like Kerns. I don't know how I let you talk me into this harebrained scheme. I certainly never expected anything to come of it."

"Shh." At least three librarians raised their fingers to their lips in the universal demand for quiet.

"Wait, please. I don't know why he didn't come. Perhaps he was suspicious of Miss Forbes." Sam put a hand on the judge's arm, but the man immediately pulled away.

All three men eyed Emily as if they thought Kerns had the right idea.

The judge shook his head. "I know you had good intentions, Sam, but this is foolishness. You never should have dragged us into your tiff with Kerns, whatever the cause." He led the way from the library, with the other two close on his heels.

Emily took a seat at one of the reading tables. "Now what are we going to do?"

Sam shook his head and sat beside her. "I don't know. Whatever it is, we're back on our own. Do you think it's possible we got the wrong end of the stick? Maybe Kerns really is innocent."

"Or maybe he was tipped off."

"You think one of those gentlemen might have told him about our plan?"

"It's a possibility, don't you think? Or maybe a clerk in their offices let something slip to the wrong person. There are any number of possibilities. After all, if Kerns was innocent, he still should have shown up, if only out of curiosity and to keep his name clean."

"Then you still believe Kerns is behind the attacks and Alice's murder?"

Emily gave a sharp nod. "I do, indeed."

"All right, then. What do we do next, O Maker of the Plans?"

Emily had to admit that nothing came immediately to mind. "Why don't we sleep on it? I'm too distracted, with opening night tomorrow, and I won't be able to participate in any schemes until I've gotten through that, anyway."

Sam agreed, though it was clear the idea of delay didn't appeal.

He took her back to the Adelphia, where Miss Clara was avidly awaiting news. Then Sam took his leave.

Emily watched him go, a sinking feeling in her stomach. What were they to do next? And even if they managed to find proof, who would listen to them now?

⌒

Before heading to his office, Sam decided to check in on Robert. He had taken Alice's death so hard, and Sam had been unable to find anything to say that would convince him it wasn't his fault. So, he'd made it a point of visiting his friend each day. Not even the revelation that it had likely been murder had been able to sway Robert's self-imposed guilt.

There was no response to Sam's knock, so he let himself in using the latchkey Robert had given him years ago. The room reeked of tobacco smoke and stale liquor. He really needed to hire new staff. Sam picked his way among the rubbish that littered the floor—crumpled newspapers, used dishes, shoes, and empty wine bottles.

Sam sighed. Robert wasn't particularly neat, even at the best of times, but neither did he typically live in squalor. "Robbie?"

There was no response. Maybe he was sleeping off his latest indulgence. Sam poked his head into his room. Sure enough, Robert lay on the bed.

Something was wrong, though. Sam waded through the mess to get to the bedside. Robert's color was off, the skin around his mouth and fingernails turning blue. Sam put his ear to his chest and could hear no lung sounds, nor was there any chest rise, though he could hear the heart beating faintly.

"Robbie! Come around, lad. Wake up!" Sam smacked his cheeks. Nothing.

Sam began mouth-to-mouth respiration and alternately applied pressure to his abdomen. Several agonizing moments later, Robert's lips had turned pink again. He needed to get help, but every time Sam stopped, the color began to fade again. There was no one around. Just like on the battlefield.

Sam was alone.

No, that wasn't quite right. He fought back against the despair threatening to consume him. There was One, a Physician far greater than Sam would ever be.

Uttering a prayer for help, Sam completed another round of breaths and pressure, then rummaged through his bag for ipecac. If Robert had drunk so much that it had suppressed his respiratory effort, the only thing Sam could think to do was to rid his body of some of the alcohol.

He rolled Robert on his side, held his nose closed, and poured the ipecac down his throat. "You want to drink? Well, drink this up, Robbie, boy. There's a good lad."

In a moment, his friend began to retch and soon emptied out the contents of his stomach. Doing his best to maintain a detached, clinical attitude, Sam deduced from the volume that Robert hadn't ingested as much alcohol as he'd suspected.

He continued working with Robert, cleaning him up, dosing him again, then repeating the cycle. It seemed to take an eternity, but at last he was breathing on his own. When he seemed stable, though still somnolent, Sam wrestled him into a set of clean night-clothes and then changed the bedding. With every pull and tug, a twinge of pain stabbed at his side, reminding him that the man he cared for had shot him not long before.

It was while wadding up the soiled linens and carrying them away that he noticed an envelope on the table next to the bed. It was addressed "To the Authorities." Sam disposed of the bedsheets and came back for the envelope. He stared at it a long moment. On the one hand, he was no authority, but on the other hand, he was Robert's physician. Whatever was in the letter might help him understand how Robert had come to be so close to death. Sam picked it up, opened it, and pulled out the letter.

> *Dear Sirs,*
>
> *I can no longer live with my guilt. I am a murderer—first of Miss Sarah DeKlerk and, more recently, of Miss Alice Geddes. I have no justification that will suffice. But I did have reasons that were compelling to me. Still, I find the weight of my sin is so heavy that I no longer wish to inhabit this world.*
>
> *Robert Romijn*

The words blurred on the page. Sam couldn't control the trembling in his hands or the pounding in his temples. His first thought was to throttle the man on the bed. *How could he? How could he?* How could he murder Sam's sister and then pretend to be his friend for ten more years? It beggared belief. And he wouldn't have believed it, except why would Robert lie about such a thing with his dying act?

Sam left the bedroom and fell into a seat at the table in the kitchen. The irony that he'd saved the life of his sister's murderer was not lost on him. If he had the chance to do over again, knowing what he did now, he would walk away and let the liquor take Robert.

Sam raked his fingers through his hair. He had to consider this. No one knew he was here. He could return Robert to the state he'd found him in and leave. But then again, that would be giving him what he wanted.

Perhaps it was good that Sam had preserved the wretch. He could make sure Robert was brought to justice, that he had no choice but to live with his regret. Not only that, but there would be the humiliation of being reviled by his peers and stripped of his military rank. Stripped of everything that held meaning to him.

Even as he imagined Robert's downfall, a niggling sense of disquiet poked at the edges of his mind. If he was honest, something about the letter felt off. Sam reread it several times. Then he dropped the page on the table and went outside to pump water. When he got back, he put on a pot of coffee.

He drank a cup, then poured a second to take to Robert. It had been several hours since Sam had arrived, and the sun had long since gone to sleep. His patient still was not stirring. Sam sat on the edge of the bed and smacked Robert's cheek, perhaps harder than strictly necessary. Robert groaned and turned his head, trying to escape the blows.

"Wake up, Robbie."

He turned his head again and made another moan. His eyelids fluttered faintly.

"I know it's hard, but you must wake up." Sam put one hand under Robert's chin and, with the other, held the cup to his lips, tipping it until the hot, strong coffee slipped into his mouth.

Robert swallowed feebly. His eyes opened a slit, and then he closed them again. "Sam?"

"I read the letter." He looked down at Robert, the man who had been like a brother to him, and his heart broke. "Why did you do it?"

Robert's eyelids fluttered again. It seemed he was more agitated, but Sam might have been seeing things that weren't there. He leaned closer to make sure he caught anything Robert might say.

"Made me...I didn't."

The words were slurred, and Sam wasn't sure he'd heard correctly. "What was that? Who made you do what?"

But there was no response—not so much as a flicker of an eyelash—from Robert.

Sam left the room. He had some decisions to make. And as soon as Robert truly regained consciousness, they were going to have a long, honest talk.

Chapter 35

Emily woke to infernal banging. She blinked and groaned. It seemed as if she'd just closed her eyes. What in the world could be so urgent?

She pushed herself up. Out in the sitting room, she could hear Miss Clara stomping to the door. "All right, all right. I'm coming."

Emily swung her leg over the edge of the bed, and then, balancing on the furniture, hopped over to her bedroom door, which she swung open. Sam rushed in the suite door, which Miss Clara had opened a mere inch.

"Is Emily here?" His eyes were wild, and he had some sort of paper clutched in his hand, so tightly, she wouldn't be surprised if he'd squeezed the ink right off of it.

"Sam?" She reached for the nearest table and hopped out into the sitting room.

"Emily." His relief was palpable. "I'm sorry to disturb you, but there's been a development."

Emily reached for the back of the settee and hopped forward again. Miss Clara dove into Emily's bedroom and returned with a dressing gown, which she wrapped around Emily, a belated measure to preserve her modesty.

Emily worked her way around the settee and dropped into it.

"Sam, have a seat. Tell me what's wrong."

"I went to check on Robert. He was almost dead."

"Dead!" Miss Clara sat almost as precipitously as Emily had.

"I was able to revive him, but then I found this." He handed over the paper.

Emily accepted it from fingers that trembled slightly, then watched as he propped his elbows on his knees and let his head rest in his hands. This must be bad.

After reading the note, she passed it with numb fingers to Miss Clara, then stared at the fire, trying to make the pieces fit.

"Robert's the murderer?" Her voice sounded thin to her own ears.

"I don't know." Sam shook his head miserably. "I just…I stayed until he could talk to me. He said an intruder broke into his home and forced him to write that note at gunpoint. Then he was made to drink something, and that's the last thing he remembers."

Some of the warmth returned to Emily's fingers. That explanation, far-fetched as it might seem, rang far truer than the prospect of Robert being a double murderer. "Who did this to him?"

"He claims he didn't recognize the man."

"So it probably wasn't Kerns." She worried her bottom lip with her teeth. "Of course, he wouldn't do his own dirty work, not unless he was desperate."

"Then you believe him? What if, when he realized he had survived, he fed me a story?" The anguish in Sam's face made Emily ache for him.

"Do you believe that's what happened?"

"I don't know what to believe anymore. Or what to do."

At the moment, neither did Emily.

"Well, I do," Miss Clara spoke up.

Emily and Sam both looked at her.

She patted the seat cushion beside her. "Doctor, you come sit by me."

When he had settled next to her, she took his hand in one of hers and then grasped Emily's hand with the other.

"We're going to do something we should have done a long time ago," she said, with the authority of an army colonel. "We're going to pray together."

Chapter 36

Emily should have been sweating by the time the rehearsal was over, but her anticipation of the grand opening that evening had her so anxious, there may as well have been ice water running through her veins.

"Miss Clara, what if I fall flat on my face?"

"You know the staging back-to-front and front-to-back. Why would you worry about falling?"

"I meant in the metaphorical sense." Emily couldn't help a small smile, and she wondered if that had been Miss Clara's intent. "But I actually could fall, as well. My legs always seem to betray me at the worst possible moment."

The older woman wrapped an arm around her. "It's only right that you should be nervous. But trust the Lord, my dear. He has your best interests at heart."

There was a time when Emily didn't believe that. In fact, she'd believed the opposite was true—that God, if He even existed, was determined to make her life as difficult as He could. But so much had happened over the last few months: she'd been given the chance to sing professionally. She'd been snatched from the jaws of death at least three times. And she'd met Sam. There was no doubt that God had His hand of blessing on her.

"I do trust the Lord. Truly, I do. But I think I'd like to practice the opening cavatina a bit more. If I can get past that, I think I will be able to relax."

"Then, by all means, my girl, we shall practice it some more." While the other performers hustled from the theater to enjoy a few last hours of leisure, knowing they'd be there night and day once the season really got going, Emily took up her position on the stage, while Miss Clara moved to the wings.

The words of longing for her absent love welled up. "*Oh mattutini albori....*" She sang through the entire cavatina and then paused. The melody was comparatively simple. She had the skill to sing it, and to sing it well.

"Thank you, Miss Clara. I feel much better now. Can we move to the final rondo in act two, scene four?" She took her position and waited, but there was no sound from the piano. "Miss Clara?"

Still nothing.

The quietness of the great auditorium suddenly took on an ominous air.

"Miss Clara?" Emily hurried to the wing where the piano was set up.

Miss Clara lay huddled on the floor, unmoving.

"Help!" Heart in her throat, Emily called out as she ran to the woman. "Is anyone here? I need help!"

There was no response. Emily fell to the ground, ignoring the fact that once she was down, it would be difficult to get back up by herself. She reached across Miss Clara's inert form and rolled her over. Her forehead was smeared with blood that seeped from a cut near her hairline. This was no cardiac dropsy. No accident. Miss Clara had been attacked.

At that instant, a rough hand closed over Emily's mouth, cutting off her scream for help. "Come along, my dear," a male voice rumbled in her ear. "I need to know what you know."

Emily kicked and fought but could gain no purchase with her wooden leg. Still she writhed, trying to pull free of the man's grip, but he was far stronger than she was.

"Ah, ah." He hauled her to her feet and jammed something hard into her ribs. "Don't make me shoot you, Miss Forbes. It's a messy way to go. And on your big day, too."

She stilled.

"See there, I knew you could be reasonable. Let's have a seat and chat."

With the gun pressed against her spine, he pushed her to a nearby chair and forced her to sit. He came around front to stand before her, and she glared up at him. "It *was* you, all along."

Harrison Kerns' smile was as caustic as acid. "Accolades to you for figuring it out."

Emily struggled to keep calm. She had to say something, anything, just to keep the conversation going. If she could distract him long enough, someone might come. In her heart, she knew the chance was slim. None of the stage crew or performers would be back until they absolutely had to be, for the evening's performance. They'd soak up every bit of freedom they could.

"I'm not the only one who's figured it out, you know." Emily spit the words at him. "You will be brought to justice."

He shrugged out of a loop of rope that hung from his shoulder and moved to tie her to the chair. "I'm well aware of Dr. DeKlerk's prying and shall deal with him soon enough. It will be tragic, of course, when one of his crazy patients turns on him. We will all mourn. But I'm afraid it's inevitable. People have been saying as much for years."

Emily cringed as he pulled the rope tight around her wrists. "No one will continue to believe these tales. It's all too convenient for you. And we've alerted others that you were behind Alice's murder."

"Yes, your little visit to the library. And how did that work out for you? From my vantage point, it seemed as if your theory was discredited."

Emily couldn't hold back her surprise. "You were there?"

"Of course. And I enjoyed every minute." His faux smile faded. "Now, enough verbal jousting. Tell me where your so-called proof is."

"I don't think so."

He grabbed her face, squeezing her cheeks between ruthless fingers. "You will tell me, and quickly, or I shall shoot you." He released her with a sharp slap to punctuate his threat.

"You will shoot me and leave me for dead as soon as I tell you. Why should I give you what you want?" As she spoke, she toyed discreetly with the knots behind her back, hoping his gaze would stay on her face.

He raised his eyebrows. "Quite perceptive for a songstress, aren't you? I suppose we're at an impasse, then." Slowly he paced in front of her, tapping the barrel of the gun against his lip. "Except...." He drew the word out, as if he were having some sort of epiphany. "There are some choices to be had. I can kill you slowly and painfully, or I can kill you quickly, with barely any pain at all."

She sneered. "You are the epitome of considerateness."

"Talk." He aimed the gun at her.

She flinched, and all the nightmares of her parents' murders and her own injury flooded her senses. Her hands stilled. She couldn't think. Couldn't breathe.

"Tell me!" He roared the command.

Still she could say nothing. Even if she thought it would save her life, she could make no words come out. No sound. The great, empty vacuum of the theater was frozen in time, nothing moving, heavy with silence.

Kerns took aim and fired.

The moment was shattered. A scream forced its way from Emily's throat. She jerked her shoulder, trying to throw herself out of the line of fire, but all she managed to do was knock her chair over. She closed her eyes and lay there, stunned. She waited to feel blood, wet and warm, seep from the wound; to see it pool beneath her on the floor. But that didn't happen. Gradually, it dawned on her that she felt no pain. "Thank You, God," she whispered. Had Kerns missed, or was God insulating her from the fiery, burning, all-consuming pain that would come later? She needed to think while she still could.

Kerns knelt over her and smacked her cheek with enough force to rattle her teeth. "Rise and shine."

She opened her eyes grudgingly.

"Answer my question, or I shall shoot you in the other leg."

The other leg? He'd shot her in the leg?

A hysterical bubble of laughter welled up into her diaphragm, threatening to burst. No wonder there was no pain. He'd shot her wooden leg. Tears streaked her cheeks. It was ridiculous. Utterly ridiculous.

Satisfaction played over Kerns' face. Between the tears and the maniacal laughter, he must believe he had shaken her. The man was totally unaware of the reality. And Emily would use that to her advantage.

After a few deep breaths, she was able to speak. "Did you put Robert up to dueling with Sam?"

With triumph a near certainty, Kerns seemed eager to boast about his deeds. "You bet I did. But, as smart as you think you are, you don't know everything." He leaned close and hissed in her ear, "I shot your lover."

"You? But—"

"You must admit it was brilliant. I loaded Robert's gun for him, and put in only some wadding. He was too loaded, himself, to have been able to shoot a ship, much less a man."

It began to make sense. "Then you had a gun, as well."

"Indeed. I fired the shot that hit DeKlerk. It was an awkward angle, because I had to avoid all the spectators who had come down. Otherwise, I'd have killed him cleanly, and everyone would have blamed Romijn."

Emily let her head fall back to the floor. She was beaten. No matter what she did, she knew too much for him to let her live. He would kill her, and then he would kill Miss Clara, too.

No! Something rose up in her spirit, roaring like a tiger and refusing to back down. It might be Emily's time to go, but she would not allow this man to hurt Miss Clara.

She raised her head again and looked Kerns in the eye. "I will tell you what you want to know, but only if you promise to let Miss Clara live, and to do her no more injury."

She held his gaze for a long moment.

"All right." He stood, leaving her to lie, trussed and helpless, on the floor. Looking down at her, he pointed the gun at her midriff. "I won't touch another hair on the head of your loving mentor. Now talk."

Emily squeezed her eyes tight and then opened them and looked at him. How she prayed she was doing the right thing. "There are financial records showing the bribes you've taken over the years."

"That's all?" He waved the gun.

"And also an affidavit that names you as the man—"

A blur streaked across Emily's vision. She craned her neck to try to see what it was. Kerns flinched and crashed to the ground. Someone was on top of him. When he reared back, Emily's heart soared. Sam! It was Sam.

Oh, thank You, God.

An instant later, another form joined the fray. This one was familiar, too. Emily blinked. *Carter?* What was her brother doing here?

There was a sound behind her, and Emily jerked her head around to see Carter's wife, Juliet, helping Miss Clara into a chair. Blood smeared the older woman's face, and she was pale, but she otherwise appeared to be all right.

Juliet joined Emily a moment later and began to work free the knots that held her to the chair. Behind Juliet, others filtered onto the stage: Robert, leaning heavily on a cane; Mr. Jerome, lending an arm to support Robert; and Sam's parents.

In moments, Kerns was subdued, and Sam sent his father for the police. Sam rushed to Emily just as Juliet undid the last knot.

"Are you all right?" He helped untie the ropes from around her and then took her in his arms. "I was so scared."

Her fingers dug into the fabric of his jacket, pulling him close, as she released the emotions she'd been holding back. "I thought he was going to kill me. Oh, Sam."

He held her close, rocking her and stroking her hair, as tears ran down her cheeks.

Someone knelt beside her and placed a firm hand on her back. "Emily."

Her head jerked up at the deep, comforting voice of her brother. "Carter!" She flung one arm around his neck but kept her other arm tightly wrapped around Sam.

With a chuckle, Carter kissed the top of her head. "As wonderful as it is to hold you, little sister, it would be even better if we got you off the floor and into a chair."

He helped Sam pull her to her feet. Then, before she could protest, Sam swept her into his arms and carried her off the stage. Once he had her settled in the first row of the audience, he knelt down in front of her. Carter remained standing, and Juliet hurried over and plunked into the seat beside her.

Emily grabbed Juliet's hand and held it tight. "What are you two doing here?"

Juliet smiled. "Carter and I wanted to surprise you by coming up for your debut. The plan was for Miss Clara to keep you here at the theater while Sam picked us up from the station, and then we would take you all out for a meal before the show."

"We meant it as a pre-celebration party," Carter added. "But when we heard the gunshot, Sam lit out like a cat with its tail on fire, and I was right behind him."

Robert limped over, grinning broadly and looking more like his old self than he had in weeks. "I would have run in, too, but I'm slightly disabled at the moment."

"Did you arrive in time to hear his confession?" Emily asked. "He's the one who shot Sam, not you."

"Venomous snake. There isn't a punishment equal to his crimes."

She couldn't argue with him.

It wasn't long before a handful of detectives and the chief of police had descended on the theater. Carter took charge of the situation, drawing the chief aside and handing over his Pinkerton credentials. A few moments later, Kerns was being led away between two police officers, his hands shackled behind his back.

A detective approached the little group. "Excuse me, folks, but we're going to need to take some statements."

"Of course."

"Miss Forbes, if you could come with me?"

Everyone began to stand and move away, but when Sam rose to his feet, Emily reached out and snatched his hand. "Please, Officer, may my fiancé come, too?"

Fiancé. It came out of her without a second's thought. She looked up at Sam, and the smile on his face told her he didn't mind. He squeezed her hand.

When the officer was done with Emily, he turned to Sam. "I may as well take your statement now."

Emily shuddered as an unexpected chill shook her body. Sam looked at her, concern furrowing his brow.

"My statement is that I arrived in time to hear a gunshot and found Mr. Kerns threatening my fiancée, whom he'd already tried to shoot. I then subdued Mr. Kerns, and the police were summoned. This will be corroborated by Mr. Forbes, who is a Pinkerton agent." At the mention of Carter, the officer looked around and sat up a little straighter.

Sam stood. "I need to see to Miss Forbes now. I am her physician, as well as her betrothed."

"Oh. Well, all right then, sir. We can get the details later."

Sam put his arm around Emily and helped her to her feet. Then, once again, he swept her up into his arms.

"Really, Sam," she said with a huff. "I'm perfectly capable—"

"Hush. Did it occur to you that perhaps I'm using the circumstances as an excuse to hold you close? Let me enjoy myself, Miss Forbes."

Smiling to herself, Emily let her head fall against his chest as he carried her past their family and friends and into her dressing room.

⌒

Sam settled Emily gently on the settee, then knelt in front of her. "As your physician, I really do need to check your leg."

Emily looked at him with a dreamy expression. "He shot me, you know."

"I know he shot at you," Sam said, grasping the hem of her costume. "Thank heavens he missed."

"He didn't miss."

Sam frowned, but when he exposed the entirety of her wooden leg, he saw that she was right. There, straight through the middle of the limb, was a splintery but perfectly round hole.

When he looked up at her, tears twinkled on her eyelashes. "Isn't God funny? The harm I suffered in the past kept me from harm today."

Without a word, Sam moved beside her on the settee and drew her into his arms. He showered her head, her face, her neck, with kisses. "Emily, my sweet Emily. I've never been so terrified."

Her fingers tangled in his hair. "Sam." Her voice was a sweet, whispered breath.

His lips found her mouth, and he kissed her with all the force of the passion and fear driving him. His heart jumped when she met his intensity with equal fervor. In a moment, he slowed. The kiss gentled as he stroked her hair and breathed her in. Finally, he drew her head down to the hollow of his neck and snuggled it there. "I thank God for sparing you."

Though he was loath to release her, he pulled away, but he didn't go far. Back down to the floor he went, on one knee before her. He took her hand. "Emily Grace Forbes, you've brought music and laughter to my life, and life back into my dismal existence. I cannot imagine one day without you. Will you marry me?"

"I thought you already asked her."

Sam whipped his head around to see Carter, along with Juliet, Miss Clara, Robert, and his parents, crowded around the door he'd apparently neglected to shut.

Emily burst out laughing, and in spite of the heat blooming in his cheeks, so did Sam.

She leaned forward and kissed the crown of his head. "Yes," she whispered, "I will marry you. And neither runaway horses nor falling gargoyles can stop me."

About the Authors

Jennifer AlLee and Lisa Karon Richardson are a dynamic writing team. Jennifer believes the most important thing a person can do is find his or her identity in God, a theme that finds its way into all her work. She has published numerous novels, short stories, devotions, and plays. Over the years, she has enjoyed being part of church drama ministries and worship teams. Jennifer lives with her family in Las Vegas, Nevada. Readers may visit www.jenniferallee.com to find out more about her and her writing.

Lisa Karon Richardson has led a life of adventure—from serving as a missionary in the Seychelles and Gabon to returning to the States and starting a daughter-work church—and she imparts her stories with similarly action-packed plot lines. In addition to writing and ministry, Lisa manages medical malpractice litigation for a major health system. She lives in Ohio with her husband and their two precocious children. Readers may visit her Web site at www.lisakaronrichardson.com.

Curtain Call concludes the team's first trilogy with Whitaker House, Charm & Deceit, which also includes *Diamond in the Rough* and *Vanishing Act*. Both Lisa and Jen can be found at www.inkwellinspirations.com.